Easy Street

Easy Street

A Lillian Byrd Crime Story

by Elizabeth Sims

alyson books
NEW YORK
Celebrating Twenty-Five Years

MANUFACTURED IN THE UNITED STATES OF AMERICA.

THIS TRADE PAPERBACK ORIGINAL IS PUBLISHED BY ALYSON BOOKS,
P.O. BOX 1253, OLD CHELSEA STATION, NEW YORK, NEW YORK 10113-1251.
DISTRIBUTION IN THE UNITED KINGDOM BY TURNAROUND PUBLISHER SERVICES LTD.,
UNIT 3, OLYMPIA TRADING ESTATE, COBURG ROAD, WOOD GREEN,
LONDON N22 6TZ ENGLAND.

FIRST EDITION: NOVEMBER 2005

05 06 07 08 09 a 10 9 8 7 6 5 4 3 2 1

ISBN 1-55583-926-6
ISBN-13 978-1-55583-926-0

LIBRARY OF CONGRESS CATALOGING-IN-PUBLICATION DATA

Sims, Elizabeth, 1957–
    Easy Street : a Lillian Bird crime story / by Elizabeth Sims.—1st ed.
    ISBN 1-55583-926-6; ISBN-13 978-1-55583-926-0
    1. Byrd, Lillian (Fictitious character)—Fiction. 2. Women journalists—Fiction. 3. Lesbians—Fiction. I. Title.
PS3619.I564E23 2005
813'.6—dc22   2005049728

CREDITS
COVER PHOTOGRAPHY FROM GETTY IMAGES.
COVER DESIGN BY MATT SAMS.

Acknowledgments

Passionate thanks to my family and friends for your ongoing love, support, and belief.

To my readers, thank you for buying or borrowing my books. You're the only thing between me and a wasted life. Equally fervent thanks to all booksellers who sell my work. To those who don't: Get with it.

For special help given me in the writing of this book I'm indebted to my brother, David Sims, for advice legal; Margaret Baker MD for advice medical; Terry McKenzie for advice pharmaceutical and veterinary; and Cindi Forslund for advice Cleveland-ish.

Once again I'm obliged to Sensible Brown.

My deepest thanks of all go to my beloved Marcia.

One

I always like a good thick ham sandwich, so I was delighted to find a whole baked ham, flanked by a pot of Polish horseradish and a stack of rye bread, on the buffet table. It was an admirably loaded table: no dainties, just solid cop-fantasy food—you know, the kind of food cops talk about when they're trying to stay awake on an overnight surveillance. Besides the ham, there was a grill-your-own steak station with a guy to ensure you didn't ruin yours, a cauldron of Bolognese sauce with a platter of meatballs the size of fists, a dune of steaming pasta to ladle the stuff over, and a handsome green salad. There were boiled sausages and oven-baked chickens, mashed potatoes with some kind of wonderful-smelling cheesy thing mixed in, and the obligatory steamed vegetable medley, touched only by one or two of the younger cops who didn't know any better.

Then there was the cake, this iced slab decorated with teensy handcuffs and guns and stacks of paperwork, with "Good Riddance, Erma" beautifully scripted in pale green frosting.

My knees got a little weak as I stood looking and smelling and swallowing my saliva. I took a pull from the bottle of Stroh's I'd picked out of a cold well next to the bar.

I was about to grab a plate and get going on the ham when something struck me between the shoulder blades so hard my head snapped back. An unfamiliar laugh rang out, and I turned to see Lt. Tom Ciesla enjoying the effect his backslap had on me.

Ciesla himself was a familiar sight, of course: his thick shoulders straining his jacket just a smidgen, his large careful hands holding a bottle of Stroh's, his direct expression, his five o'clock shadow. But I realized that I'd hardly ever heard him laugh. He was a serious cop, and we'd had many a deep conversation, but I couldn't remember when I'd heard him laugh, and that was a little sad. Cops have to take life more seriously than most people.

But right now he was off duty, he'd eaten well, and he was happy to see me.

"Was the cake your idea?" I said.

"What do you think of it?" His voice was as direct as his expression.

"It's perfect. If anything could make Erma cry tonight, it'll be that cake."

"Well, she saw it."

"Did she cry?"

He laughed again.

"What else have you guys got in store for her? Is that guy from narcotics going to do Elvis again? Please tell me he's not going to put on that—"

"Lillian."

"Yeah, Tom." I was smiling, but suddenly he wasn't.

Ciesla said, "You don't look...good." He took my upper arm and pinched his fingers into my flesh down to the bone. He held me away from him and looked me down to my Weejuns. "You're way too skinny. Are you sick?" Here he'd been joking and having a good time, now abruptly he's worried about this nerdy unemployed writer.

"No, Tom, just hungry."

"You're eyeballing that ham like you think it's going to jump the fence."

"Yeah, well, I like ham. Where's Erma? I haven't had a chance to say hi."

"Those probation officers have got her cornered over there. I think they're trying to get her to sign up for bowling again."

"Can't the woman get some peace after all these years?"

"Yeah, but she's a good bowler, and the team's gonna stink without her. She threw a 290 in the finals last month."

"Wow." I couldn't help keeping an eye on that ham.

"Well," Ciesla said, "you better eat."

"Out of my way." He watched me pick up a plate and begin piling food on. When I turned from the buffet table, he'd taken off.

This ballroom, the Crystal Grand in the Marriott, was surely the safest place in the city that night. A hundred cops in every flavor—off duty, most carrying a weapon—plus a few badges who'd stopped in for a few minutes between calls, all of them bullshitting and laughing and eating and drinking. The room hummed with the pleasant chaos of it.

I saw this towering black lady detective who'd cracked a major car-theft ring last month by calling the main crook's girlfriend and posing as a telephone psychic. She got the girlfriend to tell her everything, which was a lot more than the boyfriend thought she knew. There was a white homicide cop whose face had gotten carved by a prisoner who'd slipped out of his cuffs and reached a razor blade he'd stuck in the edge of his flip-flop. The cop's face had healed in a half-grin that gave him a crazy look, which reportedly made him a much more effective interrogator. Then there was the Chinese-American vice cop who was addicted to Little Debbie snack cakes; he'd sit down to write a report, and half an hour later you'd have to climb over this barrier of Little Debbie wrappers to talk to him.

Most of these party guests gave me a good feeling. I'm a resolute believer in the basic goodness of cops. Only a few of them crept me out—the ones who'd tampered with evidence (or so I'd heard) and never got nailed, the ones who were always on the make somehow, the ones with a quiet rep for using smack or for shaking down stupid people who couldn't figure out how to stay out of their way. You just hope you never have to deal with cops like them.

I found a seat at an empty table. I wanted to concentrate on eating, on filling my belly with as many solid calories as I could, and I wanted to thoroughly enjoy the experience of eating food that was not only free but good. The smoky-peppery ham was succulent between the firm slabs of bread. It's easy to find food that's good and expensive, and relatively simple to find food that's awful and more or less free, but good *and* free—that's the combination for me.

I chewed and swallowed, and a little sunburst of horseradish rose to clear my sinuses. So good. It felt so good to eat well.

I finished my sandwich and pickle, and a busboy came by and took my plate. I set my coordinates for the meatballs. I stopped, though, seeing Det. Erma Porrocks disengage herself from the probation officers and head toward me. I met her for a hug.

"Congratulations, Erma. You made it."

She smiled widely, showing her even teeth that formed a friendly arcade between her postmenopausally fuzzy pink cheeks. Probably the smallest cop in the department, Porrocks was nevertheless fearlessly herself. She wore her gray hair in a style that made you think of moms on 1960s-era television: a simple smooth style, but styled. She liked cardigan sweaters. There always was a little something soft and retro about Porrocks, which somehow never represented a handicap to her in the testosterone-soaked world of the detective division.

"Man, Erm, twenty-five years. How does it feel?"

"Funny. It feels funny." She tugged at the waistband of her skirt. "I started on the force late in life, for a cop. I was thirty-two. Now I can't believe I'm pushing sixty."

"Just think, you'll be able to do stakeouts only when you really, really want to. Hey, thanks a lot for inviting me. Fabulous spread—you can tell the department thinks highly of you."

"Yeah, I got the twenty-five-year spread. I'm glad you're enjoying it."

"Well, what're you going to do?"

"I'll take some time off, you know. Then I might go into private investigation."

"Yeah? That sounds good. You'd be a great gumshoe, Erma."

She started to say something, then bit her lip, and I saw she was feeling emotional. "I—I'm going to miss all these jackasses."

I touched her arm. "Yeah."

"Uh, have you had a bite to eat?"

"Mm-hmm, I was about to go get some more."

"Lillian, can I talk to you?"

"Sure, what about?"

"Why don't you get some more food and come back here?"

I grabbed two fresh bottles of Stroh's on the way back with my steaming plate of pasta.

She thanked me and took a sip of beer. "I bought a house a few weeks ago."

"You're moving?"

"Just to the waterfront. Wyandotte, actually."

"Oh, yeah?"

"I've always wanted a view of the water, and you know there's nothing like that in the city except for high-rises. Now that I'm retiring, well, I got an opportunity to buy this place—rather suddenly, actually, and it was such a good deal I went for it. It's a nice house; it's got good bones, like they say in the magazines. But it needs work—quite a bit of work. I think somebody with a temper lived there."

"Yeah?" I wondered what her point was going to be. In a prompting way I said, "Is it one of those bootlegger places?"

During Prohibition, smugglers ran so much illegal Canadian booze into Detroit and all its shoreline communities you couldn't spit into the river without hitting some guy in a fast motorboat. And you couldn't toss a daisy into a police squad room without hitting somebody on the take. It was a high time all around.

"Oh!" said Porrocks. "Well, I don't know. It does have a boathouse."

Smugglers coveted the houses on the waterfront with private docks for obvious reasons. The boss smugglers would buy these places for cash from some prosperous haberdasher or car dealer, then do the modifications in the dead of night. You'd hear about places with secret passageways from the waterline into hidden cellars, then tunnels to the alley or a neighboring house. I'd always hoped to get a look at a place like that.

Porrocks got a little more intense. "How have you been, Lillian?"

"Well—fine, Erma. Just fine."

"Really. What are you living on?" Porrocks had a little dry voice, but it carried authority. I haven't yet mentioned that she was a high-level judo expert, so good at leveraging her modest weight and strength that she taught special classes at the police academy on how to subdue obstreperous suspects without bone-breaking violence. Now and then I'd wondered about her private life.

"Yeah," I said, "I'm—I'm working on some, uh, some ideas for—for all these magazines that are interested in my work, you know. And, uh, I'm into my music."

"Yes, I've seen you playing on the streets." She was looking at me so steadily that I got a little nervous. "Lillian, why don't you get a job?"

"Oh, God, Erm." A hot blotch of shame crept up my neck. "Look, I just have to go my own way. You know. I'm trying to—I have some things going." How fucking embarrassing. I hadn't thought my circumstances showed that much.

"Your clothes are shabby." She was looking at the cuffs of my jeans.

"But clean. A lot of people wear frayed clothes. It's the style."

"Come on. Even your *shoes* are frayed."

It was true, my Bass Weejun penny loafers had been resoled three times now, and yes, the tongues lay soft as mushroom gills. But they were clean.

In fact, I'd tried. My freelance writing just wasn't bringing in enough money, so I'd applied to several management training programs, one at Comerica Bank, one at J.C.Penney, and one at Midas Mufflers. The tests revealed that I had good verbal skills (news flash there), was lousy with numbers (ditto), and dismal on management skills, however the hell they quantify those things.

Somehow I couldn't hook into anything solid. I considered trucker school; I considered bartender school; I even considered cosmetology.

Cops excel at letting you dig a hole for yourself.

"I'm doing fine, Erma. Really." I sank my cutlery into a meatball and lifted a steaming morsel to my mouth, my saliva almost spurting out to meet it. I wolfed the thing down. "I mean, I'm paying my rent and keeping Todd in bunny chow." I didn't mention that my landlords had reduced my rent so I could afford to stay there, and that I was foraging in people's backyards for leaves for my old sick rabbit. "It's not that I think I'm too good to flip hamburgers or pull weeds, okay? It's just that I'm, I'm just, I'm—oh, hell."

"No, you're not fine."

"Well, what, then? Have you been opening my bank statements or something?"

"Look, Lillian, I can't believe you've let yourself get into such dire straits. You're actually going hungry."

"I'm a fussy eater."

"You're not getting enough to eat. Are you depressed?"

"Jesus, what is this? No, I'm not depressed. I'm happy as a goddamn lark." I kept eating. I hadn't gotten to the point of borrowing money from anyone. I just kept thinking things would turn around. Something would come up. I kept expecting myself to think of a new thing to do: a business to start, or some fabulous idea for a book everyone would need to buy. Something.

As I sat there talking to Porrocks, what I really wanted to do was burst into tears and wail, "I've wasted my life! A newspaper job I blew, a few crummy freelance bylines, a couple of half-assed warehouse jobs where they didn't even let me drive the forklift, a couple of dollars a night busking on the streets with my mandolin—that's been it! That's been fuckin' it!"

Two

Sure, I'd had some fun along the way. Snooping into dark places, eluding murderous maniacs, chasing down scummy felonious wretches. Big deal. I'd had a sexy, famous lover for a while, then things went rotten. My spirits were lower than whale shit. And I feared my beloved rabbit was not long for this world. Yes, I was facing the endgame with Todd. He was almost eleven years old, and he was creaky, plus he had whatever kind of rabbit coronary disease his species gets. I pictured his little arteries going all stiff, his brave, cherry-size heart beating ever slower. I couldn't think about it without crying.

Accusingly, I asked Porrocks, "Have you been talking to Tom?"

"He's concerned about you too."

"I knew it."

"Well, I'll come to the point, Lillian," she said. "I'd like to offer you some work."

I instantly visualized myself with a pocketful of business cards that said PORROCKS & BYRD DETECTIVE AGENCY—WE KNOW WHAT WE'RE DOING. I'd carry a small but potent handgun and go undercover to help Porrocks expose corrupt heads of state, rescue kidnapped heiresses, and apprehend smug serial killers. I visualized myself kicking in the door to a motel room to snap a picture of some upstanding public leader balling a hooker or stuffing his pockets with payola.

"Yeah?" I said.

"See, like I mentioned, I need some work done on this house I bought."

"Oh."

"Now, I know you're no contractor, and I'd guess you don't have much in the way of carpentry skills. Or tools, probably."

"Stop with the flattery."

"But you could *prepare* the place for the real workers, couldn't you? There's this miserable carpet I need ripped up and thrown away, and there's this rotted tile and linoleum. I need wallpaper stripped, that kind of thing. Think you could do that? There's a ton of work in the boathouse alone."

"Sure, Erm, I have primal demolition skills."

"But carefully, though?"

"Of course. I'm a very neat worker. But I was sort of hoping, uh."

She read my face and said, "You know, private investigation these days is largely a matter of searching databases. It's not very exciting, like in the pulp novels."

"Yeah," I said glumly. "I know." Of course I knew. I'd gotten hold of the latest book in the Calico Jones series, *Encounter in Borneo,* to feed my bedtime reading habit. I'd actually found this copy abandoned at a bus stop on lower Woodward—abandoned, can you believe it?—and had considered it a good omen. An omen of something—of riches soon to come? I was beginning to get very superstitious, seeing things as omens, and the omen was either riches soon to come, or some hot girlfriend soon to come, so to speak.

Anyway, *Encounter in Borneo* starts out with Calico Jones—the beguiling, gorgeous, competent, brilliant private eye, on a train from Bombay to Singapore, where she's to meet clandestinely with a

Swedish biophysicist named Ingrid Something, who's supposed to fill her in on her next mission. You just know this Ingrid's going to be a knockout. You just know it.

Calico Jones's investigations are *never* ordinary. You don't catch *her* sitting in some Internet café Googling bad guys and taking notes. No sir, she's out there with her .45 semiautomatic and her sports car and her custom-designed clothes and her unerring powers of deduction and her nerves of pure tensile steel. She is so courageous.

I came back to Porrocks saying, "Do you have your own crowbar at least?"

"I do, in fact." One of the few possessions I hadn't yet hocked.

"Well, how does fifteen dollars an hour sound?"

"Fifteen an hour? Sounds great, Erma. Excellent. When can I start?"

She said thoughtfully, "There's at least a few weeks' worth of work. Maybe more, maybe even a month or two."

"How big is this place?"

"Fairly large. Four bedrooms—larger than I need, really, but I just fell in love with it. You know how that can happen."

I did, though it had never happened to me. People I've fallen in love with, animals I've fallen for, but never a building.

"My nieces and nephews can come visit, and now there's plenty of space for them. The house has only been vacant a few weeks, but I've had a little trouble, a couple of break-ins."

"Oh."

"That dismays me." She cupped her neat chin in her hand. "But I know the neighborhood's really okay—I think it's just kids. There's nothing in it to steal. Maybe they wanted to use it as a hangout. I was going to delay moving in till I got all the refurbishing done, but I think it'd be wiser for me to get in there right away. So the movers are coming on Monday, and I'll put the condo up for sale immediately. Hey, want to clean the condo once my stuff's out of it? Same rate?"

"Absolutely. I'll make it sparkle." Come to think of it, I have fallen in love with inanimate things: cleaning products. A sustaining force in my life will always be Spic-n-Span. Provided you do your part of using a decent rag and bucket and really hot water, it'll meet you more than halfway.

"Lillian, I want you to take better care of yourself."

"I don't mean this to be funny, Erma, but I never knew you cared."

"Well, I do. Tom cares about you too. I mean, we haven't seen you in a while, and well—it's not just that you're bonier than ever, and your car looks like it's held together by twist ties. There's something in your face that worries me."

Porrocks had lived alone in her condo overlooking the Lodge Expressway for years and years, had never married (I once asked Ciesla), went birding on the weekends, read all the police journals, worked late on thankless cases, never complained of sexual harassment on the job. I don't think she encountered much harassment; Porrocks seemed impervious to that shit anyway; I wondered what ever really got to her.

My antennae are pretty good, and I tuned them in to try to see if she was trying to show—how shall I put it?—special interest in me. I tried several frequencies but came up clear. She was just sincerely wanting to help somebody she thought needed it.

I said, "My rabbit is sick."

"Do you need money for vet costs?"

"Uh, no, I'm fairly current on that bill. Look, if I can just do that work for you, that'll help me out quite a bit. You'll have done me quite a favor. Thanks, Erma."

A drunken vice squad cop came up and put a gentle hammerlock on Porrocks, who remained seated and slipped out of it as if she were shrugging off a sweater.

"You'll have to do better than that, Duke," she commented.

"Everybody wants cake!" he hollered.

"Okay, where's the machete?" Porrocks got up and murmured to me, "I'll call you in the morning."

And that's how quietly this one got going.

Three

The next morning I pulled my shuddering, noble 1985 Chevrolet Caprice into the driveway at Porrocks's new digs. The house, one of those dark-red brick old beauties with three floors and a mansard roof, looked solid at first glance.

The day was shaping up majestically: A glittering autumn sun arced into a crystal sky filled with cold, happy air and the occasional skein of southbound geese. We were in the second half of a fine October.

On second glance I noticed the ancient copper gutters on Porrocks's house pulling away from the eaves, a few shingles missing, tattered window frames, and overgrown shrubbery around the front porch. There was a fabulously huge maple tree smack in the middle of the front yard, and its leaves had turned a van Gogh yellow. They were gently dropping in the breeze, like golden rain.

A good omen, I thought. *Golden rain.*

I saw Porrocks at the front door.

"Stay down," I said to Drooly Rick, who was lying on the backseat.

Yeah, I'd sort of sideswiped the job already, but I had to. Or I felt I had to.

Before leaving Porrocks's party around eleven, I'd filled my pockets and shoulderbag with snacks for the street people I'd gotten to know all too well busking with my mandolin downtown over the last few years. I wrapped a few sandwiches in paper napkins and scored some slices of cake. On the way back to my flat in Eagle, I detoured to Greektown and handed out the stuff.

I came across Drooly Rick and his longtime girlfriend, Young Brenda, huddled next to a row of garbage cans in the alley behind the restaurant Pegasus. It was a working alley behind that row of restaurants, dirty and dark but not cluttered with a lot of junk; trucks came through regularly. Rick was crouching over Brenda trying to get her to drink from a paper container of orange juice he'd gotten from one of the street missions.

She looked like hell, her skin pocked and gray like old snow, her eyes sunken far back in her skull. Her hair was matted and sparse, her hands shook, and although she spoke coherently, I thought she couldn't be far from a real medical crisis. Her clothes were soaked with vomit and urine. I breathed through my mouth, though that seemed risky. Brenda liked methamphetamine a lot.

Drooly Rick, by contrast, appeared to be reasonably straight, and I remembered that this was their pattern: When one floundered, the other hung on and stayed in control enough to minimally look after the floundering one. Switching back and forth like this they'd built up some staying power on the dirty, sad streets.

Rick told me, "I want Brenda to go home before winter comes."

"Home? What do you mean?"

"Her sister in Tennessee said she could come and stay for a while." He wiped his nose along the sleeve of his greasy black wool overcoat. "I ain't invited, though."

"Oh."

"If she could hang out with her sister, I bet she'd feel better after a while."

I offered Brenda a sandwich, but she muttered, "I can't eat. Got 'ny money?"

"No."

"I need some shit," Brenda said.

"Shit is right," asserted Drooly Rick, who favored fortified wine and malt liquor. He took the sandwich. "If I could just buy her a bus ticket to Clarksville, everything'd be okay."

"How much would that ticket cost, Rick?"

"Dunno. Maybe a hunnerd dollars."

"I bet not that much." I took another look at Brenda, who was only in her late twenties, I guessed. The expression on her face was a vacant sort of longing. "Would you like to see your sister?" I asked her.

"I don't care," she said in a dead voice.

Rick put the juice to her lips again. She pushed it away. "But you gotta get well," he told her. She had on a ski jacket that appeared to have once been mint green with white fake-shearling trim. It was now a mottled moss gray, somewhat like camouflage, and the trim looked like strips of dead coyote.

Rick stood up and motioned me aside. He muttered, "I don't know what to do. I love her. We've been thinking about havin' kids. I'd like to get us a ranch in Montana someday."

Dear God. "Look, Rick," I said, "if I could get you a little work for a few days, would you do it? Basic labor. I'll pay you cash—let's say seven-fifty an hour."

"Seven-fifty?"

I looked at him in the sparse light from the restaurant's security bulb. His teeth were brown but his chin was dry, and it looked as if he'd managed a shave within the past week.

"Yeah," I told him. "In ten hours you could have seventy-five dollars and put Brenda right on that bus. Work a little bit more, and you'd have a hundred."

"Couldn't you just let me have the seventy-five bucks now?"

"Lord, I don't have it. I've got about twenty dollars, and I need it for gas and stuff until more comes in. I've got work and I'll share it with you, okay? It'll be easy work, ripping up carpet and stuff in this old house."

"I could do that kind of work. Used to run a salvage yard."

"Well, you'll have to tell me about it someday."

"Inneresting work. Very responsible position."

"The big question is, can you stay sober while you're doing it?"

"Yeah. Yeah, I can."

"Because I can't work with a drunk."

"Okay, okay. Yeah."

"You're pretty straight right now, aren't you?"

Sorrowfully, he said, "Yeah."

"Well, stay that way until morning, all right? I'll come find you as soon as I hear when I'm supposed to show up."

So now Rick stayed down in the backseat while I went up to talk to Porrocks. I thought she might be okay with Drooly Rick working in her home under my supervision, but I wasn't at all sure of it, and I just couldn't have coped with a problem right then.

We chatted there on her front porch for a minute, then she invited me in to show me the place. She said all the new-house stuff people say. "So here's the view to the river. I just love it; it's so serene."

"It is."

"I hate this paint, but this oak floor is beautiful, isn't it? Look at this built-in buffet! That's the original finish."

"Very nice," I said. "Terrific place, Erm." She'd been measuring rooms and closets and deciding where to put her stuff. She looked energetic but a little uneasy. You'd expect it, really: someone retiring after such a long time and then changing her environment to boot. I wondered if she'd feel lonely.

"Then today I'm going to pull out some broken shelves in the big upstairs closet," she said. "Then after that I'll have to go back to my condo and get things organized for the movers." She had a radio tuned to a sports program; the announcers were yammering about the football game between Michigan and Notre Dame that was going to kick off in a couple of hours. Their sharp voices bolstered the getting-things-done feel in the house.

"Would you like me to get started in the boathouse?" I asked.

"That'd be good. If I can make that livable I might stay there while I'm getting the work done in the main house."

We hiked back there and she showed me what she wanted. The boathouse had a newer roof, and the pilings it rested on looked solid. Wavelets sloshed pleasantly through the pilings, and that organic clean river smell came up to our noses. Part of the building was the actual boat well, with a winch lift and a roll-up door to the river. The winch was rusted up pretty badly.

"You gonna get a boat?" I asked Porrocks.

"Maybe. I don't know."

It was dim in the boat well, the only light bouncing in from the space between the water and the start of the walls, about two feet of open space. Blots of reflected light danced on the plank walls and ceiling.

The other part of the building was a guest cottage, with a kitchenette and a dining area and two rooms for sleeping. The tiny little bathroom needed a hefty dose of Spic-n-Span. The place smelled musty but fortunately not pukey. Porrocks pulled back a filthy curtain, letting in daylight and saying, "In all its glory." Some crummy furniture gave the place a depressed atmosphere: a couch that looked like a raccoon had raised a family in it, a rickety dinette set that someone about twenty years ago had tried to resurface with pink contact paper. The carpet was beyond cleaning, as was the peeling linoleum. I couldn't tell the original color of the carpet.

"I hired a couple of guys to tear down two of these interior walls," Porrocks said, pointing, "but they quit halfway through the job, and I haven't seen them again."

"Huh," I remarked. "Well, you've got quite a mess here, Erm."

"I should have gotten the floor coverings out first. I'm not sure now whether I want that other wall down." We looked at it, covered in dirty wallpaper with a cutesy flower-basket print.

"Well, it doesn't matter," I assured her. "I'll fix everything up. Don't you worry."

I decided I didn't need to bring up the subject of Drooly Rick at all, since we could hide out and work here, down at the end of the long driveway.

The neighborhood looked quite okay. Even around Detroit waterfront property is costlier than most. The trouble is, since there's no elevation past the riverbank, a house on the opposite side of the street has practically no view, and houses on the next block have views of each other, and that's it.

Porrocks's new neighbors kept up their places nicely—nicer than hers had been, so I imagined they'd be glad to see her sprucing up 201 Adderly St. I noticed a small apartment building directly across the street from her, so there were rentals in the neighborhood, but again the place was neat. Yep, it looked as if Porrocks had made a good choice.

Porrocks returned to the house, and I pulled the Caprice down the long drive to the boathouse.

"She said she's gonna work in the house upstairs," I told Rick. "So let's just be cool." We unloaded the few tools I'd brought: a wrecking bar, a claw hammer, a utility knife, a pair of pliers.

"What happened here?" said Rick, looking at the stubble of a wall.

I told him about the couple of workers who'd preceded us.

"She want this other wall down too?" He looked at it hungrily, and I felt what he was feeling—a sort of exhilaration at having a license to destroy.

"No, now she's not sure."

"It'd make the room a lot bigger. Real nice."

"No. Listen to me, Rick. We're just gonna rip up these floors, okay? This carpet here and this linoleum. Then we'll pry the tile off these kitchen walls, see? That'll be fun. We're gonna leave the walls in place and just rip the *tile and wallpaper* off them. We're gonna leave these kitchen cabinets up, too." They were nice oak cabinets with green glass knobs.

I'd smelled Rick's breath when I picked him up downtown, but I had another thought: I wasn't going to be able to keep my eye on him all day. I already realized that we could use a second wrecking bar, which I could get at the hardware store for a few dollars. I said, "I know you're sober now, but—do you have anything on you?"

The insulted look on his face told me.

"No!" he shouted.

"Mind if I check your pockets, then?"

"Go right ahead!" He glared at me as I patted his left coat pocket, then the right. I guess he was hoping I wouldn't be thorough, but the pint of Mad Dog in his right pocket was hard to miss. I pulled it out.

"I'm gonna lock this in the trunk for you, okay?" I handled the bottle as if it were a valuable camera or something. "Wouldn't want anything to happen to it."

"Thank you," he said humbly.

"Remember, Rick, you're doing this for Brenda. You gotta get that bus ticket."

"Yeah, I really got to."

"Now, if the lady of the house comes in, let me handle it. You don't have to say anything. You can take your coat off now, by the way."

Drooly Rick's customary outfit was this black overcoat with about five assorted shirts underneath it, this outrageous pair of bright blue plaid golf pants, and several socks on each foot. The shoes varied—street people tend to be hard on shoes. This day he was wearing a dignified-looking pair of cordovan oxfords with almost no heels left. He preferred to keep his coat on.

I had on blue jeans and my Wayne State T-shirt, plus my brown nylon windbreaker and my black Chuck Taylor basketball sneakers. Rick and I were a motley team, all right.

"Will she pay us today?" Rick asked.

"I sure as hell hope so, but she might wait until next week. I dunno. Today's Saturday. Well, let's get going." We moved the furniture out to the boat well, where there was just room for it on the narrow walkway. Then I decided we should pry the baseboards away from the walls so we could get at the carpet. "We gotta be careful not to mar the wood, okay?" I gave Rick the wrecking bar, which had a tapered end, and took the claw hammer, and we started in opposite corners of the kitchen area.

I realized knee pads would have been a good idea, so as soon as I got a corner of carpet up, I cut two pieces and folded them over to make kneeling pads for us. The carpet was blackish with old mildew beneath. In such a damp environment you're going to have that kind of problem. That funny, half-chemical, half-plant smell of mildew came up, but not bad. The autumn breezes had dried things out.

It took only about an hour to get all the baseboards off and stacked out of the way on top of the furniture in the boat well. The carpet was tacked down tightly. We pulled and grunted and got into a rhythm of working. Rick was strong.

After we'd been at it a while he said, "Lillian?"

"Yeah?"

"Do ya s'pose she'd love me more if I was rich?"

Now, how the hell do you answer a question like that? I thought for a minute. "Well, you guys might be quite a bit more comfortable if you were rich. But when you really think about it, Rick, what's that got to do with love?"

"I'm never gonna be rich," he muttered.

"Well, neither am I. But the real trick is to be *not poor*. See? Help me roll up this piece now. Let's put it—yeah, good. The cool thing is not to get wasted all the time, so you can string together some kind of regular income. Then you can live under a roof and have heat and a refrigerator with food in it and quarters for the Laundromat."

"Mmm."

"Doesn't that sound nice?"

"Oh, I guess."

"You remember what it was like, don't you?"

"Yeah." And he told me about when he had the job running a salvage yard in Taylor. "I knew where everything was. You couldn't stump me, because I remembered where we put everything. People try to cheat you in the junk business, y'know."

"Uh-huh," I nodded.

"I handled money. Chased off thieves. Sonabitchin' drug addicts try to steal everything. I owned a car and lived in a room and ate in diners. Went to the strip club every other night. It was nice."

"And then?"

He heaved an enormous sigh. "And then one thing 'n' another. I got sick, had a hernia, had an operation. I never felt good since."

"You're doing great work now."

"Yeah, but my insides don't feel right."

"The booze helps?"

"The booze helps."

Perceiving how little actual distance there was between Rick's life and mine, I felt a chill, a serious chill that ran from the back of my head all the way down my spine and deep into my butt and stayed there.

Four

After three and a half hours of steady work we'd denuded the floors in all but the bathroom. Beneath everything was the original planking, quite nice, but now covered more or less evenly with that skim of hard, old mold. A good bleach scrubbing would take care of it, I judged. "I could go for a sandwich and a cup of coffee," I said.

"Me too." Rick's eyes were looking rheumy.

I wanted to forestall Porrocks bringing anything out to us, so I went up to the house and found her. "I gotta go to the hardware store for something, 'n' thought I'd pick up something to eat on the way back. Hungry?"

She had her hair in a black-and-white polka-dot scarf and was wearing stiff new jeans and a red sweatshirt without any logo or cartoon character on it. I liked the polka dots. I saw a small toolbox in the kitchen and figured she must be about to get going on some demolition herself.

"Oh!" she said. She had a habit of saying "Oh!" like that when you asked her a question. "What do you need?"

"Some blades for my utility knife. I have to cut up that flooring in pieces small enough for me to roll up and lift. Thought I'd stack it in the front room until you get a Dumpster or something."

She checked in her toolbox and didn't have any blades, so she fetched her purse from the foyer.

"This place must've come as is," I remarked. "Nobody even vacuumed."

"Yes, the seller was in a hurry. They did at least clean the house—it's just the boathouse that's so dirty. Here, let me give you some money for those blades." She held out a five to me.

I looked down and shuffled my feet and said, "Thought I'd pick up something to eat on the way back."

"Uh, of course." She put the five back and took out a twenty. "Why don't you get the two of us some hamburgers from the White Castle on Fort Street? And some fries?"

"Sounds great. Thanks, Erma." I folded the bill into my pocket and went out. As I backed the Caprice out to the street I looked back at the boathouse, just part of which was visible from the house due to a large weeping willow between the two. The boathouse window that faced the house was small and dirty; I doubted she'd see Drooly Rick moving around in there. Anyway, I thought, he probably sat down to rest as soon as I shut the door.

The hardware store was mobbed, it being Saturday, and they were shorthanded as well: Just one old guy was running around helping people. Watching him, I thought he might be the owner, the way he grabbed stuff almost without looking. He was piloting the cash register too, with these arthritis-knuckled hands. The customer before me wanted four gallons of interior flat paint mixed to match a tiny beige chip he had taped to an index card. If I recounted the entire back-and-forth between him and the old guy, it'd take an hour. Every try the old guy made and daubed on a paper strip, this customer would fault it. "It's too seashell. It's way too seashell," he said after the first try.

The old guy tried again, his knobby painful hands working the color device, not spilling, doing it right. It took about ten minutes per try.

"Now it's not wheaty enough."

The old guy tried again.

"Now you've got it looking more like ginger."

The old guy said, "You want beige paint, right? That's beige."

The customer exhaled impatiently. "I would not call this chip beige. That's where we're having a miscommunication." He glanced around, eyebrow up, at the rest of us customers as if he expected us to applaud his outstanding wit. He turned back to the old guy. "I'd call it a very pale burnt umber—an umber about four shades toward a cappuccino, if you know what I mean."

"Oh, for God's sake," I said.

The guy turned to me. He was wearing one of those Burberry jackets with the plaid on the outside. That was about all I needed.

"Just buy the paint, man," I said. "Buy the paint." I heard the by-now five or six other customers do a collective throat-clear, just a little catch of a throat-clear that conveyed their gratitude.

Burberry Boy got instantly huffy. "Who are you?" he said in a snotty voice. He wore a pair of mirrored sunglasses pushed up into his suntipped hair.

I said, "Either you are a pussy-whipped husband who's afraid to take this paint home to your wife no matter what the fuck shade it turns out to be, or you're just starting out in the decorating business and think that being an asshole is part of the job. This is not a paint boutique; it's a neighborhood hardware store. The man can give you beige. Either take the beige paint or go the fuck away. Please."

My God, what a hassle.

Eventually, I was able to pay for my blades. Burberry Boy waited while I did, then followed me into the parking lot, trying to decide how to insult me. His face got redder and more desperate until I was unlocking the Caprice. Then he got it. "Nobody wears sneakers like that anymore!" he hissed. "And your car's a piece of shit!"

"Fuck you very much," I answered, and cranked the engine. I

gunned it to the floor in a deafening display of the V-8's power as a vast cloud of black smoke poured from the tailpipe. I threw the car violently into reverse and stepped on it, and the guy leaped back even though he wasn't in the way.

The line at the White Castle drive-through was long, but it moved fairly quickly. I kept checking my mirror, half expecting the guy to have followed me. He was probably a vegan, anyway.

When I got back Porrocks met me in the kitchen, where I handed her the receipts and change. "You bought three coffees," she observed.

"I really need the caffeine," I parried.

"I'll come out to the boathouse with you. Let's take a break together."

"Oh, uh," I replied. "Uh."

She looked at me. "What is it, Lillian?"

"It's just that I'd really like to get back to work right away. I'm just—I'm just really stoked to be doing this. I'll just gobble as I work, you know? Here." I dumped half of the burgers and fries on the countertop and dashed out.

I strode quickly down the driveway, my mouth watering. The drive was gravel, pleasantly crisp to walk on, though I thought Porrocks might want to pave it to make snow removal easier. Oddly, there was no garage on the property. Porrocks had left her new Dodge Stratus on a parking apron next to the main house.

I opened the boathouse door and went in, cradling the food and drinks. I'd shoved the package of knife blades in my back pocket. I had decided against investing in a second wrecking bar just yet, since I'd been doing pretty well with claw hammer.

Drooly Rick wasn't in the front room. I set the stuff on the counter. "Rick, food!"

Silence. No sounds of working or snoring or toilet-flushing.

A funny dust hung in the air. I sniffed, but it wasn't cigarette smoke; it smelled like chalk, like dirty chalk.

Then I noticed the wall, the one Porrocks had said not to take down yet.

It was about half demolished, having been torn into from the main room. The heavy plaster and its lath underpinnings had been bashed and pried away, revealing the stout studs and the backside of the laths and plaster on the other side. As the blood rose up to my eyeballs, I noticed furthermore that it was an insane job. Any ordinary person would have begun from one edge, the archway to the next room, and taken down the whole wall from left to right.

"Fuck!" I spat. "Oh, fuck fuck fuck fuck! Rick!"

He didn't come.

I stripped off my windbreaker and threw it down. "Rick!" I stomped through the rooms, yelling curses. He'd understood me all right; he'd just gotten giddy with the power of deconstruction. "Goddamn it, come here, you son of a bitch! You stinking moron son of a bitch!"

But he wasn't anywhere.

I scanned the front room again, hoping that the wall wouldn't look as bad as all that, but it did. I saw the glint of something: a liquor bottle, sitting upright on the floor in the middle of the plaster debris. A film of dust was settling on it as I picked it up: an almost empty fifth of DeKuyper's peach brandy. Where did he get it? I crossed to the kitchenette cabinets and started flinging them open. I found a few plastic dishes, some mugs with pictures of fruit on them, and in the corner cabinet, a collection of half a dozen liquor bottles.

It was the kind of liquor people give you when they move—no good regular beverages like whisky, vodka, or gin, just oddball shit people buy in order to make a new drink they want to try and then never use up: ouzo, crème de menthe, crème de cacao, vermouth, Galliano. I can't tell you how many half-bottles of Galliano I've been given over the years.

"Oh, goddamn it." Why hadn't I thought to sweep the place for liquor? Because I hadn't. I'd thought I'd made the day safe for Rick by confiscating his Mad Dog.

I opened the door to the boat well, ready to find him cowering behind the stuff we'd piled in there. But no Rick.

"Son of a bitch! Stupid fucking addict shit-for-brains!" I stood with my hands on my hips in the gloom of the boat well.

I saw a shoe floating in the water.

I bent down to look more closely and sure enough, the shoe, a cordovan lace-up with a rundown heel, was positioned at the end of a floating pant leg.

Five

"Rick! Shit! Oh, man!" I dropped to my knees and almost fell in trying to grab the shoe, which was moving slowly in the current. All the stuff we'd piled into the boat well was in my way as I tried to belly down on the planks. I gave a shove to the dinette set. The table, delicately loaded with the long strips of baseboards, scooted and wobbled. The wood crashed down onto me and into the water. But I was able to flop down flat and plunge my hand into the cold water to reach the shoe. I got it, then hiked my hand up to the ankle. I tugged, and the leg sloshed up into my face, but with nothing solid to anchor my grip I couldn't pull the body out of the water; it was too heavy. I wedged my foot against the wall to try to gain leverage, but it wasn't enough.

I lay there on the board walkway of this boathouse, this little covered dock, holding a dead guy by the ankle.

"Dear Jesus," I said.

The body was trying to sink, weighed down by Rick's sodden clothes, especially the heavy wool overcoat. I couldn't see his head at all in the dimness. The current was tugging on him, pulling downward. My arm was stuck awkwardly over the edge of the planks.

"Erma!" I shrieked. "Erma! Help! Somebody! Help! Aw, Rick!" I yelled his name down at the water as if I wanted him to know I was trying to do something. "Rick!"

I hung on and hollered for what felt like an hour, though it was probably only five or ten minutes. Nobody came. My arm got tired. I hollered hopelessly. The boathouse was at least a hundred feet from the house on that deep lot, and its walls were built of thick planking. The willow tree, though leafless, was standing there absorbing sound waves, even the ones that made it out through the gap between the planks and the surface of the river. The houses on either side were shielded by fences and shrubbery. If someone had been near, I'm sure I would've been heard, but I guessed everybody was inside watching the Irish pummel the Wolverines on TV.

I had to let Rick go and hope they'd find him after I ran for help, or else I had to find a way to secure the body where it was, then go for help.

I'd scratched the inside of my arm on a nailhead that stuck out from the edge of the walkway, and now I felt for it with my free hand, trying to judge whether it'd hold Rick if I could snag his pant cuff on it. I tried that, but the cloth kept slipping off the nail's short shank.

Still holding Drooly Rick's ankle, I sat up, then hooked my left leg around Rick's, trapping his leg against the edge of the walkway. I pulled off my T-shirt and ripped the hem to the neckhole but not through it. I worked Rick's foot through the neckhole, then crawled along the walkway towing the body until I reached the single mooring cleat at the end. I tied the shirt to the cleat. The body swung around and down, but the T-shirt held it.

In my jeans and sports bra I sprinted to the house and burst in at the side door. "Erma!"

Hearing her muffled voice upstairs, I thundered up the staircase to find her on a stepstool fiddling with the cover of the ceiling fan in the bathroom. She stepped down from the stool.

Still somehow believing the situation was urgent, I blurted, "We gotta call 911. Do you have phone service yet?"

"What happened? Are you all right? Where's your shirt?"

"We gotta call 911!"

"The phone's not on yet, but my cell phone, uh, I think I left it in the car. Lillian, *what* happened?"

"I hate to tell you this, Erma, but there's a dead body tied to your dock in the boat well. I used my T-shirt to tie him so he won't sink. It's a guy I know."

Porrocks went into cop mode. "Are you sure he's dead?"

"Yes, I've been out there with him for maybe fifteen minutes."

"*What?*"

"I was trying to get him out! I called and called for help, but nobody heard me. His name is Drooly Rick. He's a street guy I subcontracted to help me do the work for you. Come on, I'll show you."

"Oh, Lillian."

As we hurried down the stairs, she said, "What else do you know?"

"It happened when I was gone," I panted. "The son of a bitch found some liquor in the cupboard. He got excited and probably drank a lot all at once, and then he did some unauthorized demolition, then he passed out and fell into the water. That's what had to have happened. I mean, I was gone at least an hour. I don't know his real name—everybody calls him Drooly Rick. Which seems disrespectful now, considering."

We reached the boathouse. Porrocks threw her arm out, barring me. "Lillian, wait. I'll go in first."

"Oh, God, Erma, you're gonna kill me."

"Go find my cell phone. It must be on the front seat of my car. Wait." She began to pull up the hem of her sweatshirt but stopped. "Oh, hell, I don't have anything on under this either."

"I don't care!" I ran to her car.

Porrocks's Dodge was neat inside, but I didn't see her cell phone on the seat. I lunged around, feeling beneath the seats, opening the glove compartment, but didn't see it.

"Shit!" I slammed the car door.

An elderly woman shuffled into the entryway of the apartment house across the street. I bounded over and up the concrete steps.

"Ma'am, ma'am!" I shouted.

She turned and saw me.

"Please, I need a phone."

Had I said, "Ma'am, I want to slash your face off," I'm sure she couldn't have moved any faster than she did right then. She accelerated as if she'd been shot out of a howitzer and disappeared into apartment 1D.

I followed her and knocked. "I'm sorry if I frightened you! I'm half naked by accident! Will you please call 911 for me? We need some help across the street. Your neighbor heeds help!"

Silence from behind the door.

"Goddamn it!" I returned to the small lobby with its bank of mailboxes. There was no pay phone.

I heard someone on the wide staircase at the end of the lobby. The footsteps were measured, unhurried. I waited.

A pair of legs in bright-red tights appeared. They descended. A somewhat reedy voice said, "If you yell fire, you get more attention."

Appearing one by one atop the tights: an extremely short, extremely pink fuzzy skirt, then a white pullover sweater housing a round, nicely separated pair of breasts, then a neck curved slightly sideways to the left—a graceful curve it surely was—then there was a head inclined according to the angle of the neck, with a pleasantly inquisitive facial expression. The chin was small and pointed, the eyes frank, the damp-looking dark hair grabbed up in a tiger-striped plastic clip.

She looked at me. I looked at her.

"Fire," I said.

"That's better," she said. "What's wrong?"

"I need a telephone."

"Come on up."

Her apartment, 2B, was bright with light pouring in from windows facing the street. That's all I noticed then. She handed me a cordless phone and I braced a hand against the wall while 911 rang. I told the dispatcher the basics, and she promised help right away.

Red Legs had left the room, and now she stood before me with a glass of water in one hand and a white shirt in the other.

I drained the water and reached for the shirt, a guy-type. She said, "I actually hate to give you this, but…" She stopped, staring at my midriff and what boobs I had, flattened as they were by my sports bra. I put on the shirt and moved to the door.

"Thank you. I'll return the shirt."

"It's okay. I'm sorry there was trouble."

"I'll tell you about it when I bring the shirt back."

"Please do."

"Oh, God," I said, thinking about Drooly Rick's last miserable moments. "Oh, God. Oh, God."

Red Legs's face was like a smart little schoolgirl's—enthusiastic, fascinated, concerned. That valentine-point chin, those tendrils of hair creeping naughtily from their clip. She stuck out her hand. "I'm Audrey Knox."

"Lillian Byrd, how do you do? Thanks a million, Audrey Knox."

I dashed back to the boathouse, where Porrocks was inspecting the remnants of her wall.

"Did you find him, Erma?"

"Yes. He'll stay where he is."

"I couldn't find your phone, but one of your neighbors helped me."

"Lillian, tell me what the hell you're up to here."

"What I'm up to?"

A cop car pulled into the driveway and she said, "You can tell me and the officers at the same time."

The cops were basically okay, and definitely respectful once they understood that Porrocks was a retired cop. They went to look at Drooly Rick's body, and they looked around and asked Porrocks and me questions. I confessed my plan of trying to help Drooly Rick buy a bus ticket for his inamorata, Young Brenda. That was the whole main problem, you know?—my trying to help Rick.

I was beside myself. I told the cops, "You might as well arrest me, because I as much as killed that guy."

Porrocks grabbed my arm and said, "Don't be melodramatic with cops, okay?"

"But, oh, Erma, if I hadn't brought him here, he'd be alive right now."

"Alive and eating out of a garbage can," one of the cops said in what must have been a warm tone for him.

"Well, thanks for trying to make me feel better, but I'm not sure he's happier where he is now."

I told the cops the little I knew about Drooly Rick and his habits and explained how he came to be there, how I found him, my T-shirt, Burberry Boy keeping me too long at the hardware store. I apologized to Porrocks for not having asked permission to share the work.

Then I noticed something. "The curtain is missing." I went to the window. "Wasn't there a curtain here, Erma? You pulled it back when we came in this morning."

"Yes, I guess there was."

The cops had called for a detective and a wagon, but now the wagon radioed and said they were stuck somewhere. So Porrocks and I followed the two cops into the boat well and watched them reach down and haul Rick's body out of the water. They carried him into the kitchenette, where river water ran from his clothes and puddled on the plank subfloor.

One of the saddest things I've ever seen was that body lying there.

Doubtless the cleanest he'd been in a long time, Rick sprawled there in rigor mortis, his left leg hitched up at the knee, as if he'd been felled trying to mount a horse. His eyes were open, engulfed by the terrible blank knowingness of death.

"Well," one of the badges observed, "looks like alcohol might not've been his only problem."

"What do you mean?" I asked.

"Look," he pointed to Rick's left temple, which showed an oval blue mark just above the eye.

"Oh," I said.

Porrocks reached down and flipped Rick's overcoat up, covering his face. "He could have hit his head as he fell in," she remarked.

The Wyandotte cops looked at her, then at me.

"I hear the wagon," said Porrocks, turning away.

Six

Later I went to Greektown to look for Young Brenda. She wasn't in any of the usual zones of hopelessness, and I asked around without success. There was a waiter at Pegasus who sometimes gave out stuff to the alley people; I buttonholed him, and he said he'd seen her sitting beneath the monorail when he arrived for his shift. I walked around there, but she'd moved on. At least she was still ambulatory. I had to count on the police to contact the social services agencies for help identifying Rick. He must have kin somewhere.

Neighborhoods never stay the same. Blind Lonnie, the guitarist I used to busk with, had met a woman and gotten involved. She kept him home almost every night now, and I'd heard they were planning to move to the West Coast. I missed Lonnie, the beacon of sanity among the street personalities. Listening to a few measures of Nat King Cole or Johnny Mercer would've done me some good right then.

I went home. These days I dreaded opening the door of my flat, never knowing whether Todd would be there in body, spirit, or either. You know how when somebody is old and sick you have the growing sense that they could just up and die any day? And then, of course, they do. I know the trick is to be very Zen-like about it and not dread the moment. To accept it.

The trouble is, I'm not a very Zen-like person.

My heart was all jagged when I put my key in the lock, but it smoothed right down when Todd calmly rounded the corner from the dining room.

"Hello, Toddy."

He bumped up to sniff my shoes. I wondered if he could smell what I'd been through. If he did, it didn't bother him; he rubbed his chin first on the toe of my right sneaker, then the left, as always.

"How're you feeling, friend?"

He looked up at me with his button-bright black eyes.

I got down and stroked his fur and pulled ever so gently on his ears at the base, like loosening the root of a plant. He liked that. His fur was still brown; he hadn't gone gray at all. He was an ordinary short-haired rabbit who'd been born to be a food specimen for the state fair until I took him in. Nobody would guess he was eleven. I washed his dishes, put in fresh water, and gave him a few timothy nuggets. Although I'd been finding green leaves for him from people's berry canes and so forth in the neighborhood, the autumn frosts were bringing that to an end. I'd have to buy timothy for him through the winter.

"I'm cold, Toddy. Are you cold?"

He followed me to the bedroom where I unbuttoned the white shirt Porrocks's neighbor had lent me, slung off my bra, and put on my blue cotton turtleneck and my red wool sweater over that. They were good colors: The blue was the true, saturated one that children in art class select for the sky, and the red was rich yet quiet, like a tomato muted by the thinnest skim of garden dust. I changed my jeans for my heavy cotton sweatpants. Before I dropped Audrey Knox's white shirt into the hamper, I stood there holding it, turning it over in my hands, feeling the cloth.

I prepared a hot-water bottle and placed it beneath Todd's bedding in case he wanted to warm up. Then we could both be cozy.

A pan of leftover beans and rice confronted me in the refrigerator. This would make the third night in a row for beans and rice. I tried to make my hand reach for them, but couldn't. I got out my frying pan and put in some oil. I sliced up a potato and set the pieces to cook, then cut up some broccoli. When the potato was soft I pushed the pieces to the side of the pan and threw in the broccoli. When that was hot I cracked in an egg and scrambled everything around with salt and pepper. Some cheddar cheese grated in would have been nice.

I got out one of my carefully rationed bottles of Stroh's. My little conservative voice said, *You've only got two left, and you have to make them last until Porrocks pays you, if she ever does after what happened today.*

Fuck it, I need a drink.

I ate my dinner, drank my beer, and thought about what had happened.

If I'd been Porrocks, I'd have been furious with me. But I guess I acted so furious with myself that she didn't feel right piling on. She wasn't crude enough to tell me she didn't need the hassle of a dead guy on her property, plus the damage Rick had done before he died.

She did ask me why I hadn't so much as mentioned Drooly Rick to her. I tried to explain, but it was like talking to a teacher who wants to know precisely why you decided to apply streaks of warm tar from the playground asphalt to your arms and legs at recess.

You did it because you wanted to. You didn't know the tar wouldn't come right off; you wouldn't have thought to discuss it with an adult before you did it. And why is that? Well, you knew that adults didn't go around digging warm tar out of the cracks in asphalt and applying it to their bodies to see how it would feel and look. But you didn't know *why* they didn't do it. For all you knew, no adult had ever thought to try it. For all you knew, adults would see your tar streaks and say, "Wow! Neat! What a kid!" For all you knew, you and your tar would go down in history.

Yet you also knew from experience that adults generally gave new ideas the thumbs-down. And you didn't know, but you sensed that their feeling for interesting things and sensations had grown dull. So your brain naturally shied away from trying to deal with the adults on their terms, because you knew they'd have you whichever way they wanted you. You didn't bring things up.

And most of the time—most of the time!—your approach worked. You did stuff, and no one was the wiser. But on those occasions when things turned to shit, you saw the fallibility of your system. Still, it's hard to let it go.

I didn't try to explain all that to Porrocks. All I said was, "I thought everything would be all right. Erma, I'm sorry."

She said she'd talk to me tomorrow.

Porrocks had brought her sleeping bag to her new house and told me she intended to use it for the two nights until the movers brought her stuff. I thought of her now, lying in it on the floor of her new bedroom.

After I finished eating, I washed up the dishes and sat on my living room rug with Todd. The vet had told me there wasn't much he could do for my pet, who, with his stiff little joints and failing heart, acted like an old man who knows his strength is ebbing but is determined not to save any. Every now and then he'd stop whatever he was doing and tremble. Then he'd get on with it, moving with more alacrity than you'd expect. Whenever I got down on the carpet, he'd come right over, ready to sit and be petted or play a game. We invented some new ones that weren't quite as intense as the ones we enjoyed when he was younger.

One current favorite was Nudge the Duck, which involved me placing my toy bathtub duck between us. I would give the duck a nudge with my finger, then Todd would nudge it back toward me. It was a simple, comforting pastime for both of us.

This night we played quite a long round of it, and afterward we just sat together, and I thought some more about what had happened to Drooly Rick.

He got drunk, went to hang out in the boat well, perhaps wanting to relax on the couch we'd moved out there, and he stumbled and fell, hitting his head on the way down. He tore into the wall before or after he found the peach brandy. Okay, I hadn't forced him to drink that alcohol. I hadn't tripped him into the water. If I'd asked Porrocks about Rick in advance, she probably would have said yes. It's likely nothing would have happened differently.

So I should let go of feeling guilty about Rick, I should let go of feeling guilty of having brought trouble to Porrocks. The cops, after talking some more to Porrocks and me, sent Rick's body away for autopsy. Porrocks's wall could be fixed. The rest of the house was all right. The police weren't going to bother her.

My brain stopped there. The police weren't going to bother her. I looked at the night sky out the window, the stars mixing themselves through the branches of the horse chestnut tree.

My brain got going again. *Well, what if Rick* didn't *die by accident? What if somebody killed him by bashing him in the temple and pushing him into the water?* Porrocks had been the only one around. I said, "Pft," into the empty air of my living room. Why the hell would Porrocks want to hurt somebody like Drooly Rick? "No sense," I said to Todd. He snugged his hindquarters deeper into my lap, and we sat quietly until it was time to get ready for bed. No matter how troubled I was, Todd always made me feel more centered, more competent.

Before turning out the light I read a ways further into *Encounter in Borneo*. It was absolutely excellent. Calico Jones meets up with Ingrid, the Swedish biophysicist—and wow, I was right: This Ingrid's a babe, just an incredibly radiant woman with that fiery Swedish beauty. So the basic thing is, Ingrid is part of a team of scientists funded by the socially and environmentally conscious nations of the world. This team is working on a project to reverse global warming and return the world to its normal climate. It's a machine they're working on, this astounding machine that will produce certain weather effects. The machine requires large amounts of activated charcoal, and the charcoal's got to be mined, of course, and that's another whole problem—extracting all this activated charcoal gently and caringly from the earth—plus then the charcoal has to be mixed with tiny, tiny synthetic emeralds. It's going to be a large machine—naturally, you'd expect that—and it's going to be stationed on a decommissioned supertanker and be able to go all over the world, then from remote ocean locations it's going to be switched on and gradually save the planet.

So where does Calico Jones come in? Well, one of the scientists working on the machine goes crazy and steals all the emeralds and sells them to a corrupt government. (Guess which country it was. I'll give you a hint: one of the North American ones that *didn't* get on board with the Ottawa Climate Petition—and it wasn't Canada.) And he's decided to make his *own* machine because he wants to hold the world hostage to his insane demands for profit and power, and the horrible complication is that he isn't using safe, clinically tested materials like activated charcoal and synthetic emeralds—he's using a strain of genetically modified insect larvae! He's developing it in Borneo, where the warm, damp weather suits these larvae. Can you imagine the danger—if those larvae got loose they'd overrun the earth! Because they're genetically modified!

So these scientists call on Calico Jones to find and stop this guy. Ingrid's the go-between. She is *hot*. You just know Calico's going to have the adventure of a lifetime, plus save the world. I never can remember the name of the author of these books, but I stand in awe of her talent.

In the morning I decided I wanted to give Porrocks a token of friendship, something that might make her feel okay about continuing to know me. I wanted to keep on working for her. I wanted that money.

I rifled my cupboards for baking ingredients and came up with half a bag of sugar and a canister of white flour, which I hadn't opened in quite a while. I did so now and peered in, the telltale black pinheads of weevils instantly informing me I'd left it for too long.

My landlady, Mrs. McVittie, was an excellent baker and cook. I went downstairs and knocked, and she invited me in.

"How are you, dear?" She was the kind of elderly woman who always asked other people about themselves and never complained about her own troubles. She was married to the oft-crabby Mr. McVittie, she was well into her eighties, she had Parkinson's or some kind of tremor-producing chronic illness, she was diabetic, and she had a hell of a time keeping weight on. She frequently shared food with me, in sort of a skinny-girls' solidarity.

"I want to bake something for a friend," I told her. "I want to make a little gift. What would you suggest?"

Her eyes lit up. "Why don't we make a pan of gingerbread, dear?"

"You mean you'd give me your recipe?" Her gingerbread was out of this world. Although her diabetes made her forgo sweets, she loved to do cakes. She did cakes for all the family birthdays, showers, funerals—you name it.

"Sure, but let's just make up a pan together right now!" She tottered off to her kitchen, I followed, and after about fifteen minutes of concentrated activity her dinged-up baking pan was in the oven, and about two minutes after that the smell in her kitchen was extraordinary.

She made coffee, and we sat down and chatted until the timer beeped.

Due to some new drug, her tremor had stopped getting worse. I'd handled all the delicate tasks like cracking eggs and measuring the spices.

"Where's Mr. McVittie today?" I asked.

"Jeff needed help with one of his cars, so Emmett went over." Jeff was one of their sons. With both hands, she lifted her coffee cup to her lips and sipped. Though her lips were seamed and thin, her chin was strong.

I asked, "Have you tried any of these new sugar substitutes they have in the stores?"

"You mean in my baking?"

"Yes."

"Oh, I did try one kind but Emmett didn't like it, and to tell you the truth, I didn't either. I thought it tasted all right, but I just could not enjoy eating that cake. It felt wrong to eat cake after having avoided it for so many years. I started to feel a little sick! Isn't that silly?"

"Not at all, I can understand that."

"Force of habit."

"Yes."

We talked about the weather, and she asked about Todd.

"Oh, the little guy's doing okay, I guess. You know."

"He's my favorite bunny of all. He is just so good."

"He is. He is, Mrs. McVittie."

While the gingerbread cooled on a rack, I went out and got the rake from their garage and tidied up their yard. Inches of oak and horse chestnut leaves had fallen in the last few days, and I raked them all over to a big pile at the curb. The city would come by and scoop them up next week.

I took the gingerbread over to Porrocks's house with a couple of coffees from McDonald's. She let me in and protested about the cake, but once she smelled it, she couldn't wait to have a piece. I saw in her eyes that she felt sorry for me. I didn't care. We ate and drank together, and everything was all right between us.

Seven

Porrocks didn't make me ask to keep working for her; she seemed to take for granted that I would.

"You know, Lillian," she said as we sat on her dining room floor finishing our coffees, "except for the wall, the work you guys did yesterday was well done."

"Yeah, thanks. I tried to keep us on track. Oh, God, poor Rick."

"Yes, well." She drummed her fingers on her jean-clad thigh.

"I wonder what the autopsy will show."

She made no comment, and my sentence hung in the air. After a minute she said, "Lillian, you shouldn't need to be told this, but there's not going to be much, if any, interest in this Rick's death."

"What do you mean?" I asked, like a moron.

In her precise, dry voice, she said, "The Wyandotte police have plenty to do looking after the people who live here, who pay their salaries—assaults, property crimes, all of it. Think about the headline: "Street Guy Found Drunk and Dead." Now, if you're a cop you've got these other headlines every day: "Estranged Husband Beats Up Wife for Filing Divorce Papers," "Armed Robbers Hit Jewelry Store," "Car

Thieves Target Church Parking Lot," "Rival Fans Threaten Rumble at High School Homecoming Game," "Speeder Ignores New Traffic Light, Kills 3." Okay? Do you think those cops care about Rick? They *resent* Rick for having bought it on their shift. They resent *you* for having brought the guy here from an alley in Greektown. Even if somebody did sneak up on him in the boathouse and conk him on the head, what are we looking at? A serial killer?"

"Yeah, but—"

"Did you expect them to call the crime lab to dust for fingerprints? For the apparently accidental death of an unemployed bum? You want every cop to treat every report with the same level of urgency? Come on, Lillian, even you know that's not real."

"I know it, but I don't want to know it."

A line from *The Grapes of Wrath* ran through my head: "Vagrant foun' dead." *Yeah,* I thought, *who cares?* Helplessly, I said, "But once they start the investigation—"

"Lillian, I'm trying to tell you the investigation is *over*! They investigated! They came and looked around and asked questions and wrote it down and left."

I sighed.

Porrocks said in a gentler tone, "Why don't you get back to work out there, get started on that kitchen tile?"

I rose to go.

She said, "I'm going back over to my condo for a couple of hours now. I'm almost ready for the movers tomorrow." She picked up her purse and keys. "I'll be back before dark. I'll stop at the ATM and bring you some pay. How about that?"

"Sounds good, Erm. See you later."

"Oh, wait," she said. "I forgot to ask you something: Are you handy with things like computers and stereos?"

"Uh, well, not very. I mean, if you need somebody to hook up your stereo system for you, I'm sure I could do that. But computers and me:

bad medicine. I don't know why—maybe an adding machine tried to attack my mother while she was pregnant with me or something. What do you need?"

"Well, the stereo system, but it's kind of tricky because I want it to connect with a new TV I'm buying, one of those plasma screens."

"Wow, cool."

"And then, yes, my computer. And I have to decide on connectivity. Do you know anything about DSL and satellite and all that?"

"No, but I know somebody who'd love to handle all of it for you. 'Member Lou, my friend the animal control officer?"

"Lou?"

"Big hefty gal, she's the one who saved my bacon when I got shot by that—"

"Oh, yeah!"

"She's an electronics genius. She's the one who put that radio beacon on my car, you know, so she knew where to find me when—"

"Yeah!"

"And she's got a PC and stuff. She links into all this esoteric NASA stuff and all this complicated shit, and I know she's savvy about satellite TV and all that. Want me to call her?"

"Please. Could she just stop in when I start to unpack?"

"I'm sure."

"Ask her to come by tomorrow evening, if she can. I'll pay her for her time, of course."

"Okay."

My palms started to sweat the moment I began walking to the boathouse. I'm not usually hen-hearted, but I had to force myself to open the door. My mind's eye started up the whole movie of me finding Rick and getting help and him lying sopping on the floor.

The boathouse was empty and silent, of course, but for the lapping of the water beneath. I'd brought my tools. I took a deep breath.

"Well, Rick," I said, "if your ghost is here, give me a clue as to what happened. Like, what I really need is reassurance. Porrocks is acting strange, don't you think? I mean, the way she doesn't seem to be all that shook up about this. Well, maybe that's just a cop for you." I set my stuff down and turned to the kitchenette, where my tile demolition job awaited.

And, oh, dear God, there he was. If I'd been the fainting type, I'd still be out cold.

Yes, there was Rick, on the floor there in the kitchenette, exactly as the cops had placed him when they pulled him out of the boat well.

All right. It wasn't the *body*—it was the silhouette of the body, imprinted there in the layer of black mold on the plank subfloor. The wood itself was hard and intact, but when the cops laid Rick's body down, his wet heavy body made a grayish imprint that stayed after the river water had dried. His torso, head, his arms and legs—the one cocked up at the knee—were very clearly marked. Evidently the floor had sagged over time; the water that streamed from him had collected near an outer wall.

I heard Porrocks's car leaving.

The picture on the floor looked as if a man had been shot or stabbed. He'd fallen, and his blood had flowed away. The cops' footprints were visible as well, as they stepped in and out of the wet places.

I wondered if the imprints could be cleaned away. I scuffed one of the cop marks with my sneaker; it remained.

Someday Porrocks would put new vinyl down on that floor, and cover over the impression of Rick. Or she'd have the planks sanded and treated with urethane, and the man's last mark on the world would be gone.

I turned away, not wanting to work in the kitchenette just yet. I remembered that Rick and I hadn't broken out the tile floor of the bathroom, so I picked up my wrecking bar and started down the little passageway to it. I stopped.

The wall that Drooly Rick had torn into looked so bad, like the ragged mouth of a bomb hole. Of course I couldn't fix it, but I thought maybe I could even up the job somehow, at least bring down the last bits of plaster to the floor. Then a carpenter could drywall it up again in no time.

I worked my pry bar into the plaster between the laths. Satisfyingly large chunks popped off, raising the same kind of dust I'd coughed on just before I found Rick. My ears liked the cracking sounds better than the silence. I watched the dust settle.

"Rick," I said, "you must have bashed your ass off here and then *run* out to that boat well to die. Because the dust hadn't settled when I walked in."

I pried more plaster off, working now in the very bottom corner. My bar struck something that softly went *chink*. I stopped and peered into the dark space. I put my hand in and felt around. My fingers closed on something hard and cold, resting on what felt like a bed of leaves, papery and rusty.

I pulled the cold object out, set it on the floor, and looked at it.

It was metal, four bars about two inches long by one inch wide and maybe an eighth of an inch thick. The bars were drilled at the ends and connected by round links.

And the bars and links were unmistakably gold.

The color was right, but most of all the weight was right. I picked them up again—yes—that remarkable heaviness of solid gold—and saw a rough clasp, and realized it was a bracelet. It was crude and heavy, too big for a woman's wrist, it seemed. My hand passed through it easily. There was nothing fashionable about it. I reached into the wall again and grabbed the rustly stuff. It was currency, of course, and I brought it out in handfuls.

"Holy hell," I murmured. "Loot." Reflexively, I glanced over my shoulder toward the window and door. I got up and peered out. I was alone.

I knelt and thrust my hand in again, feeling the sill board of the wall. There was no more. I popped off the last few inches of plaster just to make sure.

In the pearly wash of light coming through the window I inspected the bills, and saw that some were American and some Canadian, which was momentarily exciting: bootlegger loot! But there was Queen Elizabeth's picture on the Canadian, and none of the dates on the U.S. stuff were older than twelve years ago, so they couldn't have been put there by a Prohibition-era rumrunner. All the bills were at least three years old, which narrowed down the time frame a bit, not that I knew the time frame of *what*. There were twenties and a few hundreds with the newer Ben Franklin picture.

I straightened the money and counted it: $120 Canadian and $560 American. Not a fortune, but more money than I'd seen in a while, boy.

Kneeling there with my hands on my thighs I blew out a stream of breath. I picked up the bracelet again. A distant bell was ringing in my head.

My mind wandered around all the outlaws I'd known. It free-associated through my life, pausing at the murderers and thugs: a woman who liked to kill women she liked, a guy who tried to get even with his old girlfriend by throwing acid at her, a trio of insurance fraudsters and arsonists, a kid who stole hubcaps and saved the hock money for college. My mind wandered farther still, away from criminals, to a friend who imported handmade art papers from Oaxaca—rolling papers, marijuana—a stanza from "Singin' in the Rain," then a rainbow, then Judy Garland's oddly thick eyebrows as she leaned against the hay bales and sang before the twister came, Mrs. Gulch trying to smuggle Toto in her basket to the sheriff, smuggling, contraband, drugs, marijuana again, a girl I hitchhiked to Galveston with one time in the hope that romance might lie south of everything else. A Tex-Mex bar there where I got happily drunk on Dos Equis with a bunch of strangers who didn't try anything on me.

One guy that night was wearing a bracelet just like this one. I hadn't thought about that guy or that bracelet in all the years since. Another guy at the table told me it was a drug smuggler's bracelet. I looked at the guy wearing the bracelet. He looked mean and smart, so I believed it. The other guy, more of a weenie type, a groupie-type guy, whispered to me, "Each bar weighs an ounce, see? And there's four of them, which makes a quarter-pound of gold on your wrist. The pilots carry money this way. So if you have to bail out or run, you've got your money on you. Down in South America that's how they do it. I had one of those for a while, but I—I gave it to a girl." He watched for my reaction hopefully.

"How did you get it?" I asked, intrigued.

He winked. "I can't tell you."

"I see." I sat back and sipped my beer.

"Because I'm with the CIA."

"Oh."

"So I can't tell you."

This guy looked dense enough to have joined the CIA—I mean, he had a GATLINBURG IS FOR LOVERS T-shirt on—but my bullshit meter was squawking, so I dismissed everything he said. I forgot the guy, and I forgot the bracelet.

Whenever a guy in a bar tells you he's with the CIA, it's automatic bullshit. Automatic.

The bracelet in my hand looked just like the one that the mean-looking guy had been wearing. I perceived that a great many of these bracelets, cached with a great many handfuls or bundles of currency could have fit into the space inside that wall. A stash of drug money? Yes, indeed. For that matter, bundles of drugs could have been hidden in the wall. Robbery loot too, maybe. I'd come across the mere residue of whatever had been there.

I leaned into the broken wall and sniffed, but did not detect the heavy fragrance of marijuana. It wouldn't have made sense to stuff pot in there anyway, no matter how well-wrapped: Pot's pretty bulky and more or less perishable, losing potency with age. A bolt of cleverness shot into my mind: I licked my finger, touched it to the dust that had settled all over everything, then to my tongue, as Jack Lord used to do on *Hawaii Five-O*. It tasted like dust. Not knowing what cocaine or heroin was supposed to taste like was a drawback here.

"Okay, now," I said to the imprint of Rick, "the question is, did you find the loot or did somebody else? After we figure that one out, we want to know who has it now."

Rick remained silent, and I began one of my Lillian-to-Lillian discussions.

Me: The next step is to show this stuff to Porrocks, right?

Me: Um, well…

Me: What is it?

Me: Porrocks acted funny about Rick. She didn't wonder what happened, like cops are supposed to do.

Me: How do you know what she wondered?

Me: Well, when she flipped up his coat and said he could have hit his head falling in, that was just adopting the easiest explanation.

Me: Well, he could have.

Me: I know, but plus she didn't really respond today when I talked about Rick. Then she gave me that speech about how busy cops are.

Me: Well, cops do have to prioritize, like everybody else.

Me: All I'm saying is she ought to be upset about this and at least somewhat open to the possibility of a crime here.

Me: Would *you* be eager to have a murder investigation going on in your house?

Me: That's hardly the point. Cops are supposed to want to get at the truth.

Me: What if Porrocks already *knows* the truth?

I paused.

Me: Go on.

Me: What if *Porrocks* did Drooly Rick in?

Me: Oh, my God.

Me: Remember she said there were two guys who came and broke down that one wall, then left?

Me: Yeah?

Me: There were no two guys! That was Porrocks breaking up walls in her own house to find the drug loot she knew was there!

Me: How did she know?

Me: That's what I'll have to find out. Rick got drunk when I went out, forgot that we weren't supposed to break the wall down, then Porrocks walked in and found him looking at all this booty that spilled out, and killed him! She wanted to do me a favor, but then she wound up having to kill this guy to keep things quiet.

Me: Wow.

Me: So really, should I show Porrocks this little bit of stuff I just found? Given what she said to me about cops being busy, should I tell the police about it?

Me: No and no.

Me: Not yet, anyway.

Eight

I gathered the money and tucked it and the bracelet into the zip pocket of my windbreaker, then rolled up the jacket and set it next to the canvas tote bag I'd carried my tools in.

I began demolition on the bathroom tile and strategized about how I would conduct my investigation of Porrocks. One or two ideas came to me, centered on learning the history of the house. When you start poking around in other people's business, one thing invariably leads to another. You don't have to have a thorough plan in advance. This is good.

I imagined myself as Calico Jones—zooming about the expressways of Motown in my turbocharged sports car, checking in with my contacts in the underworld, arranging dates via satellite phone with several incredibly attractive women all in one weekend, respectfully consulting with local law enforcement yet far surpassing them in courage and ruthlessness, gently helping downtrodden people gain vengeance and self-esteem, reluctantly but graciously accepting public recognition in the form of medals, framed certificates, and reward money.

Calico Jones doesn't have to spend days on her knees chipping out broken tile with a wrecking bar for fifteen bucks an hour. She has people for that.

Over the course of the morning I got tremendously absorbed in my work. I figured out how to leverage my pry bar in the small spaces around the toilet and under the sink. In the absence of my excellent portable AM-FM radio which I'd long ago hocked, I began humming. I hummed this tune I'd heard two street guys playing on accordion and drums, this punkified German folk song. It was dottily energetic and I hummed it twice. I hummed "Blue Skies" and "Standing at the Crossroads of Love" and "Maxwell's Silver Hammer."

I tried to prevent myself from wondering how much that gold bracelet was worth, but wonder I did. What was an ounce of gold going for these days? What carat gold was the bracelet? I became lost in a cocoon of fantasy and rhythmic work. I got down on my side to reach a shard of tile that had flown into a crevice next to a vent. I was stretched out full length, my feet sticking into the passageway, my arms over my head, reaching, humming "Dance Ten, Looks Three," when someone touched my waist and said, "That's a familiar tune. What is it?"

"Whuff!" I cried, and bashed my elbow on the toilet. "Ow!"

"Whoa there, slim girl," Audrey Knox said as I scrambled to my knees, then to my feet. I caught a glimpse of myself in the bathroom mirror: I needed more than a haircut. My ordinarily smooth bob was sticking out in sweaty quills, my overly long jaw was thrust forward tensely, my eyes were panicked, and my nose looked pointier than ever.

"Hey, beautiful," Audrey said.

"Goddamn," I said.

"Did I scare the hell out of you, Lillian? A little ticklish there?"

"Yes! No! What are you doing here?"

She smiled as if she'd just been painted by Rubens, her cheeks gathering like buds. "Thought I'd see if you were all right."

"I *was*," I said, rubbing my elbow and eating her up with my eyes.

My visitor was wearing a butt-hugging black-and-gold wool plaid skirt with a black velour turtleneck that outlined her plump arms and swelling chest, little soft-soled black shoes, sparkly fishnet hose, pink lipstick, and that incredible smile.

I said, "It's a song from *A Chorus Line*: 'Dance Ten, Looks Three.' Known informally as 'Tits and Ass.'"

"That's it!" Audrey licked her lips.

I waited.

Eagerly, she said, "Quite a bit of activity over here yesterday!"

"Yes," I said. There was this awkward moment when I tried to figure out what to do. My nerves were zinging. I set my wrecking bar on the toilet tank. "Uh…"

"Well, can you take a break for a few minutes?"

"Yes, of course."

We went out to the front room. My rolled-up windbreaker with the cash and the gold bracelet glowed with a guilty brown aura. It was only this simple bundle sitting on the floor but I glanced at it as if it might shout something.

Audrey strode across the imprint of Rick and hopped up on the kitchenette counter. She perched there, legs crossed, little shoes swinging.

"Did you," I wondered, "watch the cop cars and everything from your window?"

"Yeah, I've got a great view of this place."

Audrey Knox was a femme for sure, with the soft curls and the clothes, but underlying all that was something a touch hard-bitten. She was young, in her twenties—late twenties, I supposed—but there were these very faint stress lines around her mouth, curving downward. Maybe early thirties. And there was a little counteracting upward tilt to her chin that wasn't saucy; it was a fighting-the-dark tilt. I wondered when we would kiss.

She said, "They took a body out, didn't they?"

"Yes."

"Well, what happened? Do tell!"

I felt horrible all over again about Rick.

"You can tell me," she urged. "Oh, you poor thing, you're still upset. I'm sorry." She hopped down and came to sit cross-legged with me on the floor. I began talking, and she stroked my back as I told her most of it: being broke, Porrocks's generosity, the street people in my life.

"I—it shouldn't have happened," I tried to explain. "I feel responsible, and there's the possibility that his death wasn't an accident. I mean, that bruise on the head. The police really don't give a shit. He was only a bum, you know."

"But he was your bum."

"Yeah, he was my bum." I said nothing about the money and the bracelet. Our voices rang in the empty space.

Audrey said, "I'm impressed by your—that you know so much about the streets. All those street people."

"Well, I don't think it's something to boast about."

"You look so worn-out. Why don't you come over to my place for a few minutes and let me take care of you? I'll give you something to eat."

I was hungry but said, "You're very kind, but I ought to keep working. I should get back to it in a minute. Thanks just the same. Oh! You're probably wondering about your shirt."

"No."

"I haven't gotten to the laundry."

"Please keep it."

"Oh, no, I couldn't, I'll just—"

"You looked really good in it, you know," and she flicked up an eyebrow. "Trim and strong." I suppose she could have rented a billboard that said AUDREY KNOX IS FLIRTING WITH LILLIAN BYRD. That would have made it very slightly clearer.

I asked, "Who are you, Audrey Knox?"

She laughed a laugh that was somehow tinkly and hearty at the same time, like wine bottles tapping together. "Let's see, who am I? I'm the third great-niece of a Hungarian countess, and I'm hiding in America from a gang of microchip manufacturers who think I sabotaged their factory in Patagonia."

"Have you ever read the Calico Jones books, by any chance?"

"The who?"

"Never mind."

"And tomorrow I might be a sex-toy inventor who needs a subject to practice on!" She showed me the tip of her pink tongue.

"My goodness." How pleasant this all was.

"I'm not very worldly, in fact. I've led a very sheltered life."

"I see." I wasn't sure why she said that.

"Um, so, you still want to stay here and work?"

"Tempted though I am, I'd better. Porrocks is counting on me to get this stuff done. Have you met her by the way—your new neighbor, the woman who bought this house?"

"No, not yet." My visitor lifted her arms and fluffed her hair away from her neck. Everything she did was alluring.

I swallowed. "Well, I'll introduce you. She wants to get to know her neighbors—go to block parties, do candelaria on Christmas Eve, crap like that."

Audrey Knox said, "Well, can I get you to come over later?"

I shook my head.

"Tomorrow, then?"

"Porrocks's truck is coming tomorrow, and I guess I'll help her unpack. Maybe I can stop over afterward. Or we could just get coffee sometime."

"She's moving right in, then? Good!"

"Yeah, she told me there were a couple of break-ins while the place was vacant. Have you noticed anything? Anybody prowling around the neighborhood?"

"Hmm. No, not really. Well, I thought I saw a guy one time." She stroked her jaw with the back of a finger.

"Yeah?"

"I dunno, just a guy walking around."

"She thinks kids are breaking in. Well, the place'll be safe enough with her in it, given her line of work." I got to my knees, which were sore but not enough to make me wince.

"What is that?"

"Porrocks is a freshly retired cop. She knows all about dealing with trouble."

"She must be going to install an alarm system, then," Audrey Knox decided.

"No, no, those things are junk. She doesn't need them. I'm talking about her judo certificate and her small but well-tuned collection of firearms."

"Oh, I see. That'd do it, wouldn't it?"

"You said it. She'll be back later to spend the night in her sleeping bag."

"And you'll continue to work on her place? For how long?"

"Yeah, it's a pretty good gig: fifteen bucks an hour, cash. I'm not really sure for how long, but there's weeks' worth of work to be done in that place."

"She must like having you around—quite a lot!"

"Well, I think she's just—"

"Did she give you keys and stuff—I mean, are you *really* good friends?"

"Oh, no. I mean, we're on good terms, but I don't have keys. She's left the boathouse unlocked because I've been coming and going, you know."

Audrey Knox wasn't the sort of blowhard who's always yakking about herself. She listened to me and was interested in me and her new neighbor Porrocks. Yes, I liked Audrey Knox. And she sure as hell seemed to like me.

Nine

Porrocks the next day demonstrated admirable control over the chaos of moving. I'd started work in the boathouse early, then stopped when the truck came and pitched in to help her organize boxes according to her labels. At lunchtime she opened a cooler full of sandwiches and Cokes for the movers, herself, and me.

I monitored her for suspicious behavior. When she handed me a chicken sandwich I thought, *The sandwich of a killer?* When she laughed at a joke one of the movers made, I thought, *The laugh of a gangster? The crazy chuckle of a double-dealing cop?*

It was hard to be fair.

Her cell phone rang in her pocket, and she answered it by just saying, "Porrocks." She used to answer the phone, "Detective Porrocks speaking."

She turned away from the movers and me and spoke for just a minute or two. "Uh-huh. Yeah? Was there any—right, I see.... What does Bob think? Yeah.... Well, thanks very much."

We all chowed down, then the movers got back to work. Porrocks didn't want my help then, so I went back to the boathouse. Before turning to go down the driveway I looked up at Audrey Knox's windows. I couldn't tell whether she was home. I'd laundered her shirt.

A few hours later I heard the moving van start up and leave, and I went back to the house. Porrocks was already unboxing stuff, flattening the cartons and stacking them neatly, cramming the packing paper down into one carton.

"I'd like you to open some boxes for me," she said, "but first I want to talk to you."

She stepped around a stack of boxes toward me and I went instantly tense.

"They did the autopsy on the John Doe—your Rick," she said.

"Already?"

"Yes, the M.E. called today when we were eating." She looked at me. A wisp of her fine gray hair had escaped her dotted kerchief, and she brushed it out of her eyes. "I can still pull a string or two."

I relaxed. "Why did you, Erma?"

"I knew you were anxious to know."

I was taken aback. "Wow, Erm, thank you. Thank you. What did they say?"

"Very high blood alcohol: over two. No surprise there." Porrocks spoke matter-of-factly, her thumbs hooked in the belt loops of her jeans, her posture straight. "The blow to the head happened before death, but not much before. Linear fracture of the temporal bone. Do you know that that bone is the thinnest bone of the adult skull, right here?" She reached out and touched my temple. I almost flinched but held still. "There's a blood vessel right there, and the cracked bone tore it, just enough to make him hemorrhage into his brain, which probably killed him quickly. They did find water in his lungs, but not a lot, which indicates he was dying when he hit the water. The blow wasn't delivered with crushing force, which counterindicates an attack."

"But doesn't rule it out." I sat down on a box.

Porrocks bent to put her hands on her knees, stretched her back, and straightened up with a small grunt. "Correct."

"So essentially we're talking inconclusive."

"Correct, technically."

"What do you mean?"

Porrocks pulled off her kerchief, smoothed her hair, and put it back on. "You can only prove that a crime happened; you can't prove that a crime did not happen. You can't prove a negative, right?"

"That's right."

"No empirical evidence of foul play was found. The absence of evidence is significant, do you see?"

"Yes, I see. Thank you, Erma. How can I find out if his identity has been established?"

"I'd call the Wyandotte PD."

"Okay."

"Now, how about unpacking those? My electronics. Lou's coming soon, right?"

"She said she would."

"And do you have an interior decorator in your pocket as well?"

"Huh," I said. "I do know a good one, but he's out of town on a job. He's more of an architect-slash-designer, but he sure decorates great too."

"Would that be your friend, um, Don?"

"It's Duane. Yeah. Get this: He's in New York City redoing Minerva LeBlanc's place."

"Really!"

"Yep, I hooked them up."

Minerva LeBlanc, the true crime writer, was a friend of mine too, more or less. We'd started up a romance based on a couple of mutual investigations, but then she came out with a book about how my parents died by mistake in this arson case that also involved first-degree murder and insurance fraud, and I kind of couldn't deal with it. She changed the names, but still it was upsetting to me to have my family history sitting there on people's laps in airplanes and book groups. Our relationship cooled to nothing.

Now, lifting Porrocks's stereo components out of their cartons, I wondered what Minerva would make of what had happened on this property in the last couple of days.

A little past five, Lou rang the bell. I reintroduced her to Porrocks in the foyer; then she stepped in, wearing her Detroit Department of Health animal control officer's uniform and equipment belt. She stood in the room solidly, feet apart, and said, "Good to see you again, Detective Porrocks," in her rock-crusher voice.

"I'm not a detective anymore!" Porrocks said uncharacteristically liltingly, which showed how uncomfortable she was about that—and how long it was going to be before she'd be able to move on.

"Once a cop, always a cop," Lou said firmly, and I could tell Porrocks appreciated that. "I just got off my shift," Lou added, gesturing at her outfit. "So." She unbuckled her equipment belt, which she could have left in the truck, but I'm sure she wanted to give the first impression of her full ensemble. I understood that. Lou looked exceedingly competent in her uniform. She'd grown heavier over the years—a bit of jowliness, a bit more fat spilling over her belt—but her brown eyes were clear and earnest. You'd expect such a butch to wear a buzz cut or at least a mullet, but Lou kept her salt-and-pepper-gray hair in a long ponytail, which she invariably secured with a black elastic band. She was rather old than me but younger than Porrocks.

"Now," she said, "what can I do for you?"

Porrocks explained about her components and stuff. "And the PC can go right here on this desk."

"Processor on the floor, like here?" asked Lou.

"Good idea," Porrocks said and then began asking Lou a series of questions about digital TV and dedicated lines and all that. She hunkered down and watched Lou work while they talked. I saw Lou's meaty face smiling as she unkinked cables and methodically lined up remote controls. Lou did not smile broadly, her smile was more of a general facial uplift, which some people would take to be an ordinary neutral expression, but for Lou it definitely was a smile. Lou loved to do things for people—well, for women. I wondered if she was seeing anybody. I got the feeling she wasn't.

"Erma," I said, "I'll see you a little later tomorrow. I've got a couple of things I need to do."

"Okay."

I bid the two of them adieu and took off.

I'd stashed my little bundle in the most remote crevice of the Caprice's trunk, rediscovering in the process the unopened pint of Mad Dog I'd confiscated from Drooly Rick. I fired up the Caprice and drove it around the corner, parked on the street, and walked up to Audrey Knox's building with the bottle of wine under my arm and her shirt folded in my hand.

"How come you moved your car?" Audrey said as she opened the door to her apartment. "What's this?"

"It's the stuff winos drink, Mogen David 20/20. It's fortified. I moved my car because if Porrocks looked out and saw my car still in her driveway after I'd said good night and left, she'd be confused."

"So you haven't mentioned me to her?" Audrey Knox gave me a little sly look. Sexy. Boy, the woman was sexy.

"I like things to be simple," I said. "Here, thanks for the shirt."

This evening she wore yet another wool skirt outfit, this one an elfin-green mini with a magenta jersey top, close-fitting and smooth over her torso. "You're looking lovely this evening," I told her.

"Aren't I, though?" she laughed.

I laughed too.

"Here," she said, "I'll get a couple of glasses. Have a seat."

I evaluated the seating choices and decided on the couch. It was a no-brainer, to be honest, since she didn't have much furniture—just a bright amber-colored rug, a couple of folding camp chairs, and then the couch, a worn, thinly padded thing but comfortable enough.

"Ah, that's it," said my hostess, returning with two jelly glasses and a can of mixed nuts. I unscrewed the MD with a flourish and poured, and she popped the ring on the nut can.

I didn't realize how tense I'd been until I let down. We drank the horrible wine and nibbled the nuts, and I relaxed. My mind was still working on everything, but I did begin to relax.

"I can call out for a pizza," Audrey said. "Shall I?"

"Great idea."

It turned out we liked our pizza the same way: cheese, pepperoni, mushroom. Porrocks had paid me some money, so I felt okay. I could chip in.

While we waited for the delivery, Audrey tuned in WDET on a little boom box she had, and we listened to a bluegrass program and talked.

"Do you play softball?" I asked, noticing a couple of bats propped in a corner.

"I did, in the summer."

"On a team?"

"Naw, just pickup with friends."

"What position do you like to play?"

"Pitcher." She offered me her forearm.

"Oh, yeah?" I reached for her arm and felt the muscle. "You must be good." I wanted to go on holding the lively, firm arm, but set it down on her lap with care.

"I only throw strikes."

What can you do but just smile at that?

Audrey wanted to discuss Rick and Porrocks again, but I wanted to get my mind off all that. "Audrey Knox, where do you come from and what do you do for a living?"

"Didn't I tell you that I'm a refugee from an orphanage where they made us dance to Billy Joel songs for our supper?"

"You told me something like that, but seriously, do you, like, work?"

"I'm a hostess in a brothel."

"Really?"

"No, babycakes, but you wish I were. Here's the pizza guy."

We ate the pizza from the box perched on a plastic Parsons table and sipped our wine.

"You know, Mad Dog goes pretty well with this," Audrey observed.

"How do you know it's called Mad Dog?" I asked, amused.

"I thought you called it that."

"Maybe I did."

Eating, I felt better but still troubled. Audrey picked up on it. "Is something bothering you, Lillian? Talk to me about it. It's okay. I'm serious now."

"Well, the thing is this: I think something funny happened over there."

"Funny as in?"

"As in, like, maybe Drooly Rick just sort of accidentally died, but I really feel that—maybe I shouldn't actually utter it, but—"

"Just say it, you'll feel better."

I looked at Audrey Knox, her soft eyes shining almost Todd-like in their unquestioning openness. Taking a deep breath, I said, "I think Porrocks knows something."

"Like maybe she—"

"Like maybe Rick got into something he shouldn't have, and she decided to shut him up."

"A secret?"

"Yes."

"Oh, Lillian. How could she? How could anybody?"

"Well, I'm not saying she did. Listen carefully, I'm not saying she did. It just feels peculiar to me. There's something off about the whole thing." I didn't mention the treasure yet. I didn't feel quite secure enough to.

Audrey said, "I wonder what kind of secret! What do you think it is?"

"I don't know," I said uneasily.

She suggested, "Maybe there was some connection between Porrocks and Rick that went back a long way, you know? Something nasty between them."

"Hmm. I like how you think, Audrey. Like what?"

"Like, oh, I don't know. I wish you weren't so troubled. Here, why don't you put your head in my lap, and I'll try to smooth out all that worry."

Before I could say, "Uh," she grabbed my shoulder and pulled me over. Her hands fluttered about my head, then settled at my temples. Her fingertips began circling slowly and evenly around the ridges of my skull.

"There," she murmured, "there."

My breath came easier, and I forgot everything except the sensation of Audrey Knox's small smooth hands on my head. Her fingers searched my scalp for tight places and worked on them patiently, persistently. I felt so luxuriously *liked*.

After a while she rested her hands on my forehead, and I thanked her. "I'd like to return the favor," I said, "in perhaps a slightly different way." I sat up. "Where do you feel tight?"

Audrey Knox smiled. "Well, I blew out a disc in my back once, and it's never been quite the same."

"Oh, that's too bad. I bet it just hurts sometimes."

"It just hurts sometimes."

"And I bet it's hard to make it feel better all by yourself."

"It is, it is."

"Let me see."

Audrey rolled onto her tummy on the couch and I folded her top up, exposing her fine-grained back skin. Her shape was so pleasing.

"Here?" I said.

"Yes, there."

And she sighed and purred as I worked my hands into her resilient flesh, flesh I'm almost tempted to call succulent but for the fact that I had not yet tasted it. Her body was exactly the right mix of lean and fat—firm, not bony at all, with little indulgent places of softness. Oh, what a jubilation it was to touch her.

I concentrated on that one area of her back, the upslope from low to mid, about ten inches along her spine, knowing that the anticipation of more was just as important as the more, if you know what I mean.

We spent more time on the couch, trading caresses under the guise of therapeutic healing. I had a hurty place on one thigh, and she remembered that she'd strained a shoulder not long ago. Eventually, I murmured, "I have to be going soon."

Audrey Knox sat bolt upright. "What?"

"I—I have a pet at home that I need to go and care for."

"A *pet*?"

"Yes, he's a rabbit named Todd. He has a heart condition and needs me."

Audrey Knox just looked at me.

I went on, "He's old, you see, for a rabbit, and he gets a little anxious if I come home late. I don't like to stress him unnecessarily." That sounded silly, but as you know, I was as devoted to Todd as I'd have been to a human.

"We don't," said Audrey, "have much time, then."

"Well, I thought maybe we'd save—"

But she lunged for my lips and I never did finish that sentence.

We didn't fuss with anything; I kicked the Parsons table out of the way, the pizza box skittered for cover, and we more or less cascaded to the floor in a tangle of knits and worsteds and denims that quickly got sorted into a pile.

Audrey's rug was new and clean, I smelled that furniture-store fragrance, and the room was warm with good old radiator steam heat, so we were quite comfortable. I discovered that Audrey was wearing a truly killer black bra and panties, skimpy yet serious. It was almost painful to my eyes to see her pale, buttery skin contrasted with the stark black stiffness of the lace trim, so I took care of that problem.

My mind said a little parenthetical thank-you to itself for having chosen my most unshabby underthings this day. Oh, perhaps I'd just had a feeling that morning.

Somewhere Audrey had gotten a tattoo of a bunch of yellow daffodils above her left breast, and I decided I ought to count all the petals sometime soon. But for now I focused on the two firm rosettes she'd grown on her own. My, what pretty things they were: Such rosettes could decorate a cake, and it would be the nicest cake you'd ever see.

All the parts of Audrey were just as sweet and delicate, and I breathed in her aroma, which changed marvelously as I moved along. It was like shopping on a street in Italy or some fabulous country—here was the bread bakery wafting warmth from its door, here the pushcart full of savory vegetables and light cheeses, here the stand of candies and fruits. I helped myself to it all and went back for more.

It was the most blissful evening I'd spent in a long time, and by the time I dragged myself into my clothes and picked up my keys, I realized that I'd never felt so well nourished.

Ten

After breakfast the next morning I took Todd out for a romp in the McVitties' frosty backyard grass. He bumped around beneath the cloudy sky, checking out a pile of rosebush prunings and a new gopher mound, then turned to me and seemed to heave a little sigh.

"What is it, Todd? You tired already?" Usually, outdoor playtime invigorated him. I squatted down. He was trembling, though I didn't think he could be very cold. When I picked him up his hind legs jerked convulsively against my stomach. "Oh, Toddy."

I took him upstairs and looked him over. He didn't seem to have lost any weight. In a few minutes he felt a little better, hopping around the living room as if to show me. However, when I introduced the idea of playing a quiet round of Follow the Finger, he wasn't interested. I petted him for a while, checked his water, and went out.

I stopped at the Gas-A-Rama on Nine Mile, put ten dollars' worth of regular in the Caprice's tank, bought four packs of Camel Filters, and headed for Greektown.

Morning, not too early, is always the best time to deal with street people. The ones who use drugs or alcohol—that is to say almost all—

have experienced the slight detoxifying effects, however marginal, of a night's sleep, and now they're up and out looking for a little food as well as that first hit or drink or at least a cigarette. They're the most alert you're going to find them all day.

I parked the Caprice on St. Antoine, broke open the cigarettes, and stuffed all four packs into my pockets. Wearing my Chuck Taylor basketball sneakers, jeans, and wool peacoat, I hit the pavement.

You might tell me it's wrong to give cigarettes to street people, that I should give only food. But let's be real: It's not as if lung cancer is a chief concern for you if you're living from food stamps to public toilet to garbage bin. Most street people will die from complications from their other addictions long before cancer comes around. At least smoking doesn't make you slur your words. And smoking a butt can be a real comfort on the street—something to share, something to do, something to trade. I understood that much anyway.

The street people who aren't addicted to destructive things are few and far between. Runaways tend to fall into that category merely because they haven't had enough months or years of substance abuse under their belts to qualify them as addicts.

The air was cold, not freezing, but you knew it was coming: The sky had that high, overcast, thinking-about-snow look. I walked up the streets and down the alleys and spoke to the people I met, giving out the Camels three or four at a time. Brand-name cigarettes are a luxury on the street. Everybody I talked to I invited to meet me on the steps of the church in about an hour. People asked me about Rick; naturally Young Brenda had told them all that I'd taken Rick away and nobody'd seen him since. I didn't tell them about Rick's death; I wanted to talk to Brenda first. I learned that she'd been seen behind Pegasus that morning, so I ambled over there.

I found her in a rare vertical position, leaning against a brick wall talking to a couple of Detroit foot-patrol officers. I'd never seen foot patrollers in Greektown until the casino had opened, now they were around all the time. They intervened if they saw some tourist open his wallet to give something to a street person. I couldn't blame them for this—it's their job to discourage enabling behavior, as I'd heard one of them put it.

The two cops, one a guy and one a gal, were chatting with Brenda in that neutrally friendly way cops have, and she looked about the same as when I last saw her, except her clothes had been washed. Her hair was pulled back in a rubber band, making her face look so terribly tired and drawn, yet it was animated in the meth-habit tradition of little tics and quivers.

The guy cop was saying, "If you go back to the shelter, they could help you sign up for job training."

"The shelter's a hellhole," replied Brenda.

"What do you call this alley, then?" said the other cop.

Brenda looked down at the filthy concrete. "It's not so bad," she muttered, her cheek twitching.

I said good morning to the cops, who eyed me.

"I'm not giving out money," I told them. "I just need to talk to Brenda here for a minute." I invited them to meet us at the church steps later.

"What for?" the guy cop asked.

"Just a little…gathering."

The cops walked on without saying anything else.

"Brenda," I said, "I'd like to buy you a coffee and a bun or something, okay?"

"Where's Rick?" she asked suspiciously.

"Let's go, okay?" I turned toward the mouth of the alley.

She followed me into a café where we sat at a little table and I ordered coffees. She said she didn't want anything to eat, but I got her an egg and toast anyway. As we talked, she did eat a little, pricking the yolk of the egg and dipping the corner of her bread into it. Her eyes were slits against the bright restaurant light.

"I'm sorry to tell you that Rick's dead," I began.

She turned her slitty eyes up. "I knew it."

"How did you know?"

"He—he." Brenda touched her forehead with her sleeve. "How to tell you. I was talking to a little kid at the shelter, and I was saying I like French fries a lot too, when Rick came around the corner by the bulletin board and showed me his stomach."

"His stomach?"

"Yeah, he opened his coat and there was a ball of sticks, like sharp sticks, where his stomach was supposed to be. And he said, *I'm dead for good.* Then he walked away."

"Well, I don't know what the bundle of sticks is about, but—"

"A ball of sticks, like a ball of sticks." She interlaced her fingers, cracked with dirt and grease, to show me.

"Okay, well, whatever. The fact is, Brenda, he had too much to drink and fell into the river."

Brenda's mouth kept moving all the time even when she wasn't talking, and when I talked, she uttered little syllables under her breath, like *buh, vee, vee, buh,* over and over. She flicked a fingernail at the tabletop, then at a sore on her face.

I asked, "Did he say anything else, when he talked to you? Did you get an impression of anything, like whether he was alone when it happened?"

"No."

"Okay. Do you know his last name?"

"Yes." Brenda seized the sugar server and did about a five-count pour into the half-cup of coffee she had left.

"Well, what is it?"

"I can't remember."

"Brenda, do you think you'd like to see your sister in Clarksville?"

"I dunno. Yeah, I guess so. Tell her to send a limo! Hah!"

"I can buy you a ticket and help get you on the bus. There's one leaving at one-thirty."

She agreed but wouldn't tell me her sister's name so I could call ahead. I told her I wanted to do one more thing before I drove her to the station. We made a circuit of Greektown together, giving out more cigarettes and issuing the church-step invitation. "There'll be more cigarettes," I added.

When we got to the steps, there was a knot of half a dozen street people, plus the two cops.

I gave out cigarettes, which the cops didn't object to, and passed around a book of matches. Everybody lit up, including the cops. I mounted the stone steps and stood before the carved, pretty, locked doors.

"This is as close to God as the likes of us can get at short notice," I began. I tapped out a Camel for myself, lit it, and took a good long hit. Exhaling, I said, "I have an announcement to make. Our friend Rick has passed away. Some of us knew him as Drooly Rick."

The cops looked at each other, then nodded to me.

"And some of us," I went on, "might have known him as Rick the sorry unfortunate bastard." Some other heads bobbed up and down.

The street was fairly quiet—nobody much else out, just delivery guys unloading liquor and linens for the restaurants. Pigeons pecked around in the gutters.

"I don't know yet if Rick has any family, or even his last name. Does anybody here know?"

My congregation shrugged and puffed their cigarettes hungrily.

"Well, I thought people might want to, uh, share their memories of Rick today."

A guy with one good eye and one empty socket tugged on his beard and said, "Rick never hurt nobody."

"Amen," said another guy whose face and hands were so dirty you could only tell he was white by the part in his hair, which oddly was nicely combed.

A woman who looked fairly okay except for a squirrel tail hanging from her coat pocket cleared her throat. Everyone turned to her. She said, "I just want everyone to know I never stole that tape deck."

"Amen," said the dirtiest man again.

"Well," I said, "I think Rick was a decent guy who just had a few hard times in his life. Things were looking up for him a little bit."

The guy cop spoke up. "Rick tried to be a good citizen."

Young Brenda began to cry. "I loved him!" Her voice pitched upward, making a pigeon scoot away in a ruffle of molting wings. "Oh, how I loved that man! Now he'll never see our son!"

"Your son?" I was flabbergasted. "Oh, my God—are you pregnant?" Brenda sobbed into her coat sleeve.

"She could be," said the lady cop.

"No," Brenda said, snuffling, "but I wish I was carrying his child."

"Oh," I said. "Well, unless somebody has something else, let's wrap it up."

Another guy said, "One time Rick. One time Rick." We all waited, but he couldn't get any further.

I concluded, "Thank you all for coming. God bless Rick, and God help all of us."

Eleven

After putting Brenda on the bus, I swung over to the Detroit Public Library and spent a little time online, surfing around the Wayne County sites in the property records departments.

To my mild surprise, Porrocks's purchase of 201 Adderly St. had been posted. And she'd gotten a hell of a good deal: $125,000 for a house I'd have guessed would've cost twice as much—I mean, the waterfront location, the size, the boathouse, the nice deep lot. The work it needed plus the extras Porrocks wanted wouldn't set her back more than another fifteen or twenty grand, I judged.

The seller's name was Mrs. Helen B. Donovan. To find out how long she owned it, I would've had to search the sales records year by year, so I looked up the tax records. Mrs. Donovan, evidently along with her husband Jeffrey J. Donovan had paid the taxes on the place for twenty-six years. Before that, there had been a string of four owners over about fifteen years, then another owner who'd paid taxes for almost fifty years, and it appeared he was the one who had built the place. Since Mrs. Donovan's name was on the record of sale solo, it was likely that she was a widow or divorcée.

So, given the dates on the money I'd found in the wall, this Helen B. Donovan was where I needed to start. I went back to the record of her sale of the house to Porrocks and found that the proceeds went to her at an address in Ohio, evidently not a private residence. The address line said, "Erie Shores Care Center," then gave a number and street. I wrote it all down in my notebook.

I headed to Wyandotte via I-75, the Caprice's engine laboring up the steep grade of the Rouge River overpass. Ford's Rouge complex lay below: a dark, powerful, incredibly massive organism stretching to the smoggy horizon, its towers and tanks and pipes and steam columns and waste-gas flames only hinting to the world how much goes on in there. The new model year was coming up, and I wondered whether Ford would keep on the path of retro styling, given the success of the revised Thunderbird. I longed for a car like that. The Caprice was burning even more oil these days, and although I kept adding oil as necessary and once in a while would splurge on a bottle of gas treatment, I figured the engine wasn't going to last another year without a ring job. Have you ever had to pay for one of those? On top of that, the transmission was beginning to slip under hard stress, and rust had made a travesty of the once-proud body. When I started it up or revved it, the loose body panels hammered against the frame like thunder.

I tried to do right by the car, but you know how it is. People with plenty of money and a utilitarian attitude about cars say, "Well, it finally reached the point of diminishing returns. Time to quit repairing it and get me something nice and new." Well, I needed something nicer and newer, but there was no immediate chance in hell for that. Yes, I could stop buying oil and save twenty dollars over a couple of months, and yes, I could stop paying my mechanic to coax and jerry-rig and improvise, thus saving a few hundred more over time. But where was I going to get a better car for $300?

Moreover, I loved that car. It was police secondhand, originally an unmarked detective car, and I believed that its law-and-order karma had lent me a low-level, unnameable sort of protection at critical moments. I thought about the Caprice, and I thought about the distance from Detroit to Cleveland.

The lieutenant who agreed to see me for five minutes at the Wyandotte PD was a walrusy guy, cheerful in spite of being so busy. I asked about the results of Rick's autopsy, and he told me readily enough what the report said, which jibed exactly with what Porrocks had told me. Yes, it had occurred to me to double-check that. The cop said they still didn't have any information on Rick from the social services people.

"Are you gonna run his prints?" I asked.

"We did that already, and nothing." He looked at me kindly.

"I guess he was a law-abiding guy, then."

"Prob'ly was."

My afternoon at Porrocks's was quiet for the most part. She worked on her unpacking in the house, and I continued work in the boathouse, attacking that kitchen tile. By this time I'd generated a few knee-high piles of rubble in addition to all the old carpet and linoleum, plus there was the scuzzy old furniture. When I took a break, I went to the house and offered to haul the junk away.

"What would you haul it in, your car?" Porrocks asked.

"No, Erm, I'd rent a pickup for a day, make one or two trips to the dump, and you'd be all set. I'd do it as soon as I finish ripping everything out."

"Good idea. Okay."

"Say, did Lou do a good job for you?"

"Oh! I'll say. She's great. Everything's working perfectly, and there wasn't a question I asked that she didn't know the answer to." Porrocks started telling me about what kind of satellite dish she'd ordered that morning, and I tuned out.

Late in the afternoon I was standing in the kitchenette, panting after having wrestled the heavy electric stove away from the wall and out of the way near the window. I heard a little tapping noise on the glass and turned, hoping to see Audrey Knox, but it was Lou pecking at the pane with one finger, in the most delicate gesture I'd ever seen her make. I let her in.

"Where's Erma?" she said, her face so openly emotional that I almost ached for her. I'd seen that look before.

"She's not at the house? I guess she went on an errand." I wiped my hands on my jeans. "Yeah, come to think of it, she said she needed some stuff from the store—shelf paper or something. Do you need to talk to her?"

"Oh, I just came by to see how she was doing, how everything was. I'm off duty."

I looked at my watch, and it was indeed after five already. "Well, she said you did a wonderful job."

"She did?"

"Yep. What's that behind your back, Lou?"

"Oh, it's just—I was gonna drop this off, uh, for, uh, her." With a little chuff of embarrassment, she showed me a box of candy.

Ordinarily, when you want to give a girl a box of candy, you buy a pound of dipped chocolates. You know, an assortment of chocolates in brown crinkle papers nicely arranged in a candy box. But Lou had bought for Porrocks a retail-pack carton of Baby Ruth bars, a dozen of them, which I knew to be Lou's favorite kind. Lou was like a third-grader in some ways: What she liked she thought everyone else would naturally like too. Lou had once been in love with me.

"That's very sweet," I said. And while being in love with me, Lou had saved my life. "I'm sure Erma will like this gift very much."

In spite of my gratitude, my feelings for Lou had not been reciprocal, and we were fortunate to work things out to be friends instead. We had a good understanding.

"Well," Lou said anxiously, rocking forward on the toes of her thick black duty boots, "did she—did she say anything else? About me?"

"Uh, I don't think so."

She heaved a dopey sigh. "She's quite a woman, isn't she?"

I knew it. "Yes, Lou, Erma's terrific."

"Well, when d'you think she'll be back?"

"I really don't know. You want me to tell her to call you?"

"Oh, no, no, no." Lou stood gnawing her lip in frustration.

I picked up my wrecking bar and said, "Well, I ought to get back to it here, so—"

"Oh, right, right. Hey, Lillian! I brought something for you, too." She pulled a small object from her pocket and handed it to me.

"What's this?"

"It's a laser pointer."

"Oh! Well! How nice. Thank you."

"It's for Todd."

"Uh, that's very thoughtful of you, Lou, but he hasn't been doing presentations lately, and I'm not sure his future schedule is going to permit—"

"It's to play with."

"Lou, explain it to me. I don't get it."

"You turn it on and make a dot with it on the floor, and you move it around and Todd chases it."

"Oh!"

"He'll love it. I do it with my cats all the time. You should see them, they're so funny. That's a very good laser pointer. I got it at the Gibraltar Trade Center—a guy was *giving* them away for five bucks."

Knowing Todd, I doubted he'd give more than a contemptuous glance toward such a high-tech, insubstantial toy, especially one liked by cats. But I politely thanked Lou again. Pleased, she turned to go.

"Wait a second, Lou."

She swung back to face me.

"Uh," I said, "you know, I'm not at all sure that Porrocks is—"

"My type?"

I paused. "That's one way to put it, yes."

Lou didn't want to hear it. She pressed her lips together.

I said, "Lou, I don't want you getting hurt, is all."

"How do you know I'll get hurt?"

"I don't. I don't. I'm just saying I don't even know if there's a first base to get to here, you know?"

"Yeah. Well!" Lou squared her shoulders and tossed her iron-gray ponytail. "I'm not a little piece of china, Lillian. I'm not a little baby bird. You don't have to worry about me."

It wasn't only Lou I was worried about.

Twelve

That night Audrey Knox came over with a bag of food from Good Fortune 2, the Chinese place up Woodward. I'd offered to cook, but she said she was in the mood for their Szechuan chicken. Something spicy sounded good to me too, if you know what I mean. Tonight, Audrey was wearing a pair of black slacks and these extraordinary little black shoes with white vamps with green four-leaf clovers embroidered into them. They were cute and amazing shoes.

I introduced her to Todd. He wasn't feeling well; he sniffed her pretty shoes and turned away, bumping over to have a sip of water. I noticed he'd hardly touched his timothy nuggets. I got out a carrot top, which appealed to him somewhat.

Audrey looked like a happy sparrow, her eyes alert, head high, as she gave herself a tour of my apartment while I unpacked the food and set the table. She looked at all my stuff, my books and mandolin, my stovetop percolator, with the right amount of interest and appreciation.

"This is the coolest coffeepot in the world," she said. "Where'd you get it?"

"Goodwill," I said. "Let's eat."

I don't consider myself to be sluttier than most people, but I do tend to get involved quickly when it's someone I really like. This has made for good times and bad times, but at least they've been times, you know?

Audrey and I ate the savory food at my kitchen table, drank Stroh's, and talked. I wanted to know more about her, but she joked away my questions about her family and livelihood. She'd flick her eyes down with each joke; some pain going on in there, I sensed, old trouble, most likely old wounds she wanted to keep covered up. It would be a matter of time, I judged, until she revealed everything to me. I could be patient until then. She did open up, however, about her unusual footwear. I was really curious about those shoes.

She stretched out her leg and carefully placed her foot on the edge of the table. I admired the expertly worked shoe.

"Well," Audrey said, "a guy I used to know back home was a cobbler."

"Really? They're custom-made?"

"Yeah, he took my measurements and asked what I was in the mood for, and I said something lucky and old-fashioned."

The shoes were retro for sure, with the two-tone thing and the embroidery.

"What are they made of?"

"Kidskin."

"Must've been expensive."

"Yes" was all she said.

I couldn't make out any exact regional accent in her voice, so I decided to use a ploy that always works. "You know," I said, "I've been listening carefully to how you talk. I'm pretty good at guessing where people are from based on their speech habits."

She smiled and leaned forward, resting her chin in her hand.

"Well?" she said.

"Southern Indiana," I suggested.

"Nope. Guess again."

"Hmm. Am I warmer if I say the greater Philadelphia area?"

She laughed her funny little laugh. "No!"

"Mountain states?"

"Now you're warmer."

"Denver?"

"No."

"Cheyenne?"

"No."

"Billings?"

"You're getting closer."

"Boise."

She smacked her head. "Bingo! Lillian, you're amazing!"

"What's Boise like?"

She sipped her Stroh's, and a soft light crept into her eyes. "It's beautiful. The town itself, well, Boise's Boise—know what I mean? But all you have to do is walk a mile in any direction, and, oh."

"Mountains like on TV, huh?"

"And the Snake River—rocks and water forever. It's so wild. You can relax there more than you can anywhere else."

She brought up the Porrocks thing. We were alike in that way, both of us with a taste for the morbid. She wanted to know if I still thought Porrocks killed Drooly Rick.

"I didn't say I think she killed him, I said I think she might know something."

"What's the difference?"

"Maybe not much. I don't know. I'm looking into the background of things."

"What do you mean?"

"Oh, God, Audrey." I sat and thought. Finally, I said, "Can you keep a secret?"

She got very solemn and very excited. "I can keep a secret in a place it'll never escape from."

"Well, will you put this one there?"

"Yes. It's a good one, isn't it?" Her eyes sparkled. "Lillian, tell me before I explode!"

This is what was going through my mind: Maybe I could crack this dead-Rick-with-hidden-treasure thing by myself, but maybe I couldn't. I realized that Audrey Knox's proximity to Porrocks's house could be valuable. She could watch comings and goings if we wound up doing long-term surveillance on the place. We could join forces and solve a bizarre crime nobody else thought mattered.

So I described how I found the money and gold bracelet in the broken boathouse wall. When I finished, she was quiet, her index finger on her lips. Then she looked up and said simply, "You know Porrocks killed him."

"Audrey, I *can't* think that. I can't let myself think that."

"But you're thinking it."

"Unh!"

"Because you know it."

I peered into the neck of my Stroh's bottle.

"And she knows you know it."

I looked at her. "I don't think—"

"She knows it, and therefore you're in danger, Lillian."

"If I make her uncomfortable, why wouldn't she just tell me to forget the job? Pay me off and tell me to get lost? It isn't as if I witnessed anything."

"You didn't see a thing, didn't hear anything?"

"No, I wasn't there."

"Can you prove it?"

"What?"

"Do you have an alibi for where you were when it happened?"

"What in God's name are you talking about?"

"If she thinks you're onto her, she could try to frame you for it."

"Oh, my God."

I don't know if you'll understand this, but there was something tremendously sexy about this conversation. We were both excited—talking, speculating, being scared and thrilled together. Audrey Knox's eyes bit into me like power drills and it felt great. I had this suspenseful smile on my face.

"Do you suppose there's more treasure?" Audrey said.

"I wouldn't be surprised."

"Would you—would you show me what you found?"

I left the room, retrieved the loot from the bottom drawer of my bureau, shoved the Chinese food cartons aside, and spread the money and bracelet on the table.

"It isn't much compared to what must've been there," I said, "but—"

"It's beautiful, isn't it?"

I picked up the bracelet, which caught the kitchen light like a key in a hallway. "It's ugly compared to you," I said.

That really got her. She reached for the bracelet, hefted it just as I did the first time I picked it up, and draped it over her wrist. I remarked, "The gold looks good against your skin."

She tried to fasten the catch, and I had a sudden worry that she wished I would give it to her. But after fumbling for a second, she said, "Oh, it's so clunky," and put it down.

I would have given it to her except that it really wasn't mine to give, no matter whether it was crime booty or something else. If I was going to investigate this thing, I might need to show the stuff to some critically important individual.

We decided to move to the living room, where I lit a couple of candles and we lounged on some cushions I arranged on the rug. I played my mandolin for her. The mandolin is the perfect instrument for an audience of one: Its natural voice is sweet and reserved, yet it'll respond to sudden energy. You can be as agile on it as you want.

Audrey slipped her shoes off and lay back on the cushions, eyes closed, chest rising and falling to the simple rhythm of "Come Rain or Come Shine." It was very pleasant.

"That's a lovely sound," she remarked, "from such a plain little thing."

I paused. "It is plain." I looked at the flattop instrument in my lap: yes, a simple design, nothing fancy. "Over years of playing," I said, "a mandolin becomes richer and mellower, if they used good wood in it. That's happened to this one. I don't know why—something about the vibration that makes the wood molecules line up better or something."

I played until she sat up with a big smile.

"That boathouse would be a fun place to make love," she suggested.

"Well, maybe, my little cupcake," I agreed, "if it gets fixed up. You saw what a wreck it is now."

"Ever made love on an actual boat?"

"No, have you?"

"It's nice. When the waves are right, you get a womb-like experience."

"Huh."

She noticed my copy of *Encounter in Borneo* on the floor next to the couch. "Didn't you mention something about this book to me? Calico Jones. What's the significance?"

Enthusiastically, I told her all about Calico Jones. When you go mad for someone new, don't you always want to share the things you like? "You'd love her. She's just tops." And I told her the story, as far as I'd gotten, of *Encounter in Borneo*.

You'll remember that Calico has met up with her go-between, this tremendously beautiful Swedish brainiac scientist who makes every other woman she stands next to look like a dog, except for Calico, of course. She and Calico have to meet in this out-of-the-way hotel in Singapore so as not to arouse suspicion. But I tell you, other things get aroused.

See, Calico has got to stop the rogue scientist who's doing the experiments with the mutant insect larvae in order to take over the world via climate control, and Ingrid fills her in on the relevant facts, and as she does so she falls in love with Calico—who wouldn't? And suddenly, she desperately wants to go *with* Calico on this dangerous journey to Borneo.

But Calico knows things are going to get really dangerous and violent, and she just won't put this amazing creature in harm's way. She says no.

So Ingrid tries to *persuade* Calico to take her along. During the days in this hotel, she briefs Calico on all the science and geography she needs to know for her mission, and during the nights she works on Calico to try to get her to take her along. I mean, consider it: five nights in a row of this gorgeous scientist who happens to be an expert in human anatomy, especially the *sensory systems*, throwing everything she's got into making Calico not be able to leave without her. Oh, my God. Calico is very aware that Ingrid is absolutely essential to the project to stop global warming, once new emeralds have been synthesized (which takes at least a week and a half), so Calico simply will not agree to let her come along. The safety of the world is more important to Calico Jones than a dozen incredible orgasms with a future Nobel laureate.

I read a couple of pages aloud to Audrey Knox, who lounged against my knee listening intently, her face turned up to mine, her lips parted in a small perfect smile.

When I paused, she said, "So, Calico, won't you take me with you?"

I put the book down. "My dear, I can't."

"Please."

"No, you beautiful Swedish brainiac."

She began stroking my legs. "Oh, please. Please, Calico Jones, I must go with you."

Instantly I was aflame with passion. "No, my intellectual lass, I cannot expose you to the kind of dangers I must face."

Audrey got into it. "But don't you see? That is exactly why I must go. I cannot let you face such dangers alone."

"No, it cannot be."

"I'll help," breathed Audrey Knox softly into my ear. "I'll be so helpful, you wouldn't believe how helpful I'll be."

"No," I said firmly, my diaphragm quivering.

"We'll see about that."

"I must repeat, no."

Audrey Knox twined her fingers into my hair and let them loose down my neck. "I'm not going to let you sleep until you promise you'll let me come with you."

I squirmed in ecstasy. "But, my dear, you must realize how much I care for your safety and that of the world."

For half the night we played Calico Jones and beautiful Swedish brainiac, and I thought I could never be so happy and wrought up.

Over coffee in the morning, all Audrey wanted to discuss was Porrocks. "Do you think she'll be happy in her new home?"

I was still glowing from last night and had to work to focus on what she wanted to talk about.

"Uh, yes, I think she's a pretty resilient person. She told me she's started taking long walks in the early mornings all the way to St. Edward's Park and back. Good for her health. She says she intends to make a habit of it. You know, I could stand to get more exercise myself—I ought to do something similar. Want to go for a walk with me now?"

"Oh, I don't think I have the energy." She smiled, remembering last night.

I smiled too. "Want some eggs or something, then?"

"Sure." She watched me open the refrigerator. "Imagine," she murmured, drumming her fingers on the kitchen table, "if you could get her arrested!"

"Oh, wow."

"Wouldn't that be something! You'd be a real-life Calico Jones!"

I fixed us toast and eggs, and we chatted about other things. I wondered about Porrocks. Everything about her seemed suspicious to me now—the way she engineered my working in the secluded boathouse, the way she wanted to go eat hamburgers with me when Rick was floating there in the pilings, the way she acted when she saw his body.

Even if the police decided to suspect her, how could they tie her to the death of Rick? First of all, there was no evidence Rick was hit or pushed into the water. If somebody went looking for clues, what could there be?

Porrocks's fingerprints would be irrelevant. Fibers from Porrocks's cloth-ing would be irrelevant. The boathouse hadn't been secured as a crime scene; I'd been coming and going and busting the place up. No, there was no way I was going to get hard evidence against her or anybody. All of this was distressing.

Audrey and I finished breakfast.

"I better get over there," I said. "But first, may I ask a favor?"

"Sure, Calico, what is it?"

My heart pounded with pleasure at that.

"Would you take a picture of me and Todd?" I'd been thinking about it, and realized we'd never been photographed together. It was something I wanted, and Mrs. McVittie was too unsteady to do it. I got out my Canon SLR, set it up, and showed Audrey how to frame the picture and click the shutter. I called for Todd, and in a minute he came bumping in from the bedroom.

I took him on my lap and sat on the living room floor, my back com-fortably against the couch. He snuggled down, but I made sure his face was turned toward the camera.

The strobe popped.

"There," Audrey said.

After she left, I got on the phone and confirmed that the Erie Shores Care Center, evidently Mrs. Helen B. Donovan's residence, was a nursing home. I asked to speak to Mrs. Donovan.

"She doesn't have a phone in her room," said the brainlessly coopera-tive administrative person, who sounded like a young version of my Aunt Rosalie with a cold, a little whiny but polite. "She's in the Reminiscence Wing."

"Ah, yes."

"Are you calling from a doctor's office, or—?"

"Uh, no."

"Well, may I ask what this is regarding?"

"Of course, I'm sorry! I'm Mrs. Lee with Merrill Lynch, and I need to secure Mrs. Donovan's signature to disburse some dividends. Simple matter of getting a form to her to sign."

"Oh, well, she doesn't sign anymore. Her daughter-in-law has power of attorney, so you'd need to talk to her."

"Of course. Could I trouble you for her information?"

She gave me the name, Lisette Donovan, and a phone number. I asked for the address as well, but she wouldn't give it, saying that if I sent something to the nursing home for Mrs. Donovan, it'll get forwarded to this Lisette and she'd take care of it. I thanked her and tried Lisette Donovan's number. There was no answer, and I decided a road trip ought to be in my immediate future.

I remembered that Audrey and I hadn't gotten around to eating the fortune cookies that came with our meal. I opened the packet and broke the first cookie I touched. There was no fortune in it.

Thirteen

Today was Wednesday, the day salaried folk call the hump of the week. I've never felt that way, though, seeing the work week as level all the way until Friday, when you get your unmistakable downslope into the weekend. It felt good to be working.

After greeting Porrocks I worked steadily in the boathouse until there was nothing more for me to do except haul trash. When I reported this to her she had me start removing old linoleum and tile in the upstairs bathroom of the main house. I'd gotten faster at the work and made good progress, and as I went along I thought more about Porrocks and the treasure. Without more information I truly was stalled. Casually, I tapped on the walls upstairs but couldn't tell a thing.

At the day's end before I unlocked the Caprice, I looked up at Audrey Knox's window. It was dark.

What to make of her? Was I in love with her? She was on my mind, sure, but there was so much else on it that I couldn't tell whether I was thoroughly infatuated, or just responding to her prettiness. I liked the feelings she stirred in my pelvis. I did a heart check: inconclusive. Well, I'd get to know her better. We hadn't yet done a life-story dump.

Usually, those come on the second date, the first being the date where nobody wants to monopolize the conversation for as long as it takes to tell her deluxe version, which is the only version worth telling.

When you do finally get the life story out of the way, then there's the compatibility part where you compare major likes and dislikes: politics, religion, hang-ups, goals, and so on. Then the day-to-day reality sets in, and that's where you learn the important stuff: how considerate? how receptive? how honest? how passionate about things other than sex?

For now, I wanted to keep my relationship with Audrey Knox in the fling category, though I didn't know how long I could. On some sub-skin level, she was working on me. I was beginning to feel protective toward her, though it seemed she believed I needed protecting—checking up on me over at Porrocks's, bringing food to my place. She seemed so vulnerable, really. Her guardedness about her past must have kept her pain—or shame, perhaps, same thing—at bay. Maybe I could ease her pain somehow, with patience and back rubs and long walks on drift-wood-strewn beaches.

One thing I wondered: gay or bi? Because with a butch, let's face it, you know. But with a femme, you can take nothing for granted. Why should I care? I didn't, exactly, but I wondered. I felt I could stand up to any female challenger, but if somebody decides to go for a guy over you, then it's not specifically personal, is it? So it's out of your hands, you have less to do with it, frankly. And if you really care for her, you want to be able to compete apple-to-apple.

I wanted to take care of Audrey Knox as Calico Jones would take care of someone special, if she ever had one for long. Her girlfriends kept getting killed by bad guys, or they'd fail to withstand the rigors of the Calico Jones lifestyle. I mean, you need to know how to rappel and clear a jammed cartridge and analyze trace elements if you're going to hang very long with Calico.

As I say, Audrey Knox was working on me. After I fantasized about solving with her what I was convinced was the strange crime in the boathouse, I daydreamed about the two of us going grocery shopping, a sure sign I was in deep. I decided to try to cool it emotionally for a little while, just sort of chill down my heart at present so I could concentrate.

When I got home I spent time with Todd, petting him and trying out the laser pointer. I made the garish red dot dance on the floor in front of him, but he just turned and gave a little sideways blink. The game was ridiculous compared with, say, Find Punkin', which we played with our usual enjoyment after I put away the pointer. To play Find Punkin', you take the potholder with a pumpkin embroidered into it that Aunt Rosalie made and gave you for Christmas ten years ago, and you tuck it into the back waistband of your jeans, and you say, "Where's Punkin'?" Todd, nobody's fool, hops around to your rear bumper, periscopes slightly on his hind legs, seizes the potholder, gives it a good chomp, and heads down the hall with it. You follow, get around in front of him, retrieve the potholder, and begin the game anew at that spot. You cover quite a bit of ground this way, so it's good exercise.

After that, I prepared a little dinner for the two of us, then played some old comforting songs on my mandolin, "Wildwood Flower"—Todd's favorite—"Shepherd's Hey," "Greensleeves," "Captain Jinx." Todd listened, his black button eyes shining up at me.

I showed up for work at eight the next morning, but Porrocks didn't answer the door. I waited and rang again, thinking she was in the shower or something. She didn't come to the door. Her Dodge was parked in its usual spot. Maybe she was out for her morning walk.

I sat on the front porch and waited half an hour, then tried the doors: locked. I went to the boathouse and looked around for something to do, but I'd picked the work clean there. I noticed some robust weeds growing around the shrubs in the backyard, so I got down on my hands and knees and pulled them, making a pile on the gravel walk. I went to the water's edge and picked up some rocks that were slumping from Porrocks's breakwater and repositioned them, kicking them more solidly into place. I cut a twig from the willow tree with my pocketknife and tried to make a whistle, but it was the wrong time of year; the bark was too tight on the pith. I found a moldering stack of split firewood next to the fence line, and two baby mice under one of the chunks. I left them alone, telling them, "Mama'll be back soon." And sure enough, the grass parted and there she came, tail high, hurrying to them with cheek pouches full.

At noon Porrocks hadn't come. She'd said, "See you tomorrow," so this absence wasn't planned. I inspected the house more carefully but saw no jimmied window, no scarred doorjamb. I drove to the White Castle, got some lunch, brought it back, and ate it in the boathouse. At around one o'clock I heard an engine in the drive. A man got out of a blue truck and said, "Satcom. I'm Andy."

He was there to put up Porrocks's satellite dish; when I told him she wasn't here, he said, "Well, I'll go 'head and put up the dish, she said chimney. Then when she gets home I'll run the wire in." So he got out his ladder and started work.

I crossed the street to see if Audrey was home; she buzzed me in.

"I have a funny feeling about Porrocks." I told her Porrocks hadn't shown up and asked to use her phone. Immediately she was concerned too.

"Of course," she said, and withdrew to the kitchen as I dialed Lieutenant Ciesla's direct line.

"Oh, hello," he said. "You got my message?"

"No, Tom, I'm calling about Erma. I'm afraid something—"

"That's what I called you about. She's in the hospital. Somebody barreled through a stop sign and ran her over at six o'clock this morning. Hit-and-run."

"Oh, my God. Is she gonna—"

"She's gonna be all right, but she's banged up pretty good—broken leg, broken pelvis. They're gonna operate on her."

"Oh, God, how terrible! Oh, Tom. Where'd it happen? Have they picked up anybody yet?"

"No, nobody saw anything. It happened at a crosswalk at the gate to this park down there—"

"St. Edward's?"

"Yeah. They don't have a plate—they don't have anything, just Erma's description of the vehicle, which isn't much."

"What did she say?"

"Black Chevy Blazer, she thinks, late model."

"The driver?"

"Didn't see the driver or any passengers. Listen, I gotta run."

"Where is she?" I asked.

"Wyandotte General."

"Okay, I'll go right over."

I turned to Audrey, who had come back into the room as I hung up, and told her what happened. She said exactly what I'd said, "Oh, my God."

"Yes, poor Erma."

"It sounds like she's really badly hurt. Very serious." Audrey bit her lower lip and shook her head, her eyes drooping with sadness.

"I'm afraid it is. I've got to go and see what I can do for her." I picked up my keys.

"Do they know how long she'll be in the hospital?"

"Well, I don't know—I mean, it just happened! I guess if they have to—what difference does it make?" I opened the door.

"Come over when you get back, okay?"

"Okay."

They'd patched Porrocks up in the ER and moved her to a regular room to wait for her surgery the next day.

She lay almost flat, very quiet beneath bandages and medical equipment and IV things, in a pool of soft light from the oblong fixture above the bed. The air in the room smelled of the standard hospital chemical mix: antiseptic, slightly bitter. Evidently, Porrocks had gotten some bad scrapes and cuts as well—swaths of gauze bound her forehead and most of one arm.

"Erma." I laid my hand on her nonbandaged arm.

She turned her head a tiny bit, painfully.

"Lillian." She licked her lips and swallowed.

"I'm so sorry."

Slowly, she murmured, "I'll be all right."

"Are they gonna put some pins in or something?"

"Yes." Her voice was weak, her skin gray next to the white sheets, but her eyes were fairly clear.

"Have they given you enough for the pain?"

"Yes."

"Look, don't talk. I'll just sit with you for a while, okay? And I'll do anything you need, okay?"

But she wanted to talk. "I don't know how it happened."

"Tom said you didn't see the driver."

"I looked both ways, started across. Then I realized there was something bearing down on me. Not going very fast, maybe twenty-five. But accelerating."

"Goddamn." *Accelerating.*

"I tried to jump out of the way. Guess I'm not as agile as I used to be." The bandages crisscrossing Porrocks's forehead somehow gave her a wise look, like a nun who's seen a lot. She looked tinier than ever in that be, her shoulders so narrow beneath the blanket.

"Black Blazer, right?"

"I just caught a glimpse. Black for sure."

"And not little, like a Jeep Wrangler?"

"No, a big one. I think it was a Blazer, but it could've been a different SUV."

"Oh, dear God, what a terrifying experience for you."

"I'm glad I'm alive."

"Yes. Do you have any family around?"

"My sister and her kids are in Wisconsin. Tom called her, I think. She probably won't be able to come. I'll be all right." She licked her lips again.

"Would you like some water?" I reached for the pitcher and cup on her table and helped her drink.

I heard heavy, hesitant footsteps and turned to see Lou standing at the door, looking pale and distraught.

"Lou!" I exclaimed. "Well, come in."

Tears rolled down her cheeks when she saw Porrocks.

"How did you hear about this?" I asked quietly, still holding the cup of water.

"Police radio. I got off duty as soon as I could." She looked at me with undisguised jealousy.

"Hi, Lou," Porrocks said.

"Detective Porrocks," Lou said, her voice cracking, "I swear I will kill whoever did this to you." She moved toward the bed, her face twisting in anguish.

I stepped back, and Lou sank into the chair next to the bed and sobbed.

Porrocks pressed her lips into a line.

"Lou, Lou," I said, "take it easy." I handed her Porrocks's tissue box.

A nurse came in to check the IV, ignoring Lou, who began to pull herself together.

"Erma," I said, "is there anything I can bring you from home, and would you like someone to stay with you here overnight?"

She shook her head slightly. "Would you do something special for me?"

Lou started to speak, but Porrocks went on, "Stay in my house while I'm in here, Lillian."

"Of course. I'll look after everything. The satellite guy was starting work outside when I left."

"All right. I think my keys came here with me. They were in my pocket."

"I'll ask the nurses."

"My purse is on the kitchen counter."

"Don't think about anything but getting through that surgery and getting well. I'll see you tomorrow."

She closed her eyes.

"I think she needs to sleep," I murmured to Lou, who didn't move from the chair. She gazed mournfully at Porrocks. I motioned to her to follow me into the corridor.

"You can do a lot to help her, okay?" I said. "Like the satellite guy's going to need some direction inside. She'll *need* that satellite dish when she gets home. Want to come with me and deal with that?"

"Yeah. It'll be really important for her to have her connectivity when she's at home recovering."

"That's right. You can come back tomorrow, okay?"

I got Porrocks's keys and Lou followed me over. The satellite guy was still working, having had to drill into the chimney masonry, so I unlocked the doors for Lou and went over to fill in Audrey Knox.

"I'm going to be your neighbor for a while," I announced.

"What?" She looked at me as if I'd touched her with an electric wire.

"Porrocks asked me to move in while she's gone."

"Oh." She took a measured breath.

"I was hoping for a little more enthusiasm."

"Uh, well, it's just so sad. You know."

"Yeah. I guess she'll be in the hospital for at least a few days. Then she'll need a lot of help at home while she recovers. Well, I'm going to go and get some of my stuff and Todd. Lou'll wait until I get back."

That night I changed the sheets on Porrocks's bed, found clean towels, and laundered everything from her hamper in her nice new Kenmore machines down in the basement. I put newspapers in the corners of one of the spare rooms, since Todd liked to mark new territory, and got him settled in there. The room had a window seat and a nice shaded lamp.

I felt peculiar in that big empty house, furnished so sparsely with Porrocks's condo stuff. I walked all around, restlessly turning on lights, my breathing sounding exaggerated. The more I tried to breathe normally, the more exaggerated my breathing sounded. I tapped on the walls and ceilings, and wondered whether a metal detector would prove anything, given all the copper wiring and plumbing. I looked out the kitchen window at the backyard. The blank black night looked back at me. Out on the river a buoy pulsed a pinpoint of white light, on and off, on and off.

A dog barked on the street, and I practically bit through my tongue. I looked for beers in the fridge; there were none. I was too cowardly to go out to the boat-house in the dark and retrieve the Galliano. I checked on Todd three times; he hunkered peacefully in his box, seeming to enjoy the change of scene from home.

I went to the living room picture window and pulled back the drape. Silhouetted in her window, Audrey Knox looked down at me. Golden light surrounded her. I lifted my hand, and she lifted hers. I beckoned to her, and she turned from the window.

Fourteen

As soon as Audrey crossed the threshold from the shadowy porch into Porrocks's gloomy living room, my heart strengthened. She brought light with her. I suppose it was her smile, her quick sparkling eyes, so glad to be there. Suddenly the house wasn't gloomy at all. She wore her elfin-green outfit tonight.

"You weren't," she said, "scared to be alone here, were you?"

"Of course not. I'm especially not scared now that you're here."

As soon as we kissed hello, Audrey wanted to see the house, so I gave her the tour just as Porrocks would have done. "And this is the dining room. Look at that built-in buffet, original finish. And aren't these oak floors beautiful?"

"Yes." In spite of her good humor, she seemed tense. There wasn't anything obvious enough for me to question her about it yet, though.

I showed her the work I'd been doing in the upstairs bathroom.

"Nice job," she said. She picked up my wrecking bar and turned it over in her hands.

"Ever use one of those?" I said.

"Uh, no, not exactly like this one." She hefted the bar, then set it down with a thoughtful expression.

"Is something wrong?"

"No, far from it."

"I like using tools. You get such a satisfaction."

"I agree."

"Well, there's no pressure to finish this bathroom now, Porrocks won't be using it for a long time. I'm going to see if Lou and I can carry her bed downstairs." Talking to myself now, I said, "I ought to bring some books for her—some books and CDs."

We finished the tour back in the living room where I'd left the drape askew. A black triangle of night sliced in on us. I nudged the drape closed.

We lounged on the couch. Audrey nestled into me and said, "Don't you think Porrocks is a killer anymore?"

"She might be. But I feel so goddamn sorry for her, lying there so racked up. Moreover, if that accident was in fact an assault, she might be as innocent as Drooly Rick was. If someone hurt her deliberately, it means someone wanted her out of this house."

Audrey looked up, her deep brown eyes wide. Slowly, she said, "I hadn't thought of that—at all. Lillian, you're—and I don't mean this sarcastically, I mean this sincerely—you're a genius."

"Well, thank you, but although I feel quite smart at times, I know I make bad judgments. I'm not always a good judge of people, for instance."

"Oh, I can't believe that!"

"It's true," I insisted. "You'd be amazed at the mistakes I've made."

She laughed, "Ha ha ha!"

"But you, you're so easy to talk to, you're so easy to be with. I really enjoy your company. Did you notice how the house went from cold to warm as soon as you walked in?"

"You make me blush."

I was secretly pleased to be called a genius—who wouldn't be? Yes, being called a genius gives you a feeling of savoir faire.

I kept thinking about Mrs. Donovan in Cleveland, and I thought about the fact that Porrocks wouldn't need anything from home tomorrow. The surgery would take hours, and then she'd be doped up. If she'd been run over deliberately, then this thing was escalating, whatever the hell this thing was. Why waste time?

I buried my lips in Audrey's soft curls and kissed the top of her head. Holding her close, I said, "I have an idea. You know how I said I was looking into the background of all this?"

She nodded into my arm. I could feel that she was tense, all right, and I didn't understand why. Maybe something about Porrocks's place made her remember some old pain.

"Well," I said, "I want to go and talk to somebody out of town, and sooner is better than later, I think."

She looked up. "Who?"

"Audrey, honey, it's just too—I mean, I'm embarrassed even to go into it. I might be being just a stupe here. I'll tell you all about it when I come back. Now I'm getting ahead of myself. Here's the plan. I promised Porrocks I'd look after the house. And given recent events, leaving the place vacant overnight, even just for one night, would be a bad idea. The trip I want to do might just be a one-nighter, but I don't know for sure. One thing might lead to another, and I could be away for a few days."

I felt her relax; she sort of sank into my arm; she knew what I was going to ask now, and she felt good about it. She really wanted to help.

"I want to hit the road early tomorrow. Would you look after this house while I'm gone? If so, you'd be doing me—and Porrocks—a tremendous favor. You'd have to sleep here alone at night, but during the day I'm sure you could come and go, and things'd be safe enough. If you get scared at night you could call my friend Lou. She'd be glad to come over and hang out with you." Would she ever.

Audrey smiled and sat up.

I said, "I don't know whether any of this would interfere with your—work or whatever. Your life."

She said nothing.

"You're a very private person, Audrey Knox," I said.

Her smile grew broader. "So," she said, "you'll leave the key with me and take off in the morning?"

"If you're up for it."

"Count me in. I'll treat the place like my own."

Considering the tidiness of her apartment, that was a good promise.

"But," she said, "what if Porrocks—"

"Porrocks is never going to know about this. I'll be back in a day or two. Even if there's more for me to learn and I have to go off again, I'll come back just to reassure her. I might have to get Lou to cover for us, you know, which she would do. It'll be all right."

You just can't worry yourself to death over logistics. This was a serious investigation. Last night I'd dreamed about Drooly Rick and Young Brenda. They'd come over to my flat to play three-handed euchre with me, and somehow we all decided to go into business together importing penny candy from Argentina. Drooly Rick's clothes were dripping wet. Then we were at the old Tiger Stadium, the Tigers were playing the Oakland A's, and the three of us were trying to talk George Kell into letting us into the press box. My dreams never make any sense. But I feared I'd have more visits from Drooly Rick's restless ghost if I didn't act on what I knew.

"What about Todd?"

"I'm taking him with me."

Either Porrocks was in danger from another person, or I was in danger from Porrocks (not that she was in shape to act against me herself now), or possibly both. That last possibility made my brain hurt. "Hell," I muttered.

"What?"

"Nothing."

Our evening was lovely enough, but it didn't include sex, to my disappointment. I found myself deeply turned on by Audrey Knox, and although I'd vowed to myself to cool it with her, I found the prospect of being away from her for a couple of days disquieting. I tried to steer us in the intimacy direction, but she lolled on the cushions and said, "Sometimes I find it more exciting just to look at each other."

"Oh," I said. I'd never heard that exact version of no before.

I rose early, packed my gym bag with a change of clothes, placed Todd in his travel case on the Caprice's passenger seat, added a bag of supplies for him, and kissed Audrey Knox intensely. "Thank you," I said. "Together we'll get to the bottom of this."

"I know we will," she said. "I can't wait to see you again."

"I hate to leave you." She looked so cute I felt like pinching her cheek.

"Well, you'd better get going."

Fifteen

The Erie Shores Care Center squatted in the middle of a long block on a dreary avenue miles from the lake. The building was an institutional thing from the fifties: two flat brick wings connected by a parabolic concrete entrance. But it also appeared as if someone had tried to make it look like a bowling alley or a motel: Swaths of artificial green grass lay uninvitingly between the parking area and the frostbitten flower beds next to the entrance, and silver metal starburst decorations splayed themselves at intervals along the brick facings.

In general, Cleveland is a nice-enough Midwestern town, rooted as most of them are in industry. The same water molecules that tumble along the Detroit River eventually cruise past Cleveland's lakefront 170 miles away. Like Detroit, Cleveland saw a lot of European immigration, a lot of Poles, Germans, and Swedes in the white communities, while the blacks made their way to factory jobs from Dixie. Cleveland has never been accused of being overly hip, although it does have its own polka sound, the Cleveland Style, which includes banjo and sometimes makes you think of blues. That style is looked down on by the harshest devotees of the other major style, the Chicago, which relies on accordion, clarinet, trumpet, and a fast tempo. Because the Industrial Age is essentially over in America, you could say metropolitan Cleveland looks old, you could say it looks tired, and to be sure, you'll find civic projects that look pathetic, their hearts missing. You'll find kids skipping school and shoplifting spray paint; you'll find the usual derelicts arguing in the weeds beneath the viaducts. You'll find sooty train tracks.

But the city hugs the shores of pleasant Lake Erie, and there's something to be said for the clean, cold air that blows in from the north. There's a working port and factories still, an extraordinary art museum, and a famous symphony. Plus, the place has trees. The city and the suburbs and the countryside have lovely tall good trees—maples and oaks, ashes and locusts, pines and spruces. The high-storied greenery gives you the secure feeling that you're on the planet and not surrounded by every goddamn thing synthetic.

All this makes for a population that's matter-of-fact and more factory-tough than most. Sure, wussy types are always around, but the feeling in the air here is, I work hard all day until the whistle blows. Then I go home and shovel snow or cut the grass.

Cleveland's an okay place.

The Caprice, I'm sad to say, was severely challenged by the drive. The engine ran rougher and rougher, and I had a hard time starting it after the rest stop. The battery seemed all right; I thought the starter must be going, since eventually the engine did catch. There's a sprocket thing in a starter, and sometimes the teeth break off. You have to keep cranking it until a remaining tooth catches, and you start. Plus, the engine took a full quart of oil after just 105 miles. "Not good, not good," I muttered to Todd.

I was wearing a white oxford-cloth blouse, my best blue jeans, and my Weejuns, an outfit I'd selected for its working-class neutrality. Now I put on the baseball cap Todd's veterinarian had once given me, a navy twill job with WESTRICK ANIMAL CLINIC in white letters. It looked sharp and professional. Plus I pinned to my white blouse a nameplate I'd found in the street with ROBERTA KLOTZAK stamped on it.

The drive had taken three and a half hours including a rest stop for gas and doughnuts; it was just one o'clock now, and lunchtime at the care center should be winding down.

"Come on, Todd."

Cradling him in my left arm, I presented myself at the care center's front desk. "Good afternoon," I said to the woman who looked up. She wore a pink smock and had fluffy auburn bangs and a pleasant aspect. I invested my voice with enthusiasm and good cheer. "I'm Roberta Klotzak from Westrick Veterinary," big smile, "and this is Todd. We're here for the Pet Therapy Walkabout!"

The woman, whose own nameplate said EVELYN, smiled. In her smile was the desire to relate to me and Todd, to welcome us, but she was clearly feeling a measure of confusion. "Pet Therapy Walkabout?"

"Yes!" Something bumped my hip, and I turned to see a 400-year-old man trying to shove his walker between me and a supply cart parked just behind me.

"Oh, I beg your pardon," I said, with a wink to Evelyn. "Let's get you a clear path here!" I stepped out of his way. He glared at me, then saw Todd. He stopped, and a misty look came into his eyes.

"Todd, say hello to this good-looking fellow."

Todd glanced at me, then rested his head on my wrist.

The man remained where he was, all urgency gone from his journey. He gazed at Todd. I held my breath; Evelyn rose from her chair to witness this tender moment.

The man's lips twitched. "Rabbit," he said. "Good eating. Haven't had rabbit in years." He smiled and moved on.

I turned back to Evelyn, whose face had fallen only slightly.

"He's the cutest thing," she said in an effort to counteract the man's insensitivity. "Todd, pay no attention," she added in a pretend-pouty voice.

I maintained friendliness while Evelyn said she'd check with the boss about the Pet Therapy Walkabout.

Needless to say, Pet Therapy Walkabout was news to the care center's administrator, Jennifer, too. We decided that Shawndra at the clinic had made a mistake and sent me to the wrong nursing home.

As we talked, shrill alarm sounds went off periodically and disconcertingly, indicating that inmates were trying to get out of their wheelchairs or beds. Or falling out.

"But you're aware," I said to Jennifer, "of the new state mandate on pet therapy, right?"

"Well, I—"

"The governor just signed it, so it's not actually in implementation phase yet. But from what I've been told, you're going to be seeing a lot more rabbits coming through here. When the board saw all the data on elderly peoples' heart rates, their cholesterol levels, and so on, they were like, man, we've gotta get a program going. You know?"

Jennifer asked with caring intensity, "Is there something specifically beneficial about rabbits? I mean, we have the dog people in here quite a bit, and we do the plant protocol."

I'd noticed an array of fussy-looking houseplants next to the nurses' station. "Yes, rabbits," I asserted. "The main thing with rabbits is they help older people's sense of balance and their—their respiratory enzymes. The enzyme levels of the test group elderly absolutely were in the toilet before the experiment, but you should have seen them afterward. And nobody can explain the balance thing, but there it is. They just stopped falling."

"Wow," Jennifer said, "it almost doesn't sound—"

"But look, since I'm here, why don't I just go ahead and do a Walkabout? I'll check with the clinic later. It's so nice here, I might as well stay a little while and show you how one works!"

"Well, all right, Roberta."

"Fantastic!" And Jennifer, Todd, and I moved down the corridor and into rooms, introducing people to Todd. The aides went wild for him, and the residents in general seemed amused.

In a dayroom we came upon a row of three women sitting in wheelchairs watching television. I strode in, saying, "Ladies! Let's turn off that mush and make a new friend!"

They swiveled their heads to watch me unplug the TV. "Thank you," one said in a tired voice.

"This is Todd, and he'd like to know your names," I began. We all exchanged names—none of the three were named Helen—and after careful evaluation I put Todd in the lap of the calmest-looking one. Her whole face glowed with joy as Todd hunkered across her bony thighs.

"You can pet him," I urged.

She sank her gnarled fingers into his fur and looked up at me.

"Don't you feel ten years younger?" I asked. "I think he likes you."

Jennifer was about to say something when her belt-mounted pager vibrated.

"Ooh!" she said. "Excuse me!"

I kept going by myself. The place was a typical nursing home, clean enough, yet there was that depressing end-of-the-road atmosphere that no number of plants, disinfectant, or rabbits can erase. Fortunately, there were only about fifty inmates, and people's first names were on plates next to their doors.

Helen B. Donovan shared a room with a corpse-like individual who neither spoke nor stirred from bed the whole time I was in the room. Mrs. Donovan herself sat in a wheelchair, looking out the window at the parking lot. Todd was a wonderful calling card. I introduced us and asked if it was all right if we sat with her.

"What a hell of a day this has been," she said. "Sit right down."

Mrs. Donovan's face was the sunken-apple type, worn and sweet. She had one of those old-lady potbellies and wore a polyester dress with vertical color bars that made her stomach look like a convex TV test screen. Todd seemed to focus on the magenta color over her appendix area.

I sat in the side chair and scooted it a little closer so she could pet Todd. He was being phenomenally patient with this whole show. Meeting strangers never did bother him, but this was a lot at once.

He was with me more or less by default because I didn't want to leave him in Detroit. I couldn't leave him alone in the cold car very long either, and he was so usefully appealing. People focused on him and not so much on me and my intentions.

"Well, Mrs. Donovan, I'm just a visitor to this place, just passing through. You know how it is."

"Yes. Nice bunny you've got there. Is it one of those seeing-eye bunnies?"

"He hasn't been specifically trained for that, but he's pretty smart."

Her face searched mine for some purpose, which seemed a good sign. It behooved me to get a grasp of how with-it she was before asking anything mission-critical.

"Have you had some difficulties today, Helen?"

"It's been four days since I've taken a dump!"

"Oh, my."

"And my pain is getting worse."

"I would imagine so."

"I mean this pain." She stopped petting Todd and pointed to her legs. "I've got arthritis really bad and I can't walk."

Mrs. Donovan's legs appeared to be swollen, and her feet were encased in velcro-strapped boot-style slippers. She looked bizarrely ready for action in them. She wore a wedding set on her left hand and a pair of bifocals in pink plastic frames on her nose. Her hair was long, white, and loose, and it flowed around her shoulders like Buffalo Bill's in the pictures you see of him later in life.

"I'm very sorry to hear that," I said. "Do they—"

"They tell me I'm addicted to my pain *and* to my pain medication! How do you like that?!"

"What nonsense. Don't they take good care of you here?"

"Not very. I wish I had a nickel for every time I've pushed that button and all they did was laugh."

I looked at her.

"They laugh," she insisted. "I can hear them clear down the hall."

"That's just terrible."

"Well, it's not so damn terrible, actually. You get to feeling sorry for yourself when you get in a place like this. Nobody feels sorrier for me than I do for myself, I guarantee you."

"Is there anything I could do for you right now?"

"Yeah, run down to the corner and bring me back a pack of Benson & Hedges and some little cupcakes and a bottle of Asti Spumante and a comic book and a little football I can throw around here. You think I'm kidding? What's so funny?"

"Well," I said, "I could go and get you those things, but of course smoking's against the rules here—drinking, too, for all I know."

"I don't want to smoke them, I want to smell them. I want to hold one in my hand and *act* like I'm smoking. As for the booze, well, hell, if they gave us each a pint of gin a day in this place, things'd go much smoother—*much* smoother."

"No doubt. Well, in a little while I'll go out to the store for you. Doesn't the center have things for you to do to get your mind off things, like you know, group activities or something?"

She brightened slightly. "There was a..." She searched for a word. "I'd call it a party, but it wasn't really a party. Now you see how I'm losing it."

"A gathering?"

"A gathering. I got the tangerine."

"Oh, really?"

She looked at me searchingly. "Goddamn it. This is what happens."

I said, "Did you all play a game or something, and the prize was a tangerine? Was that it?"

"She gave me the tangerine to play. Goddamn it."

"The tangerine to play."

"There was another lady who only got two sticks to hit, and she wanted to shake the tangerine, so I gave it to her. I didn't even want it anymore."

"Oh, the tambourine! You shook the tambourine. You went to a musical gathering."

"Yes! It was the goddamn tambourine! *Thank* you."

"Well, I bet that was a lot of fun."

"Oh, we had fun up the yinyang," she said grimly.

"Myself, I play the mandolin."

Mrs. Donovan said nothing.

"The nurses and helpers here all look quite nice," I ventured.

"Most of them are all right, I guess, when they're not lounging around on their asses eating gourmet sandwiches and laughing at all the people sitting in their rooms pushing their buttons."

"Say, do you have a favorite one?"

"Oh, yes."

"What's her name? Or his name," I added for the sake of political correctness, despite the fact that every employee I'd seen so far was female.

"Hmm, that's a good question."

I waited.

"It might be Susan."

"Susan?"

"I can't say for sure. She might be a Susan."

"Well," I said in a jolly tone, "that's a safe thing to say!" I noticed a framed photograph on her windowsill. "May I look at this?"

"Oh, yes!"

I brought the picture to her. "Is this your family?"

"Yes, that would be my family. That much I remember, anyway."

The picture was a color snapshot that had been blown up to eight-by-ten size. I recognized 201 Adderly Street in the background. A group of people stood on the front lawn on a sunny day around noon—there were no shadows except beneath everyone's eyes: the raccoon effect. I recognized Mrs. Donovan, younger, but with a faraway look in her eyes, a look that seems to precede confusion when a person gets older. There were two dark-haired men, thirtyish, obviously related to each other: same mesomorphic body type, same taste in NFL team jerseys.

There was another woman in the picture as well, standing next to one of the men, whose arm encircled her shoulders.

"That's my son Richard." Mrs. Donovan pointed to the slightly taller of the two men.

Richard! Could such a coincidence really be? Drooly Rick? Richard? I stared at the picture.

"And would this be Richard's brother?" I asked.

"That's the one I don't like."

"How come?"

"I can't remember. He was no damn good from the minute he was born. That much I can tell you. He was a screamer, you know?"

"I see. And who's this young lady here?"

Mrs. Donovan bent closer to the picture. She said nothing for a long time, and, afraid she might be falling asleep, I said, "Mrs. Donovan, do you remember that house very well? The one you used to own, there in the picture?"

"Hmm." She kept gazing at the picture. "It's a nice house, isn't it?"

"It certainly is. Do you remember the name Erma Porrocks?"

"Erma?"

"Yes."

"I think I used to have a cat named Erma. There were rocks in the backyard of that house."

I looked at the picture again. Could Richard really be Drooly Rick in better days? I imagined I saw a likeness. I had no idea how long Rick had been on the streets, but suddenly I speculated, what if Mrs. Donovan was mother to both Drooly Rick and Porrocks! Now that'd be a twist.

"Ma'am, did you ever store anything inside the walls of your house? Like, did you have a bank account, or did you like to keep your money right in the house?"

"Oh, I had a bank account. I'm sure I still do. I was never one of those suspicious people. I figure you've got to trust somebody, and bankers are at least clean-cut."

"Did you rent out that house ever, before you came to live here?"

"Hmm." She looked up at me, then down again. I waited with a pleasantly relaxed air. Mrs. Donovan turned to look out the window. A man in a ski jacket slammed a car door in the parking lot. Mrs. Donovan turned back to me and said, "I can't begin to tell you how bad it feels when you can't take a dump for four days."

A woman walked into the room swinging a yellow tote bag. "Hi, Helen!" Her demeanor was solidly cheerful, even though she looked very tired, as if she were just getting over a bad cold. I realized she was the woman in the photograph, older now as well, perhaps by ten years. I judged her to be in her late forties.

I, sitting at Mrs. Donovan's side with Todd, didn't give her much pause.

"Hello," I said.

"Good afternoon to you. I'm Lisette Donovan."

"Oh, Helen's daughter-in-law. I'm Roberta Klotzak, pet person."

"How did you know that I'm her daughter-in-law?" She said this with an open smile.

"Oh, you know. I didn't see all that much family resemblance, so I just took a guess. I do that all the time in my job. Your mother-in-law is a lovely woman."

Mrs. Donovan gave Lisette a triumphant smile. "I still haven't gone," she said.

Lisette upended her tote bag on the bed. "Christ Almighty," she said, "things could be worse. Let's buck up here. Look, I've got treats!" I was amused to see that she'd brought a movie magazine, a package of little cupcakes, a can of Red Bull energy drink, and several packs of gum.

I left the room and visited some other inmates with Todd, keeping an ear toward Mrs. Donovan's door. After about forty-five minutes I went and filled two Styrofoam cups with coffee from the urn I'd noticed in the TV room, and returned to Mrs. Donovan's room.

Lisette was preparing to leave. Mrs. Donovan saw the coffee cups first. "Oh, you've brought coffee! How lovely! Have you tasted it yet?"

"Uh, no," I said.

"Try it," she urged with a malicious smile.

Lisette smiled at the floor as I took a sip.

Being too polite to spit it back into the cup, I swallowed and said, "I've drunk lousy coffee all over this great land of ours, but I have to admit, this is the worst."

Lisette said, "We can't drink it at all. I usually bring Helen a cup from across the street. Today I had my hands full, but I bet you'd like a cup, Helen, wouldn't you?"

"Yeah, maybe it'll loosen up my bowels."

"Worth a try. Roberta, would you like to walk across with me and get good coffee?"

I looked at my watch, then gave Lisette a sympathetic look. I could tell she liked me; a feeling of solidarity passed between us. "Sounds good," I said. "I've got a little time before my next stop." Lisette clearly categorized me as a helping professional: someone who might want to listen to *her* for a few goddamn minutes.

So I put Todd in his travel box and carried him with us across the street to a coffee place that smelled bean-toasty wonderful. We decided to sit for just a little while before bringing coffee to Mrs. Donovan. And that was how I found out a few interesting things about her, the Donovan boys, and that house.

Sixteen

Lisette sank into a chair like a sack of flour finishing a marathon. I brought coffee and carrot cake from the counter. She thanked me for paying.

People often find themselves telling me things, just sharing the details of their lives with little prompting. I've been told I have an earnest face. Moreover, in this situation, Lisette not only was glad to have somebody paying attention to her, she was the kind of working-class person who thought that being voluble was the thing to do in social situations. Her hair was orange and bouncy, her figure pudgy, and her face creased with a variety of long-standing worries. She was sober right now, but I had the sense she could and would gladly drink me under the table at a moment's notice. I also had the sense she was no stranger to buying gas three dollars at a time and putting winter coats on layaway in July when they're the cheapest. Her coat this season was a sack-like thing with one big button in the middle.

I got things going by saying what an interesting person Mrs. Donovan was.

"You know," Lisette said, "most wives just hate their mother-in-laws, but Helen's been more of a friend to me, more of a mother than my real mom. My mom was an asshole, frankly. Helen taught me to cook. Things could've been worse."

We talked about the nursing home and Pet Therapy Walkabouts, and I told Lisette about my life as a veterinary assistant and bowling league secretary. For every personal detail I shared, Lisette supplied five of her own.

"I saw you looking at that picture in Helen's room," she said.

"Yes, looks like you married the fellow standing on the porch steps?"

"Yes, I married Jimmy Donovan. What a piece of work."

"Did you guys always live in Ohio?"

That got her going on the Michigan thing. She and Jimmy had hooked up fifteen years ago, when Jimmy worked as a sheet-metal guy in an automobile-customizing shop in Southgate. When he showed up for work, he made good money, but he enjoyed tequila and cocaine more than was good for him. Eventually, they lost their apartment and moved in with Helen in the house on Adderly Street in Wyandotte. Helen had been widowed shortly before that, her husband keeling over with the big one while changing the windshield wipers on his car.

The coffee and cake were excellent. Café sounds clinked around us, and we heard the low murmur of other customers talking and enjoying the afternoon. It was an Internet café, and a few people were mousing along with their coffee.

Richard, Helen's favored first son, took a very self-directed path in life. He saw a picture postcard of Phoenix, Arizona, that his tenth-grade teacher had brought to school, and decided that his heart's desire was to be a mail carrier in Phoenix. So he pursued that goal after he graduated from high school and was in fact now a U.S. Postal Services employee there, walking all day in the warm sunshine. Every few years he vacationed in Michigan and would stop in at his mother's house. During one such visit the photo on Mrs. Donovan's bureau had been snapped.

"I see," I said. So Mrs. Donovan was not mother to Drooly Rick. I let that one go and concentrated on Lisette's relationship with Jimmy and the house.

Jimmy supported Mrs. Donovan and Lisette for a time on a marijuana business he'd started. He acquired some good seeds from a batch of British Columbian homegrown; he purchased grow-lights, flats, pots, and electric fans and set the little seeds to germinate. He raised several decent crops of marijuana in the basement and found buyers for the stuff, but was forced to stop when Lisette let it slip to the old lady that the plants were illegal. Helen couldn't abide that, and she was willful enough to throw them out and make them stay out. So Jimmy turned to dealing cocaine, which was more easily hidden from her, then he branched out to heroin. When Lisette got bored she'd work at little jobs here and there, selling costume jewelry, doing word processing, whatever.

Jimmy always talked big, always promised Lisette that they'd be on easy street someday, have a place of their own and plenty of leisure time. When he was dealing, he threw money around but not enough to attract huge amounts of attention. Even so, Lisette marveled that he never got busted.

"I'm from Detroit originally too," I volunteered. "I used to know some kids in high school from Wyandotte."

"Did you ever know Vic Toretti?"

"Hmm. Little guy, glasses, pocket protector?" I asked.

"No. Vic Toretti was scum—a fat, crooked, cocaine-dealing son of a bitch. You would've seen his mug shot in the post office, probably. He loved to get people hooked. He was a real shit, and Jimmy hung with him for a while. They did business together. I think they pulled a few robberies. Jimmy thought Vic was wonderful—the most *masculine* dude, the best with *women*, the *smartest*."

"How come?"

"Because Vic was friends with an even bigger dealer."

"Oh."

"It's just a scummy life, drug dealing, you know?"

"Yeah."

"In fact, the drug business is a lot like this carrot cake."

"Yeah?"

Lisette had eaten about half of her cake. She pointed the tines of her fork to the layer of frosting on top. "Drug dealing looks on the surface like this sweet thing. Sweet and thick."

We both looked at her frosting.

"Then," she continued, "there's the cake, which isn't frosting, but it's still usually pretty good."

"Yeah."

"Then, see, when your cake is gone, you realize that all you've done is buy cake from the store. What if you want to make one?" She laughed harshly. "You don't know how."

I nodded wisely. "You said it."

"Things could be worse, though."

A teenager looking at a computer terminal let out a sarcastic laugh.

"So what's Jimmy doing today?"

"Jimmy's dead."

"Oh! I'm so sorry!" I laid my hand briefly on her arm.

Lisette sighed, forked up another bite of cake, washed it down with some coffee, and said, "Yeah, some guy found him in the men's room at the Sugar Shack, a knife sticking out of his neck. Happened three years ago September."

"The topless place?"

"Yeah. Before he died, he kept promising we'd be so rich. He tried to make me think he was saving money, but he didn't have a dime when he died. I never found anything: no bank accounts, nothing in the mattress. Ha!"

"Who killed him?" I bent down and extended a crumb of carrot cake to Todd in his box. He nibbled it from my fingertip, then I wiped my finger on my napkin. Sweets weren't good for him, but it seemed wrong not to even let him taste the carrot cake.

"We never found out. I think he crossed somebody higher up, one of the heroin guys. Or I think Vic Toretti might have done it. I never trusted him."

"Did they have an argument or something?"

"I don't know. I never knew."

"Tell me, Lisette, did Jimmy ever kick you and Helen out of the house for a couple of days at a time?"

Lisette looked at me. "Yeah!" I could see her mind zinging between Jimmy, the drugs, my question, and sudden memories. "Yeah. He'd give us a couple hundred and tell us to go up to Mount Pleasant, to the Indian casino, or to Birch Run. We'd take the bus and stay overnight at whatever el cheapo place and actually we'd have a pretty nice time. At Birch Run we'd spend too much money on our credit cards, you know—you can't go there and not buy stuff."

"Was there a casino there too?"

"No, just the outlet mall. At Mount Pleasant somehow we'd just gamble until our money ran out. It just seemed too sinister of a thing to do to tap into our credit cards at the casino."

"A slippery slope–type thing?"

"Exactly." She watched me drink my coffee. Her hands and fingernails were nicely shaped, but she wore two shoddy rings of fake gemstones and gold, and she'd put a muddy shade of maroon polish on her nails. "Why did you ask me that?"

"Why did I ask you what?"

"If he ever kicked us out of the house."

"Oh, I ran with drug dealers myself for a while," I said, "and they did that too. I've always been curious about it. Want some more cake?"

"No, thank you. What did your dealers do while you were gone?"

"I really don't know, that's the interesting thing. Sometimes they'd trash the place, like with a party, but other times the house was cleaner than I'd left it."

She exclaimed, "That's exactly it!"

"Those guys, you can't figure them out. I mean, they always thought they were so smart, you know?"

"Boy, do I know it." Lisette told me that she and Helen continued to live in the house, getting by on Helen's Social Security and a pension from GM. No savings, but enough to live on. Vic Toretti had come around a few times after Jimmy died.

"What did he want?" I asked.

"He wouldn't say. I mean, he acted like he was just coming to visit. He'd bring a package of Lorna Doones or something, but it was like he had something on his mind."

"Did he ever try to hit you up for money?"

"Oh, constantly. But we never gave in."

"Another slippery slope. Did he hit on you sexually too?"

"He tried." Lisette suddenly stretched her arms over her head in a ballerina-like pose that actually looked graceful, in spite of her open coat hiking up at her shoulders. She arched her back as if trying to center her body somehow. She brought her arms down with a little *uff*. "But I just didn't like him well enough. I always thought he knew something about who killed Jimmy. Besides, he had a girlfriend, this real looker who kept him on a short leash, considering. I think he was afraid of her."

"Yeah? Was she a dealer too?"

"No, she just ordered Vic around like a slave. Always carping on him to bring in more money. And he did, he did. I think she had some kinky hold on his dick, you know what I'm saying?"

"What was her name? Maybe I knew her."

"Uh, Bev, I think, or Barb. No, Bev. It was Bev Something. I met her a couple of times. Spooky little thing. She always reminded me of a little pretty vampire. A well-dressed one, though. I always felt dowdy next to—"

"Where is Vic now?"

"Oh, he got busted for possession, amazingly his first time, and his lawyer couldn't keep him out. He went to prison about a year after Jimmy died. I don't know how long he's in for." Lisette looked into her coffee cup and swirled the dregs around.

"My guy went to prison too. He's up in Marquette doing twenty. Which one's Vic in, do you know?"

"Well, they move them around, you know."

"Right, they do."

"So who knows or cares where he is now? I sure don't."

"Me neither," I declared. "Did Helen always want to retire to Cleveland? Myself, I'd prefer Florida or—"

Lisette laughed. "Helen got to be too much for me to take care of by myself. A couple of months ago I helped her sell the house. We looked at nursing homes in Detroit, but she's got a sister here in Cleveland, and she decided she wanted to be near her. Unfortunately, Jane's got liver cancer and isn't gonna be around long."

"Oh, that's too bad."

"Well, they never got along all that well, but family's family."

"Yeah."

Lisette told me that she was helping Jane now too and living in Jane's basement, which was furnished with a large-screen television and a Jacuzzi, so things could be worse.

Seventeen

After a while Lisette went back to the nursing home with a sixteen-ounce coffee-and-cream for Helen. I watched her walk carefully with the hot paper cup. Before we said goodbye she asked if I'd ever been in a support group for friends of drug dealers. I told her no, but it sounded like a helpful idea. Lisette Donovan was a good egg, and I felt sorry for her loneliness.

I spent an hour on one of the café's computer terminals surfing the Internet for information on Vic Toretti. Evidently, his drug bust had been run-of-the-mill and not made the papers. I looked for Michigan court records but found nothing online. This particular bust, a first offense, was unlikely to have been done by federal agents, but I checked some U.S. sites anyway. Nothing. Then I checked the Michigan Department of Corrections site and found him. It was a Victor Toretti at any rate, whose dates fit the time frame Lisette Donovan had given me. He'd been convicted for possession of less than twenty-five grams of cocaine, sentenced to a maximum of three years, ten months, and been paroled already. The parole date was in August of this year, barely two months ago.

There it was: Toretti could have been the one who came upon Drooly Rick with Jimmy Donovan's loot.

The prison Web site didn't show his address at the time of his arrest, so I'd need to check the court records in person to make sure this was the guy. Then I'd have to find him.

While it was certainly possible that others could know about—or suspect—Jimmy Donovan's private practice of stashing away a percentage of his drug-trafficking income, it wasn't bloody likely. Otherwise the entire house would've been leveled by now by cash-crazed drug crooks.

I supposed Jimmy Donovan was one of those guys who always intended to get out of the business. You squirrel away money. Maybe you cheat your contacts a little more than you used to; maybe you set up one last big transaction; or maybe you set up a big double-cross, where you keep a wheelbarrow of money or goods you were supposed to hand over to somebody else. In that case, you'd need to blow town immediately. Since Jimmy Donovan didn't do that, I had to figure he was a squirreler who maybe tried to do a big transaction that went wrong. Hell, maybe he'd met his end for a *small* transaction that went wrong.

If he was squirreling, he was thinking about the future. The older a drug dealer gets, the worse the paranoia gets: You leap up at every car in the driveway; you shrivel at every tap on the shoulder. You never know. Yes, Jimmy Donovan would have been tiring of the racket by the time that knife found its way into his neck.

I purchased a wrapped-up ham sandwich and put it in my pocket, then discreetly changed the newspapers in Todd's carrier in a corner of the café, using a local free paper someone had left on a table, and gave him some water and timothy nuggets. We returned to the Caprice where I loaded him in then walked the soiled newspapers around to the rear of the care center and threw them into a trash bin. I cleaned my hands with a Kentucky Fried Chicken towelette from the car's glove compartment. Now we were all set.

After five tries the Caprice's ignition caught, and we chugged out of the parking lot. It was four o'clock. The engine ran hot immediately. "Shit," I murmured. I pulled over and looked under the hood. The oil was low, as I expected, but I judged there was enough until we needed gas. Nothing else appeared wrong, but I had a bad feeling. I decided to believe that the temperature gauge was faulty. "Let's just make a run for it," I said to Todd. This time it took nine tries before starting. Hoping for the best, I pointed the hood in the direction of the Ohio Turnpike. I was willing for the Caprice to breathe its last in Detroit, our turf, and I was trying to prepare myself emotionally for that. But I didn't like the thought of being stranded this far from home.

Of course, not liking the thought never has anything to do with it.

As I threaded my way through the ghetto-ish zone between the nursing home and the I-90, which I intended to take to the turnpike, the Caprice's idiot lights started flashing like Las Vegas. You do know that the dashboard-warning lights are called idiot lights, don't you? Because they only come on when the situation is extreme and not even an idiot could miss the message. Then you feel like an idiot because if you'd done more for your car you probably wouldn't be in this shape.

I pressed on, the goal now to make it at least to the toll plaza at the turnpike where they have tow trucks and courteous employees. The sky darkened as I accelerated into the concrete chute of the I-90 downtown, or maybe it was my imagination. The weather had definitely gotten colder, and I wondered if it would snow, even though it was still autumn.

Suddenly the engine lurched and went into fibrillation, missing rapidly, shudderingly. An enormous cloud of blue smoke filled my mirrors.

"Damn, Todd," I said. "Don't worry."

I gave it full gas in the sudden hope that the problem might simply be carbon buildup in the cylinders, and visualized eight cleansing flames burning the bad stuff out of each smooth steel tube. In response, the car bucked and screamed like an insane camel. Currents of traffic swept around us, angry drivers honking as if I were trying to thwart them all personally.

Skeeee! went the Caprice.

Standing on the accelerator, I forced the car up an exit ramp and onto a surface street where the engine uttered one last waul and went silent. I wrestled with the now-stiff steering wheel and got us over to the curb. I removed the key from the ignition.

Todd shifted in his case. I reached over and unlatched it, took him on my lap, and stroked his back. Together we just breathed for a few minutes. He seemed glad it was over, and I have to confess I did too. Poor old Caprice. A small amount of smoky vapor rose up from beneath the hood and dissipated into the cold city air.

Gradually, Todd's warmth on my thighs got my heart rate down. Nothing was all that bad. Be here now. Focus and execute.

We hadn't made it into a better neighborhood. Actually, this place was not a neighborhood at all. Battered warehouses and blank-faced factory buildings stretched along the street; we were in a light industrial quarter that must have been thriving thirty-five years ago. Now nothing was happening, and everything was storm-cloud gray. The traffic was desultory and sparse. Trees would have gotten in the way of progress on such a street, so there were none.

I got out and put on my wool peacoat, which I'd luckily tossed in the backseat this morning. Man, that was a long time ago.

A kid rode past on a bike, flicking a tough glance over his shoulder.

"Yeah, you too," I muttered.

I opened the trunk and removed my gym bag and the only other thing in there, a set of jumper cables. I set them on the hood, then sorted through the junk in the glove compartment, picking out my registration, insurance certificate, crumpled repair bills, anything with my name and address on it. I ran my hand beneath the seats and pulled out my gas-pumping gloves and my Detroit Street Finder. At the last minute I remembered an agate from Lake Superior that my friend Billie had dropped for luck into the police-installed map pocket when I first got the car. I plucked it out and held it up. Agates are dull stones when dry, but when water touches them they show their gem-like patterns. This one, Billie had shown me, had tiger stripes. I decided to polish it someday, and put it in my pocket.

Next, using the short blade of my jackknife, my good old Case double-blade, I managed to unscrew the license plate at only the cost of the skin on one knuckle.

I stuffed the plate and papers into my gym bag, looped the jumper cables over my shoulder, picked up Todd's case, and took one last look at the Caprice. "So long, friend," I said. "Thanks for everything."

I couldn't afford to cry, right out in public like that. I turned and set off on foot down the dirty street.

It took me two hours, receiving vague but ultimately correct directions from the pedestrians I met up with, to walk to the Greyhound bus station on Chester Avenue by the university. No one bothered me; I even stopped at a bar when it got dark and drank a glass of beer for eighty cents, a price I hadn't paid since I couldn't remember when.

The day's last bus to Detroit had gone, and the next one was at three-fifty-five A.M. I bought a ticket from the clerk behind the counter for twenty-six dollars. I still had a couple of twenties on me, but that was it.

I set Todd and my stuff on a bench near the snack bar and, remembering the ham sandwich that was still in my bag, bought a Coke to go with it. We settled down to wait for the middle of the fucking night.

Well, what can you say about an inner-city bus station? Although this one was pleasanter than most I'd seen, with decent lighting and wood paneling from olden days, the place smelled like cold mop water. A few sorry-looking zombies—all guys, of course—lurked in the corners and in the doorway to the men's room. There was no way I could allow myself to fall asleep in that place; not that I feared for my life with the clerk right there around the corner. But you just don't want to lose consciousness in a place where people buy and sell sexual favors that don't involve lying down. You just don't.

Thank God I'd brought my copy of *Encounter in Borneo*. After making sure Todd was comfortable in his case next to me on the plastic seat, I ate my sandwich, drank the Coke, and read many soothing chapters.

The story completely took my mind away from my troubles. That's what a good book does for you. I tried to read slowly to make it last.

So Calico Jones tears herself away from the stunningly, brainily luscious Ingrid and sets off from Singapore to Borneo in a chartered vintage Beechcraft F90 seaplane piloted by a leather-jacketed deserter from the North Korean secret police. Calico, ever cool, just climbs in, hands the guy a map, and buckles her safety harness. She can tell the guy's trustworthy and a good pilot because when she asks him how fast he's going to get her to this anaconda-ridden jungle in Borneo, he merely says, "Not fast. In once piece. In Borneo, one piece is enough."

Calico, you'll remember, has to find and stop this mad scientist who's building a climate-control machine using mutant insect larvae.

So she finds herself paddling this tiny rubber raft to shore from the pontoon plane because of course there's no dock at the godforsaken lake in the middle of nowhere. En route, a crocodile snaps her paddle in two so then she's forced to get into the water and tow the raft containing her equipment and supplies to the slimy shore. She is so cool and brave. I wished the croc would come back so she could punch it in the nose.

Then Calico's carrying her stuff on her back through the rain forest, and it's hot and she's only wearing her tank top and shorts and sturdy boots, and her muscles are bulging all over the place when a band of headhunters captures her for dinner. All I'll reveal here is that Ingrid had taught her some words of headhunter language which she now uses to convince the headhunters that she's more valuable to them alive than dead, playing on a little-known Bornean superstition involving a certain species of amphibious butterfly.

She no sooner gives these guys the slip than *another* band of head-hunters grabs her, this one made up exclusively of chiefs and their queens. Now Calico's getting impatient, so she gives a major karate demonstration *on them* and escapes with the subtle help of one of the headhunter queens, who found herself getting tremendously hot watching Calico Jones send all those tribal chiefs flying ass over teaket-tle.

I closed the book. A creepy guy edged toward me, but as soon as I gave him an icy Calico Jones stare, he backed off. The station clock said eleven-fifteen. Less than five hours to go.

Eighteen

When dinosaurs roamed the earth, public transportation in southeastern Michigan was very good—all those streetcars and whatnot. Times indeed changed, but the bus system these days wasn't as bad as you might expect. You could get around, not fast or in style, but you could do it if you didn't mind walking a mile or two on either end. The Greyhound got into Detroit at seven-thirty in the morning. One DOT ticket and two transfers later, I was drinking coffee and eating oatmeal and bacon at the diner where my friend Billie worked, the Cracked Mug, on West Jefferson in Ecorse.

My good friend was busy, so we didn't talk much. I watched her speed-slide four mugs into a row on the counter, then fill them with coffee in one deft sweep. Her arms were ropy from years of heaving plates and elbowing countermen, but her face looked young because she never let the hard work get her down. Of all my friends Billie was the quickest to smile. She eyed my luggage, said hello to Todd in his case, asked if I was all right, and refused to give me a bill.

"What'll the boss say?" I asked, getting up.

"Shut up," she said. "I see you're on the move. Do you need a place for Todd?"

"Naw, but thanks. Get this—I'm house-sitting for a cop and solving a murder at the same time!" A solid breakfast makes me feel cocky.

"Good God. What's going on?"

"Way too much. I'll tell you about it soon."

I stepped up to Porrocks's front porch and rang the bell. The drapes were drawn and the house was quiet. I was a little surprised that Audrey Knox had gone out so early; I should have called to tell her when to expect me. To be honest, the thought had occurred to me, but I feared sounding pathetic. I didn't want her jumping in her car to come rescue me when Porrocks's place needed protecting.

I rang again just to make sure. I looked up at Audrey's apartment windows across the street. The sun was bright, as the day was cold and clear, and I couldn't tell whether she was home or not. Terribly anxious to tell her about all the intelligence I'd gathered, I hauled my gym bag, Todd, and my jumper cables over to her building and rang. No answer.

"Well, hell," I muttered. I crossed the street again and went down to Porrocks's boathouse, which I'd locked after finishing my work there. Of course, I'd left the key on the same ring as the house key, which I'd given to Audrey. I took off my coat and set Todd and my stuff in the marginal shelter of the doorway—there were a couple of shrubs to block the cold breeze that flowed around the house and along the riverbank. I went around to the end of the boathouse where the boat well was.

The structure had been designed in a simpler time, when barbed wire was used only on ranches, and tall unscalable fences were built for soldiers to scramble over in boot camp. A long narrow board had been nailed to the outside of the boat well as a marginal bumper. Finding that it held my weight, I set off, edging my Weejuns along it as you'd go along a rock ledge. The river lapped along inches beneath me as I used cracks in the weathered siding as fingerholds. I smelled the old familiar river smell, that cool, mossy, earthy aroma that always means peacefulness to me.

When I got to the end of the wall, I reached around and grabbed one of the handles on the garage-type door facing the river. I half expected not to be strong enough to raise that door from my one-handed awkward position. But it slid upward on what must have been well-packed, overbuilt bearings. Typical of the quality of construction in those days.

I rested a moment, then swung around the wall quickly, half-leaping to the inside walkway.

"Ha!" I exclaimed with satisfaction, brushing my hands on my jeans.

The door from the boat well to the inside had no lock. I went in, turned on the electric baseboard heat, and brought in Todd and my stuff. Now we had a warm place to wait for Audrey. Todd was asleep in his case. The ghost image of Drooly Rick lay across the kitchenette floor, unfaded.

I wandered around and thought about Jimmy Donovan's treasure. How much might he have hidden? He surely wasn't a big-time dealer, not a guy who'd routinely bought and sold huge shipments for millions. Guys like that need an entourage, and his widow, Lisette, hadn't mentioned anything like that. On the other hand, there was the gold smuggler's bracelet I'd found, which reasonably seemed an artifact of volume dealing.

If Donovan had handled $1,000 a day five days a week and put away $200 of it, he'd have more than $50,000 at the end of one year. If he'd handled $2,000 a day, double it. And a big score could have boosted that.

One thing that had occurred to me on the bus from Cleveland was this. Those walls were plaster throughout the two buildings—that's the way they built them then. Wet plaster, everybody knows, is a fussy material to work. Which is why they use gypsum board, or drywall, in houses today.

I examined the busted wall in the boathouse. You'll remember that only one side had been demolished. I took a close look at the remaining part, from the unmarred side and from the inside, as it were.

How had I missed it before? Because I hadn't looked for it. The cops hadn't looked for it. The opposite side of that wall had been patched with drywall—about a two-by-two-foot square of it at knee level, covered with a swatch of that nauseating daisy wallpaper. The spot would have been selected for its seclusion behind a piece of heavy furniture. And in fact, I perceived a faint rectangle, bureau-shaped, surrounding the newer paper patch like a halo. If you weren't looking for the patch, you wouldn't really notice it, and you wouldn't remark on it.

Now that I'd figured out the MO, I'd easily be able to find more patches, if they existed, in the main house.

Something Porrocks said way back at the party came to me. Talking about the house, she had said, "I think someone with a temper lived there."

Of course. With her cop's acuity, she must've noticed patches like this in the house, all at a similar height. And she probably deduced that some habitually angry person kicked the wall, then had to patch it, time after time.

"Ha!" I said again, so pleased with my analytical powers. I couldn't wait to get another look inside the main house and boast about it all to Audrey. "Ha!"

Two hours, however, passed with no sign of her. Restlessly, I walked over to her apartment and rang again. Nothing. I returned to Porrocks's house and stopped at the side door. Suddenly an exceptionally odd feeling swept through me: the ugly clutch of dread.

I opened the storm door and tried the inside knob. It turned smoothly, and the feeling of that cold knob turning like that with no resistance made me sick to my stomach.

Dear God. Oh, dear God, my Audrey—please, God, my Audrey. Where would I find her? Lying in a pool of blood, having been hacked to death by the same greedy, insane monster who killed Rick? Or was she at this very second crawling toward the telephone, left for dead but barely alive, rasping my name through a hideously torn mouth? Or was her battered body floating down the river now, having been callously discarded the way you'd kick away a dead rat? My dear perky one.

I swallowed my spit and stepped in. "Audrey?" My voice echoed in the silent kitchen. At first I thought everything was all right. The air was completely still and cool. But I walked quickly into the dining room, then to the living room, and that much was enough to tell me I'd made an enormous and terrible mistake.

Porrocks's home looked as if fifteen Drooly Ricks had been given wrecking bars and told to find the bourbon between the studs.

"Audrey! Audrey!" I cried. I listened for footsteps, rustling, breathing, moans. Nothing. I raced through the house, stumbling over rubble in my haste to find my curvaceous, exciting lover. Shards and chips of plaster lay thick underfoot, mixed with splintered lath, clumps of dust and dirt, like debris from an earthquake. On second thought the destruction was much more bomb-like in its violence. Porrocks's furniture had been shoved away from the walls, every single one of which had been savagely broken into. Unsurprisingly, I saw no currency or valuables lying about.

Nor was there any sign of Audrey.

I yanked on the handle to the trapdoor to the attic, which I'd noticed in Porrocks's upstairs dressing room. I scrambled up the ladder and poked my head into the gloom. "Audrey?" In the weak daylight coming in from the vents I saw bits of junk—a suitcase, a birdcage, a box of Christmas decorations—but no Audrey Knox.

I plunged down, returned to the kitchen, and flung open the basement door. The light switch didn't work, so I grabbed Porrocks's flashlight, a vintage Kel-Lite police model heavy with a fistful of D batteries, from the kitchen counter. "Audrey! Oh, damn, damn." I switched on the flashlight, thundered down the steps, and ran around throwing the strong beam across the concrete floor, along the walls, into every damp corner. I smelled mustiness but not death. Nothing. No one.

I stood for a minute with my hands on my hips, the flashlight beam shining out in front of me.

"Shit," is about all I've ever been able to say at a time like this.

I noticed something curious and went over to take a better look. It was the house's electrical box, an antiquated fuse-type one. It stood open, and every fuse had been unscrewed and dropped on the floor, where they lay scattered like glass tops.

I puzzled over that, then remembered seeing a tangle of electrical wire hanging threateningly from a gash in one wall. Sure—whoever had done the demolition had known enough to take this important precaution, especially given the age of the wiring. That clump of wire was insulated with cloth covering, safe when perfectly intact, but easily torn.

I headed back upstairs.

Where the hell was she? A completely different thought crept into my mind, but I pushed it out.

How can I describe my feelings? The ugliness of the damage was so shocking I couldn't even mutter curses, after the first few minutes. No dust hung in the air, except for what I stirred up as I moved about. My wrecking bar, which I'd left in the upstairs bathroom, lay on the living room floor on top of a pile of debris. Shoe prints slightly smaller than mine were visible here and there where the dust lay thickest. My stomach felt as if someone had chopped it out with an axe. Porrocks's fine house—what a fucking mess.

With a heavier, slower step this time, I visited every room and peered into every hole with the flashlight and groped around. No dregs of treasure today.

Looking closely and knowing what I'd seen in the boathouse, I found two gypsum-board patches on walls still standing and broken pieces of it lying in the rubble in one other place. Jimmy Donovan, then, had stashed money in three places in that house, but the person who went after it hadn't known which walls to look in and hadn't thought to look first for patches. If she had, she'd have saved herself a lot of trouble—and Porrocks and me a whole lot of grief.

Yeah, she. For it hit me at last: Audrey Knox was all right. She wasn't dead, wasn't battered, wasn't anything but somewhere safe. She was counting money and carrying out the rest of her plan, and if she was thinking one single thought about me, it was to the sound of a condescending laugh.

Audrey. My dear Audrey.

"Damn you, Audrey!" I spat, kicking a pile of rubble. "Damn you and your perky little outfits. Goddamn your sweet lips and your naughty smile and your sparkly eyes." Fury welled in me. "You little sneaking thief. You bouncy little betraying murderer."

Could she be that too?

As I hopped over a pile of trash, the floorboards creaked sharply, painfully. "Yeah, old house, I bet this hurt," I said. "I bet all this hurt pretty bad."

I couldn't begin to think what I'd say to Porrocks.

I perched on the dust-thickened arm of the couch. A sort of schizophrenia came over me; I thought at once, *I must tell Audrey Knox what happened; we must work together to solve this situation,* all the while knowing it was Audrey who had executed this destruction. It was crystal clear—she'd all but *told* me she was going to do it. As the author of the Calico Jones books so often writes, everything fell into place. Audrey had learned there was treasure here—somehow she'd learned that—and she'd taken that apartment to watch for an opportunity to get it. Why hadn't she done it during the time the house stood vacant while it was on the market? Well, Porrocks had said there'd been break-ins. Maybe they had been exploratory.

Of course. She hadn't known *where* exactly in the house the loot was. I pictured her climbing up the trapdoor to the attic and rooting through that junk, looking inside the toilet tanks, behind the stove, inside the furnace ducts, and around all the crevices of the basement. Only after she'd done all that would she begin to think about the walls themselves. And by that time Porrocks was moving in.

What about the two guys Porrocks said she hired to tear down the first wall in the boathouse? They must have found the money by accident and, unmolested, took off with it before Audrey Knox got set up in that apartment across the street, or while she wasn't looking.

I imagined the two guys: ordinary guys, workmen, finding the first batch of dough and ecstatically splitting it up. Thinking only like regular marginally dishonest, greedy people—not like practiced crooks or druggies—they'd gone their separate ways, not wondering yet whether there might be more. It wouldn't have entered their minds to savage a whole house on the chance that another glory hole might exist. I imagined them smoking cigars in Orlando, ordering surf'n'turf in Branson, testing out their Spanish on hookers in Tijuana—"Hot fuck for ten buck, chickie?"

Porrocks was innocent. All she'd done was buy a house with too much of the wrong kind of history. Just that was enough to get her almost killed.

Was I the most enormous jackass in the world? When I brought Drooly Rick to the place of his death, did I anticipate anything but a lovely outcome? But there was Audrey Knox, watching and waiting like a little spider up there in her hastily rented apartment. She was there when a scraggly dude and a scrawny chick walked into that boathouse with wrecking tools. She saw us go in and panicked, thinking we were after the loot.

It had been broad daylight. She hesitated. Eventually, she saw me leave empty-handed and figured she could take on Rick. And she did.

In his half-coherent desire to do demolition, Rick had torn into that wall. A cascade of wealth had burst forth, and he was sitting there scratching his head and trying to remember *how much* he'd had to drink, and trying to think what to do when Audrey Knox sneaked in with one of her softball bats. Even a gentle blow with such a weapon against the long-addled specimen of Rick would have hurt him enough to make him draggable the short distance to the boat well. *Man, oh, man.*

Then she grabbed up as much treasure as she could and scurried home before I came back. I remembered the missing curtain—of course she ripped it down to bundle up her bounty.

And then I, in my nerdy excitement, came over to her building, and she saw the outstanding possibilities in getting into my life. She befriended me, and I allowed her to seduce me, and she'd done so without giving a goddamn about me at all. The night we'd spent in Porrocks's house together—the night before last—she had intended to get me out of the way. A bonechill shot through me as I remembered our conversation about my wrecking bar. I remembered the way she'd hefted it in her hands and looked at it so thoughtfully, there when we were alone together in that house at night. I remembered the look in her eyes when I asked if she'd ever used a tool like that.

She'd intended to kill me, and if I'd waited an hour longer to tell her I was leaving in the morning, she would have.

Nineteen

I supposed I'd been angrier in my life, but it was hard to remember when. I picked up my wrecking bar and wiped it off on my jeans. I slipped it up my coat sleeve, then changed my mind. I set the bar on the kitchen counter and rooted in Porrocks's broom closet where I found an interesting brush, a nice soft-bristled one with a two-foot-long wooden handle. I supposed you could use it to wash a car. I left my coat on Porrocks's counter, took the brush, and went out.

I stood on the street and looked up at Audrey Knox's windows. The windows themselves were the crank-style kind, and they were old, probably as old as the building. I thought about Audrey's apartment door, which was a steel security door like all the others. I could've gotten into the building easily enough, but I doubted I could force or jimmy that door open without alerting someone.

The apartment building was red brick, with protruding sandstone blocks as details at the corners. I approached the shrubbery in front as if looking for a lost cat. I slipped between two junipers and assessed my route. Those sandstone blocks were a lucky thing. I stuck the brush into a side belt loop of my jeans and boosted myself to the first sandstone block, then to the next one about eighteen inches above. The route was fairly easy all the way up the corner of the building: grasp, step, boost, grasp, step, boost. I took the brush out at every step and scrubbed industriously at the sandstone. The scrubbing had no effect, of course, except as camouflage.

I was almost to the second floor when a voice called from below, "Hey there!"

I looked down. "Yes?"

The elderly woman who had fled from my toplessness the day Rick died said, "Would you do my windows next?" She wore a head scarf with a picture of Tahquamenon Falls on it. She shaded her eyes as she looked up.

"Yes, ma'am."

"1D, all right?"

"Absolutely."

"Because they're filthy."

"Yes, ma'am."

The crux move was from the corner block to Audrey's windowsill, which was also stone, nicely sturdy. The move was easier than my around-the-wall swing at Porrocks's boathouse, yet fifteen feet off the ground I had to steel myself for it.

I willed my brain chatter to stop for one bitching minute, then took a deep lungful of cold autumn air. I let go with both hands, sprang sideways the necessary few inches, caught the sill with my left foot, and grabbed new handholds on the metal window frame. I allowed myself a quiet "Ha!" A good omen.

There were actually three windows set into one frame, three vertical panes each with its own crank.

I inspected the frame as I scrubbingly moved the brush around. I stuck the brush in my belt loop again and reached into my back pocket for my trusty jackknife. With the long blade I easily pried away the screen, then set the screen tidily on the ledge. I was betting Audrey hadn't locked all three of her windows. Locks on windows are usually balky except if they're really new. I pantomimed scrubbing the window and then, hiding what I was doing with my body, slipped my knife blade between the window and the outer frame. The windows opened outward, so this was easy. I couldn't get much leverage, though; this window was either locked or had no play in its crank mechanism.

I tried the next window, the middle one, with better results. I was able to get my fingertips inside, and once I got a good grip, I pulled steadily, careful to keep my balance. The window edged outward an inch. Then it was simple to insert the wooden brush handle as a lever and force the window wide open. I flourished the brush and climbed inside Audrey Knox's apartment. I turned and leaned out the window for the screen and put it back in place. I closed the window.

My pretty playful lover had made a hasty, though not unplanned, exit. She'd left all the furniture, perhaps having rented the place furnished. Her bed was tousled, the linens and blankets all there, and her towels were still hanging in the bathroom. Her toiletries were gone, however, except for a lime-green comb. All that was in the cupboard beneath the sink was a bottle of Windex and a roll of paper towels.

I looked at her pillow, the indentation of her lovely head, the almost-clear body lines she'd left in the bed. The intimacy of her right now was almost unbearable.

The closet was empty of clothes, as were the drawers of a small bureau. Her softball bats were gone. She'd left behind some trash in a bag beneath the sink, which I inspected: Wendy's wrappers, a frozen-pizza box, an empty bag of spaghetti, an empty jar of Ragu tomato sauce. There were some grocery receipts corresponding to those items, as well as a drugstore receipt for candy and sunscreen. "Hmm," I said into the empty kitchen. You don't need sunscreen in Michigan around Halloween. All the bills had been paid in cash.

The refrigerator was empty except for half an onion, an apple, and a bag of carrots. There was no array of condiments, as you'd see cramming the door of anybody's refrigerator; a couple of flat bladders of McDonald's ketchup was all. This had been a short-term rental, all right.

I sat on the couch and thought. Should I report the damage to Porrocks's house to the police? If I did that, I'd of course have to tell her about it. She'd have to file an insurance claim. I couldn't even begin to imagine telling her about this, upsetting her so much right when all she needed was to get well. I looked at my watch and wondered if she was in surgery right now. It was eleven o'clock. "Oh, God," I muttered.

I had to catch up with Audrey Knox, and I had to talk to Vic Toretti, who might be with her now. She might essentially be working for him, or—I remembered Lisette Donovan's words about Toretti's girlfriend: *spooky little thing, little pretty vampire, well-dressed.*

Yeah. Lisette said Toretti's girlfriend's name was Bev, but that meant nothing. Most likely, Audrey Knox was an alias as well. Blast it all to hell. I'd never seen her driver's license, never glimpsed anything with her name on it. I could figure out a way to learn the name under which she'd rented the apartment from the building's manager, but for what good?

I took the Windex and paper towels from the bathroom and let myself into the corridor, first carefully blocking the lock open with a bit of twisted paper. I went outside to the windows of 1D and began cleaning them. The old woman appeared instantly and cranked one of her panels open to critique the job I was doing. After a minute I was able to tap into her lust to gossip by saying, "You know that little cutie in 2B?"

The old woman's eyes chirked up and she lifted a brow as if to say, *Yeah, that slutty thing—whatcha got?*

"Looks like she took off," I muttered, shaking my head. "I lent her some valuable records, which I'd like to have back. You wouldn't have heard anything, would you?"

"Huh," said the woman. "Well, good luck with the likes of her." Her blue-veined hands gripped the inner window frame like talons. "I saw her packing her car yesterday. She's long gone."

"Yeah? What's she drive, anyway?"

"I don't know. A purple car."

"That purplish Avalon that was out front?"

"Yes, that one," the woman said decisively and scornfully, as if Audrey's choice of car showed just what a lousy person she was.

"Well, do you know where she might have gone? I mean, did you ever talk to her?"

"Oh, we spoke occasionally." This was delivered coyly, and I saw that she'd no idea where Audrey went, probably never had spoken to her, but wanted to keep me engaged, wanted to keep me talking. It was a pity the woman was lonely, but I had too much to do to waste any more time with her.

A voice behind me said, "I know where she went."

I turned, wet wad of paper towels in midair.

A young man who resembled an isosceles triangle stood there with a two-wheeled shopping cart full of groceries. He wore a long black overcoat similar to Drooly Rick's, but the coat was stiff and flared out at ground level. Then it narrowed to his unbroad shoulders and relatively small but well-groomed head. His crisply avant-garde haircut and the fact that his hair was dyed white proclaimed him to be a contributing member of society—artistic species.

I understood that a young person who dyes his hair white is making an ironic statement, the opposite of what an older person tries to do with a bottle of hair color. His leather shoes were paint-spattered and he carried, slung over one shoulder, a canvas bag with a picture of Mr. Peanut on it. The dad-style overcoat teamed with the tot-style accessory—yes, this young man was a nonconformist.

"Well, where?" I finally said.

He said in a gentle tone, "Where else do lost people go?"

Oh, brother.

"What'd he say?" queried the old woman through her window.

"*Home*," the young man said intensely. "She went where we all dream of going."

He seemed a really nice guy beneath all that individuality. I said, "Do you know that for a fact, as in she actually told you where she was going, or have you just made a theoretical, philosophical statement?"

"I never theorize."

"Okay. You mean her ancestral state? Would you just sort of talk to me here, man? I'm Lillian, by the way."

He stepped forward and shook my hand. "James."

"I'm Pamela!" called the old woman.

"Okay, good to meet you, James. You know who we're talking about? This woman named Audrey Knox?"

"I think I know who we're talking about. Initially, I knew her as Beverly, but lately she was calling herself Audrey."

"How come, do you know?"

"She said it was her middle name and she preferred it. I think she did in fact go back to Idaho. Why are you interested? She's not dealing anymore, if that's what you need."

So James and I talked there on the sidewalk for a few minutes, and although his information was good, it wasn't quite pay dirt. I explained about my missing valuable records and found out he'd known Audrey slightly for a couple of years. He lived in the apartment building, painted in oil colors he mixed himself, attended classes at Wayne State, and worked at a bar called the Gridlock.

"I saw her in the neighborhood and realized she'd moved into this building. She'd come into the bar once in a while and we'd talk, not much, you know. She had an interesting gestalt—you know, her look. It was very of a piece."

"Yes, I know what you mean."

"People like that interest me. But she never really opened up to me. Last I saw her—I guess a couple of nights ago—she said she had some scores to settle back home."

A couple of nights ago. "Yeah, like what? Do you know?"

"No, she never said. She acted tough about it, like she was trying to impress me. I could tell she's a lost soul, though. Very sad underneath. Said she'll be happier at home. Maybe she will be."

"Well, I'm really pissed at her. I don't want to make a federal case out of it, but I want my stuff back."

"I'd guess that unless you go to Idaho, you won't get your records back. Were they, like, some jazz 78s?"

"Uh, yeah. In fact, I lent her some Bessie Smiths and some Little Memphis Jims."

"Oh! What a pity."

"So she actually said Boise was her home?"

"She said Idaho, which I remembered, because you don't meet people from Idaho every day. I don't know that she said exactly Boise. How valuable are those records, Lillian? I mean, one time I drove all the way up to Sanilac to hunt down a guy who owed me fifty bucks, but jeez."

I asked if he knew Vic Toretti, by any chance. He didn't, nor did he know anything more except that Audrey had mentioned that she'd dealt cocaine in the past.

I returned to her apartment. After using the toilet and washing up, I reclined on the couch and thought. Audrey didn't seem like all that much of a nature girl—no fleece jacket, no hiking shoes. Her style was urban. Yet the triangulation of James's and my information told me at the very least she had connections out West.

The apartment's walls and ceilings were painted white, and there was a motel-style picture of a millpond and a boy in a canoe on the wall. Audrey had left a few magazines on the floor next to the couch— *People, Cosmopolitan* (which disappointed me perhaps more), and a Victoria's Secret catalog, which is essentially a soft-core porn magazine.

Why had she spoken of her fondness for Idaho? Why would she tell me anything truthful? Well, she didn't know Lillian Byrd, that was for sure. Even the most calculating crooks get honest once in a while. They get careless. By this time in my life, I'd learned that a little bit of carelessness can go a long way.

I tried to sort out what I ought to do, what was realistic for me to do, and what I couldn't do.

I didn't want to upset Porrocks. Therefore I didn't want to report the damage to her house to the police just yet. I needed to find out how she was doing.

If I could find Vic Toretti, I might more easily locate Audrey Knox. Or, vice versa, if I took the Greyhound to Boise, how the hell would I find Audrey Knox if she was there? Idaho is a large potato-shaped state with hundreds of thousands of people living in it. You don't just show up in a place and start walking around hoping to bump into your fugitive.

The receipt for the sunscreen bothered me. Was Idaho sunnier than I'd thought?

I rolled onto my stomach and poked desultorily at the magazines with my finger. I noticed a letter-sized piece of paper tucked into the *Cosmo*, perhaps as a marker. I pulled it out. It was an Alamo rental-car receipt. I sat up.

Pay dirt: Audrey Knox had rented a black Chevrolet Blazer for one day. And the date was the date Porrocks was run over. The receipt documented a Michigan driver's license number and a Visa card number.

Twenty

Lt. Det. Eric Stonehauser stepped over a pile of crushed plaster in Porrocks's living room, pushed his hat back on his head, and said, "This almost beats my wife's housekeeping."

The junior cop who'd driven him to the house snickered in a toadying way. As the three of us surveyed the damage, I thought it all looked uglier than ever.

"Well," I said, "I was hoping to avoid telling Porrocks about this just yet."

"Nobody has to tell her anything," Stonehauser said. He was the walrusy one I'd met briefly when I'd stopped in to ask about Drooly Rick's identity. Stonehauser wore a plain gray fedora, which looked just right on him. Guys these days look ridiculous in hats like that, except for a few, and Stonehauser was one of the few. I like a guy who can wear a fedora. He removed it and stepped over to hang it on Porrocks's foyer hook.

He continued, "You're the house sitter. You called it in. We'll do an MDOP on this, but Ms. Porrocks doesn't have to know yet." MDOP is cop-ese for "malicious destruction of property."

"You understand my embarrassment," I said.

"Sure, if I were you I'd want to at least clean this up for her. Be a challenge to fix it so you couldn't even tell it happened, wouldn't it?"

"Like in classic *Mission Impossible* shows with Peter Graves in them," the toadying cop said. He was young and clearly ambitious but in the wrong way; he looked at the older cop with calculated adoration. "Like where they do all this construction to look like it was there all along, and then when—"

"I heard she's gonna be okay," Stonehauser said, ignoring him.

"Yes, I got word just after I called you that her surgery went great. They expect her to make a full recovery."

Stonehauser nodded. "Now, what about that rental-car receipt?"

I handed it to him. "As I said on the phone, the person who rented this car lived in that building across the street—and now she's gone."

I invited the cops to sit at the kitchen table where I went over everything—Drooly Rick, the boathouse wall, Audrey Knox, Idaho, Jimmy Donovan, and Vic Toretti. The cops wrote down notes. The name Vic Toretti rang a bell for the junior cop. He said, "I think Sherman or Leedy or somebody busted him for possession, and as soon as he got out, something happened to him. I think he's dead."

"Yeah?" I said.

"We'll check it out," he told me dismissively.

"Okay, and, well, Audrey Knox could be an alias, of course—"

"We'll check it out," the junior cop said again. Stonehauser gave him a look that said, *Don't interrupt the witness.*

I said, "I was just trying to say that she went by the name of Bev or Beverly before she was known as Audrey."

"Beverly what?"

"I don't know."

The junior cop, writing a note, let out a subtly sarcastic sound. Stonehauser said, "Bill, shut up."

Bill gave him a *What'd I do?* look, but he got the point.

"I know it's not much help," I acknowledged, "but I wanted to tell you guys everything." A twinge seized my midsection, because I hadn't told them everything. I'd omitted the gold bracelet. I'd confessed to finding the cash and said I'd bring it to the station, but I kept my mouth shut about the bracelet. Why? Because I had a vague idea I might need it.

They asked for a description of Audrey Knox, then Stonehauser wished me luck and told me it'd be okay for me to call him.

After they left, I toted Todd, my gym bag, and jumper cables to the bus stop.

Back at my apartment in Eagle, it felt good to be consolidated again. Todd seemed to appreciate being home. He used his litter box, ate, and drank a little, and generally bumped around.

"Just keep being my friend, all right?" I said. He looked up at me and thought his private rabbit thoughts.

Mrs. McVittie's tentative tap sounded at the door.

I greeted her warmly, as always. "Please come in."

"I can't, dear. I've got some soup on the stove, but"—she stood on the landing twisting her almost transparently thin hands in her apron—"I'm so glad you're all right!"

"What's the matter, Mrs. McVittie?"

"Well," she hesitated, then blurted, "are you furious with us?"

"No. What are you talking about?"

"She said you'd be furious when you got home because we wouldn't let her in." Mrs. McVittie's head and hands moved as if buffeted by a tiny but insistent current. Still, she and her husband managed to live independently and more or less safely. Their grown children looked in on them frequently, and I was usually around for backup.

I said, "Wouldn't let who in? When?"

"The young woman who said she was your cousin. It was yesterday afternoon, around three o'clock, I guess. She told us you'd gotten hurt and she had to come in and get your medical card for you."

"My medical card?" I wished I had one.

"Yes."

"Was she about five foot three, a little plump, curly hair?"

"Yes!"

"She's not my cousin. You didn't let her in?"

"No, Emmett has a policy. We don't let anybody into the rental unless the renter arranges it with us in advance."

"A good policy."

Mrs. McVittie sucked her teeth. "We were worried about you, naturally, but something about her didn't seem quite right. She wouldn't tell us whether you were in the hospital or what. Oh, she wanted something from this apartment in the worst way! Emmett finally threatened to call the police on her."

"Yes. Interesting. Well, I don't think she'll be around anymore. I'm sorry you were bothered."

"She's not a friend of yours, then?"

With a firm voice and a sad heart, I replied, "No."

It was about four o'clock when I returned to Wyandotte on the bus. I got off at the hardware store and put three pairs of work gloves, two boxes of contractor-weight trash bags, and a handful of household fuses on my credit card. Next I stopped at the party store on the corner and picked up a six-pack of Coke, one of Stroh's, and a giant bag of Doritos. I schlepped all of it over to Porrocks's and got busy.

I threw away the broken fuses and put new ones in the box downstairs, turned on all the lights, put some of Porrocks's Patsy Cline CDs on the player, and found the vacuum cleaner (with, fortunately, a stash of fresh bags), and started picking up debris.

It was from Lou that I'd learned Porrocks came through her surgery well, though she was running a fever and would have to stay in the hospital until that cleared up. Porrocks's sister told her she'd come as soon as Erma was out of the hospital, Lou added with an edge of resentment. Well, that was a relief to me. When I broke the news to Lou about what

I'd found at the house, she immediately said, "I'll be there as soon as I get off work. We can use my city truck to haul stuff."

"Isn't that against the rules?"

"Lillian, do you really care at this point?"

"No, but I thought I should make a show of it. Anyway, I think I can get Billie to come too, and I'll get pizza for us."

That was a long night. Both of my friends showed up, and the three of us set to scooping and chipping and dumping. Lou's knowledge of electricity came in most handy; she inspected the exposed wiring and tucked it away to ensure we didn't fry ourselves.

Initially, we kept up our energy with the Cokes and Doritos; it was fun to carelessly munch with no thought of crumb mess, since the final vacuuming would take care of all that.

Lou worked with ox-like determination, the stolidity of a simple honest soul in love. As she worked, she rumbled incessantly of the wonders and charms of Erma Porrocks in her gravel-pit voice until Billie and I found reasons to work in other rooms. I turned up the volume on Patsy Cline. As we worked hour after hour, Billie's copper-bright hair abandoned any idea of obedience. She kept tucking it behind her ears, then gave up and mashed down the fluffy mass with a faded SAY NICE THINGS ABOUT DETROIT cap. Billie couldn't believe the destruction, and she could barely fathom the whole goddamn story.

"Lillian, I mean, a man is *dead*, and you're talking about going to *Idaho* to help the police find some *psychopathic pixie* you still had the hots for as of *this morning*? How do you get yourself *into* these things?"

"When," I asked, "will you ever learn that my true talent is for getting myself *out* of these things?"

"That's a glib answer, sweetheart. Don't glib me."

"Well, I haven't made up my mind to travel anywhere yet. I don't— I don't have enough to go on."

Waitresses, like ballerinas, have thighs like concrete. Billie pumped along tirelessly as the night wore on—this on top of a full shift at the diner. Although most of Billie's and my dynamic had been her taking care of me, I'd actually managed to do her a couple of serious favors lately, so I didn't feel like a total shit asking for her help tonight. I'd helped her paint her garage and rototill her garden, neither a demure task, especially given the dimensions of her garden. I told her she should rent a combine when her sweet corn came in. Plus, I'd volunteered to spend three weeks bottle-feeding a baby pig she'd rescued somewhere; Todd's patience was strained by the tiny pink interloper, but he forgave me. He liked Billie too. She was a sincere animal person.

At about two A.M., we ate pizza and drank beer before gathering our strength for mopping and damp-dusting. And by four we'd done it. The place was clean, all the debris packed into the back of Lou's truck.

"Where are you going to dump this stuff?" I asked.

She winked. "Us city professionals have connections. Not to worry."

I was too tired to wonder which casino's or factory's dump bins would wind up quietly swallowing our trash.

I threw Porrocks's rags in the washing machine, and the three of us took one last look at all the cleanliness we'd wrought. We were all silently wishing we could get the walls repaired just as fast too. I offered up a prayer of thanks to Spic-n-Span.

"Well," Lou said, reading everybody's mind, "I can get some drywall and come back tomorrow night and fix it."

"Have you ever done drywall?" I asked.

"No, but how hard could it be?" The three of us were so slaphappy with fatigue, we laughed uproariously at that.

"Seriously," said Lou, catching her breath.

Billie suggested, "Maybe one of Porrocks's other friends knows how to do drywall. Like one of the guys on the force?"

I said, "Drywall is not something cops do in their spare time."

"She's right," Lou said. "It'd take us as much time finding somebody to do it for cheap as just learning to do it myself. I mean, look at the place: It doesn't look like such a big job now, does it?"

Billie and I acknowledged that, in fact, it didn't.

"Leave it to me," Lou said.

Billie turned to me. "What are you going to do next?"

I traced a half-circle on Porrocks's rug with the toe of my shoe. "Sometimes," I said, "I do my best thinking while cleaning. An idea came to me about an hour ago. Lou, would you give me a lift home? And, Billie, if I do go out of town, can you take Todd for a while?"

Twenty-One

I slept a few hours, then got up and ate a quick breakfast of toast and coffee. I retrieved my prized Canon, a journalistic tool I'd vowed never to hock, from its corner of my closet, unloaded the film, laced up my Chuck Taylors, and walked the thirty minutes to Blue Streak Photo on Eight Mile. It was another bracing, fine October Saturday in Michigan. Frighteningly, many of Eight Mile's shopkeepers had thrown themselves into harvest decoration mode, so I had to keep sidestepping pyramids of pumpkins and bundles of corn shucks. Blue Streak's stack of European art magazines kept my mind occupied as I waited for express processing on my roll of Tri-X.

And then, standing at the counter, I scanned the contact sheet until I found it. "Ha!" I said. I ordered two express prints and waited for them.

I was right. Until that moment all I had to go on with Audrey Knox was Boise, Idaho. No, I didn't have a photograph of her. What I had was the picture of Todd and me I'd asked her to snap the night we stayed up late playing Calico Jones and Sexy Scientist.

So there I was, sitting on my living room floor with this stupid infatuated look on my face and holding Todd, who always looked dignified. There was my ninety-dollar couch from St. Vincent de Paul, my throw pillow with the face of Jesus needlepointed on it by my great-aunt Alberta. There was the McVitties' mottled wall-to-wall landlord carpeting. And there sitting next to me, just as neat as whiskey, were Audrey Knox's shoes: the two-tone, shamrock-embroidered, custom-made, cute little shoes. Made for her by a cobbler back home.

The idea to develop that film had come to me as I damp-dusted Porrocks's oak mantel last night.

I hiked home with the prints and called Lieutenant Stonehauser, thinking to leave a message, it being the weekend, but he surprised me by picking up.

"Oh, a few of us masochistic types like to come in on Saturdays and Sundays," he said. "We've got some more information," he went on before I even asked. "You know that Vic Toretti?" I heard his fingers drumming on a plastic keyboard in the relative quiet of the detective division. "He is dead, just like Bill thought."

"What happened to him?"

"Heroin overdose on September 2, less than a week after he got paroled."

"Oh. Where did it happen?"

"Good question. Tom Ciesla told me you were sharp."

"He did?"

"Yeah, he called to see how we're doing on the hit-and-run, and my interview with you yesterday came up. He said if I want a peaceful life I should go ahead and answer your questions."

"Because otherwise I'll make more work for you by sticking my nose in places I shouldn't?" I asked.

"Exactly."

"Uh, well, I'm glad we understand each other, Lieutenant."

Stonehauser laughed. He liked me. Thank God he liked me—at least I amused him. You never know with cops. For instance, if his side-kick, young Bill, had been in charge of the investigation, he wouldn't've even taken my call. That guy was a pissant from the word go.

Stonehauser said, "204 Adderly Street, number 2B."

"That's where Toretti died?"

"Yes."

"That's the apartment! That's Audrey Knox's apartment!"

"Yes, I know. Actually our suspect's name is not Audrey Knox, because Audrey Knox is a student at Mercy College who had her identity stolen sometime in August. She didn't know it until this morning when we called."

"Really, now? So we're talking a credit card gotten under false pretenses, but what about the driver's license? Forged?"

"Had to be."

"Huh," I commented. "Well, what about Idaho?"

"What about Idaho?"

"You could give a description of—of the fugitive formerly known as Audrey Knox to the state police, and remember I told you about the purple Avalon and the sunscreen, right?"

"You did, but without a plate number, Lillian, it's nothing. And what'm I supposed to do with the fact that she bought a tube of sunscreen? Look, Bill's going over now to inspect that Chevy Blazer on the rental receipt. Until we have more evidence, I can't justify alerting the whole state of Idaho to look for somebody who at this point doesn't even qualify as a suspect in that hit-and-run."

"Well, she did it."

"Fine. Prove it."

"You realize, Lieutenant, I take that as a direct challenge."

He laughed again. I caught a tone from him that made me feel good. He appreciated my drive for revenge—he didn't try to shut me down. Well, I'd liked him from the first minute we met.

He said, "This person is a suspect in the identity theft and the property destruction, all right. I'll grant that, but—"

"But," I interjected, "if she broke into those walls, she stole money from Porrocks's house."

"You don't know whether she found anything in those walls. They might've been empty."

"But I showed you the patches. Somebody stowed something in there, and Jimmy Donovan was a drug dealer who handled a lot of money."

"And he might just as easily have unstashed it, using the same holes."

That hadn't occurred to me.

Stonehauser said, "The boathouse might've been the only place with money in it."

"Yeah."

"So as far as anybody knows, there's nothing missing from Ms. Porrocks's house!"

I admitted, "It's not missing if you didn't know it was there."

"All right?" said the detective.

I took a deep breath. "What if I told you I've got another clue about the fugitive formerly known as Audrey Knox?"

"What is it?"

I told him about the shoes and the photograph. He cleared his throat and said, with the hard-edged politeness of sarcasm, "That's a clue as to her name and whereabouts, right?"

"Right!" I exulted.

"But not a clue that points to anybody's guilt in anything."

"Uh, right."

"So don't bother me with it now. This is not the O.J. Simpson case. I mean, okay, I shouldn't have said don't bother me with information, but come on. A picture of a pair of shoes? What would you do, show it to shoemakers in Idaho?"

"Well, yes."

"She probably bought them in a store, anyway. Sounds like bullshit, frankly."

"Lieutenant, I sense you're running out of good will toward me here."

"I gotta concentrate on first things first."

"But these shoes really could be the—"

"I understand! Look, you know my resources are limited. Right? And so are the resources of every cop in Idaho or any other damn state. Now, if this was a murder investigation, I'd be all over that shoe picture. But I have to concentrate on police practices that fifteen years of experience have taught me will bear the most fruit—like sending Bill over to look at that car, like interviewing people in the neighborhood where Ms. Porrocks was hit to see if anybody saw anything, like talking to some of the lowlifes Toretti hung out with, people who might have known him or the suspect."

Had I been a real detective, I'd have thrown myself into all kinds of workmanlike activities just like Stonehauser described to find my erstwhile lover. As we know so well by now, however, I wasn't.

I hunkered on the floor with Todd and my mandolin. As I played "Tom Billy's Jig" and "Banks of Red Roses," he laid his head on my thigh. When I played "Wildwood Flower," he got very calm, as he always did when listening to that song. I thought about Audrey.

I kept calling her Audrey in my mind; I had to call her something, and all the other names I could think of were ever so vulgar. So Vic Toretti was dead. I pictured him getting out of prison, breathing the muggy grassy air of central Michigan, running into the waiting arms of his faithful sexpot girlfriend. They would have lived it up, partied heavily—McDonald's hamburgers, beer, all the Snickers bars he could hold. And then he overdosed. How easily that could have happened.

Had he told Audrey to rent the apartment before he got out without telling her why? Maybe. He would have hinted to her about loot, though, to keep her interested in him, to get her to agree to help him get it, and let him screw her while they plotted. All she needed was one half of a breath of a mention of hidden money, and she'd have been all over him. I could just see her, a silky boa constrictor, squeezing the information out of him an ounce at a time.

Then once she knew why she'd rented an apartment overlooking that house, what good was Toretti to her? Just a guy to fuck and argue with.

Me: Now, don't get carried away.

Me: But it would've been so easy for her to kill Toretti with an overdose. Get him good and drunk, then offer some special Mary-pure smack you got and saved for just such an important occasion. Stick it in him before he knew what was happening.

Me: Okay, fine. Now pick up the phone and find out when the next bus to Boise's leaving.

Me: Oh God, should I?

Me: Of course you *shouldn't*. What difference has that ever made to you?

Me: Right.

Me: The point is, she took you for the biggest sucker in three counties. She killed Drooly Rick, she tried to kill Porrocks, and she'd made up her mind to kill you—if you hadn't handed her the goddamn keys to Porrocks's house!

Me: I just cannot believe my error in judgment. I just cannot believe she really used me! Used me and cast me aside like a Kotex—from the very beginning! Use it once, then throw it away. I've got to believe maybe she did really care for me, really truly. Maybe she cared for me at least a little bit and regrets hurting me. Maybe she wishes she could apologize.

Me: Listen to yourself! Now you're saying you hope a *murderer* found you appealing? You're hoping a murderer felt true deep affection for you, *loved* you? Are you insane?

Me: I have to meet up with that bitch. I loved her, okay? I fell for her and I loved her! I thought she was the universe's gift to me, to make up for all the shit I've had to deal with in my life. I thought it was finally *my turn*! I can't let that go without a fight. If I can just have a—

Me: A heart-to-heart talk with her?

Me: Even I'm not that naïve. An honest confrontation with her, at least. Then I'll feel better when she goes to jail for her crimes.

Me: She has no heart, you know.

Me: How can I be sure?

Twenty-Two

You have perhaps taken a long bus trip across this magnificent continent. If so, you know that such a trip has its heavens and its hells. For some people I've met, heaven is sitting next to a quiet stranger and speaking every thought that has ever come into your head, plus all the new ones the trip stimulates. For others, needless to say, hell is being the quiet stranger.

While I generally like listening to people, smart and dumb alike, I've not been able to figure out how to shut up another human being at will. Therefore when I'm a captive of public transportation, heaven is an empty seat next to me. I love watching the scenery, which is considerable even from the limits of the interstates. You can't beat a prairie thunderstorm, the purple horizon sweeping toward you flashing and growling; likewise, a flock of meadowlarks taking turns streaking upward yellow-breasted, then coasting down to join their brethren invisible in the prairie. Or your first glimpse of the Rockies sternly and astonishingly welcoming you West.

On the Greyhound one must reconcile oneself to missing all the quaintness of the back roads. The people who live on those back roads, however, tend to be the ones who ride the bus.

If I have to sit next to someone, I like sitting next to servicemen and servicewomen who tell me about their military adventures, be they getting burned by the hot cartridge casings spewed by machine guns, or learning that knuckle pushups are easier in the long run because they save stress on your wrists, or standing on the deck of the destroyer after the locked-on alarm has sounded and wondering whether the technology that's supposed to confuse the enemy missile will work this time.

I like sitting next to people who read silently. I like sitting next to people who own their own small businesses, because they are generally agile-minded.

I do not like sitting next to people who must orally justify the choices they have made in life over and over again. I do not like people who play pocket video games that emit toothpick-like beeping sounds. How does that poem go, be patient with jackasses and the insane, for they too have their stories? That's great, but just try sitting next to one of them across two or three state lines.

I like people who use deodorant. I like people who have taken the time and trouble to teach their small children basic manners.

The first twenty-four hours of my trip to Boise more or less constituted Great Plains hell, but then a little boy in a cardigan sweater walked up the aisle and paused at my seat. He stooped and picked up something.

"Miss, is this your nickel?" he asked quietly, holding it out to me.

I nearly scooped him up in a hug. "No, young man. You're five cents richer."

That little boy sustained me for the next twenty-seven hours.

On an overnight bus trip, you work at cleanliness at the comfort stops; you try to find fresh fruit before the doughnuts and fried chicken take their toll; you sit and think a lot as the bus plows through twilight into black night. The driver dims the interior lights, and the blackness weighs on your eyes—the hard blackness of the bus window, reflecting back your own ghostly face, makes you uneasy when you know you ought to sleep.

You sit and you stare and you think. You hunch down in your coat, and you listen to other people's breathing. You think about the creases on the back of the driver's neck, and you wonder whether there's a more relentlessly nauseating smell than diesel fumes mixed with chemical toilet fumes, and you think about life and death and love and cancer and electric blankets and sitcoms and prom dates and bounced checks. You worry. You worry about your sick old pet rabbit back at Billie's, and you worry about meeting up with someone who might try to do you harm. At long last you realize that shapes are coalescing on the other side of the cold glass and dawn is coming and then the world returns, and you figure what the hell, everybody dies.

As the bus rolled the last 150 miles through the Snake River Plains, buffered by blocky mountains to the north, I saw why Audrey loved Idaho. You look up from the potato fields and hay fields and ache to smell the cleanliness of the forests as they reach up to the snow line on those mountains.

A cold thunderstorm had just passed through, and there was a feeling of relief about the town of Boise as the sun came out and the wind blew the still-heavy clouds off to the east. I saw that Boise featured the usual retail strips and noisy little airport, but the downtown part looked fairly interesting, with parks and clean streets and camping equipment stores and restaurants that looked as if they might serve olive oil and salt with their bread instead of I Can't Believe It's Not Butter.

When the bus pulled into the Boise depot and shut its motor off, I staggered slightly on the way to the women's room but got my land legs back quickly. I'd done a little research, bought a map, and made two telephone calls before boarding the bus in Detroit. Which is to say I had a plan. It was Tuesday morning.

Wearing my peacoat, blue jeans, and my Chuck Taylors and carrying only my gym bag, I hiked three quarters of a mile to a storefront shop run by a guy who called himself a cobbler in the Yellow Pages but whose dusty, stinky shop offered only such minor footwear surgery as resoling and seam stitching.

The other establishment I'd targeted occupied a loft above a health food store. Suddenly hungry, I stopped and consumed a tart organically grown Pink Lady apple, a falafel sandwich, and a bottle of ginger drink. I don't usually go in for such stuff, but I guess my body was craving unprocessed food.

The shoemaker upstairs remembered my call and introduced himself as Sajeed. I continued to use the name Roberta Klotzak, for simplicity's sake. Judging by the decorations in his shop, Sajeed was of Egyptian descent, which was sort of surprising, since Egyptians aren't exactly known for their shoemaking folkways. Nevertheless, he kept a very nice shop, with framed Egyptian blessings and woven things on the walls. You expect cobblers to be old, with Geppetto-style whiskers and so on, but this one was young, with bright black eyes and satiny nut-pod skin.

His main business was making bulky custom footwear for people with diabetes, plus he dyed shoes for bridesmaids and so on. I saw these things as he showed me around his shop. "But what feeds my soul," he told me, unconscious of his pun, "is making exquisite shoes of calfskin and kidskin for people who want something different." His voice was good-humored and spicy with the offbeat cadence of his accent.

He pointed to his photo wall. "These are examples of what I can do."

The shoes were beautiful—sleek lines and interesting patterns of leathers, lethal high heels—a lot of them—and low slip-ons. I didn't see Audrey's shoes among them, but it didn't matter; Sajeed's style was unmistakable. My heart began to pound. I forced myself to remain casual.

"The women in this town sure have big feet," I commented.

"Would you guess that transvestites make up a large portion of my clientele?"

I looked at him.

He said, "For men, it is hard to be comfortable in even the largest sizes made for women."

Mr. Sajeed's shop smelled wonderfully of new leather and shoe wax. Hundreds of wooden lasts hung on a rail over his work bench, where perhaps a dozen shoes, some half done, others almost done, lay among worn tools of steel and wood.

Steel, wood, leather—all good materials to work with one's hands, I thought.

He glanced at my ragged Chuck Taylors, then met my eyes with a look of solemn sympathy.

"Well," I said, "I bet you get to know quite a few people in this town."

"Oh, yes, I do. It is a very friendly place. Would you like to sit? What may I do for you today, Miss Klotzak?"

"Call me Roberta, please." He smiled resignedly, and I realized he was a man accustomed to civilized forms of address. I sat on a little carved chair and he took a low stool, resting his hands on his thighs. I took out the photograph.

For an instant he was baffled—*A rabbit? You want shoes for your rabbit, lady?*—then he saw Audrey's shoes and coughed softly. "Oh, yes. I made that pair."

"They're very pretty."

"Pretty but sturdy," he said proudly. "You could walk over a hundred roads in my shoes. Why are you showing me this picture?"

"Well, Mr. Sajeed, I'm trying to find their owner."

He looked at me with a little smile. "It would be for a personal reason?"

"It would, yes. It's a long story, and you're a busy man. Can you help me?"

His face lifted in remembering. Then he shot me an exceedingly sharp look, which I met with my standard open earnest expression, and I saw that he had an opinion about Audrey Knox.

He decided to give me her name, his thumbs curling back deliberately. "Miss Beverly Austin. Yes, I made a pair for her and one for her sister. A little different pattern for the sister—the decoration was a thunderbird on each vamp."

"Sister?" I leaned forward.

His face clouded. "Not that she has much use for them anymore."

"What do you mean?"

He shook his head.

"Mr. Sajeed, does Beverly Austin owe you money?"

"How do you know this?" he exclaimed. "I am very impressed."

"I too have had some dealings with Miss Beverly Austin."

"Now I understand. Well, I do not know where she is. For a time I tried to find her myself, but"—he spread his hands—"I didn't try very hard. You see, I am no detective."

"Me neither." For once, I didn't laugh nervously when I said it. "So her shoes aren't paid for."

"Not fully."

"Have you ever heard the saying, 'New shoes will squeak until they're paid for'?"

Sajeed burst out laughing. "No! I must put up that saying. Oh, I like that saying."

"Bad debts," I said. "Cost of doing business."

"Yes. It was not very much money, anyway."

"I see." The windows of the shop were clean. A starling lighted on the ledge and preened as if admiring its reflection.

"Others in this city have wished to find Miss Beverly Austin. I let them keep trying."

"Others?"

"It seems always to have to do with money."

"Always small amounts?"

"Oh, no! There is a man who—foolishly, I am sorry to say—permitted Miss Beverly Austin to load a truck with many televisions and drive away promising to pay him. He said the shipment was worth $50,000. I will make tea now. If a person sits with me long enough, I must make tea." He went over to his little tea shrine in a corner and carefully fussed with kettle, hot plate, and canister as we continued to talk.

I said, "You're very kind, Mr. Sajeed. I'd like a cup very much. What did the police do about the stolen televisions?"

"Nothing, I'm afraid. They could not find her either."

"Well," I muttered, "I could've told them where to look until a few days ago."

"With a truck she would go to Mexico or one of the large cities far from here."

"Why is that?"

He shrugged at my ignorance. "That is where one goes with stolen goods. One goes to Mexico if one has a way to cross the border without questions. Or to a large city with many dangerous areas. There such property changes hands easily."

"Yes." I thought of Detroit. "Well, what about this sister of hers?"

"I know where you can find her sister, Miss Amanda Austin. Everyone here knows Miss Amanda Austin."

"Yes?"

"She is a brave lady, a spiritual lady of good reputation."

"Spiritual? You mentioned she asked for thunderbird decorations on her shoes. That's a symbol, uh—"

"A symbol of the American Indians."

"Right, it's a power symbol, I guess."

"Do you like sugar in your tea? I like sugar in my tea. Miss Amanda Austin is known to have a special interest in the culture of the native people of this land. Some say she has learned their magic."

"Really?" How potentially useful.

The cobbler handed me tea in a red mug with SKI PROVO on it in white letters. His mug featured a sea otter holding an urchin on its stomach. The tea smelled and tasted good. "However, Miss Klotzak, she will surely not help you find her sister."

"How do you know that?"

"She did not help me. She does not help anyone who searches for her sister."

We drank our tea. I said, "She's protective, then."

"They are two very different sisters."

"Not twins?"

"No, Miss Beverly Austin is younger. The young bad one!" He laughed. "Here, I'll get Miss Amanda's address for you, I do not know it by heart. I'm sure she will not mind me doing so."

He went behind his counter. "My filing system is primitive but useful." And he brought out—what else?—a shoebox: his card catalog. He flipped through the cards, then pulled out one. "Yes, here," he said, turning it so I could read it. I copied the address and phone number into my pocket notebook.

He wished me luck.

I said, "Look, Mr. Sajeed. It occurs to me that you might call Amanda Austin to tell her to expect a visitor—and that's fine with me if you do. But I'd like you not to mention my name—at least yet. I ask this of you."

He looked at me with his smiling black eyes. "You wish to trick Miss Amanda Austin?"

"Harmlessly, I promise. And—it's a trick in the name of honesty and justice. I'm not even sure it'll—"

"I will not call her. I do not believe she can be tricked, so it does not matter."

"What is she, a mind reader?"

"Some think so, but I myself do not believe in such things."

I went down to the natural grocery and bought a bag of oranges and a package of dates and carried them up to Mr. Sajeed's loft.

"Please accept my thanks," I said.

He took the fruit with a broad white smile. "I accept your thanks."

Twenty-Three

Miss Amanda Austin lived in an apartment downtown in one of those cool old buildings with stone lintels and bronze lobby doors. I rang her buzzer and after a minute a sweet voice came over the intercom. "Yes?"

"My name is Stacy Wounded Deer." I paused. "I search for Miss Amanda Austin. I am sent by friends."

"Uh, well, what about?"

"I am sent by friends."

"Friends—who?"

"Friends of Miss Beverly Austin."

"Oh? Well, come on up."

"If it's convenient. Thank you very much."

"Oh, it's always convenient with me!" Amanda Austin's voice was upbeat, the words delivered with crisp enthusiasm.

Her apartment door stood ajar as I alighted from the elevator. I tapped on it and pushed it two inches open. A brief whirring sound came to my ears, then, "Come in!"

I stepped into a bright living room where a rush of information presented itself to me. A woman, a near-replica of my fugitive—Audrey

Knox, now identified as Beverly Austin—sat in a motorized wheelchair. Sajeed had said Amanda was older, and I saw this, but she didn't look that much older—maybe three or five years.

Amanda Austin's hair twined about her ears and neck in the same silky-curly way Beverly's had. She had the same plump pixie mouth and chin. Even the eyes were similar, though Amanda lacked the hard-life stress lines I'd noticed in her sister.

I closed the door behind me, crossed the room, and took Amanda's extended hand. "How do you do, Miss Austin? As I said, I'm Stacy Wounded Deer."

"Very well today, thank you." She smiled and looked at me with curiosity and friendliness. Her basic build was about the same as Beverly's, but her body was heavier. Her round tummy challenged the fabric of the pale pink sweat suit she was wearing, but she didn't have that weighed-down, sad-frog look that you see in other fat wheelchair-bound people. On her feet were white fringed moccasins, and I half expected them to fidget.

Because I guess if she hadn't been in a wheelchair I'd have called her hyperkinetic. Actually, it was her affect that seemed hyper—she had this active gladness about everything, *no matter what*. She wore feather earrings that tossed and swung with every movement of her head.

The hand I took felt slightly stiff in mine but not cold. I clasped it gently with both hands. "Thank you for seeing me."

She flexed her hand, and I sensed the gesture required strain, and I released it. "Technically," she explained, "I'm a quad, but I function closer to a para."

"You sustained a spinal cord injury, then."

"Yes."

"I am sorry to know it."

Her wheelchair was one of those mountain-bike ones, with knobby tires and a sturdy frame. Mud had been wiped from the frame, and the tires showed wear. She touched the toggle on the armrest, the motor whirred, and she went to a position of comfort in the room, her back to a bookcase, her view oblique to the door. The apartment was warm but only slightly stuffy. There was a smell of heated-up food; I noticed a plate with a clump of casserole on a small eating table. There were wheelchair-height counters in the open kitchen and a short hallway to the bedroom. It appeared that Amanda lived alone. She gestured toward a short couch with a questioning look and hiked herself up with one elbow, adjusting her butt more satisfactorily in her chair.

"Have you finished your meal?" I asked.

"Oh, yes, yes. I'll clear that off later."

Still standing, I opened my peacoat and carefully withdrew two brilliant red maple leaves I'd found still clinging to a branch in a park I'd cut through along the way. I also took out a black pebble and a short forked stick whose ends I'd whittled round.

"I offer these tokens of our world to you." I held them out to her.

She opened her hands gravely and bowed her head. I placed the things in her hands, and she lowered them to her lap, touching them all with reverence. She looked up at me. "Thank you."

"You are welcome, but my thanks go to you."

I played the nature gambit because my guess about Amanda, based on what Sajeed had said, was right.

There was a shopping-channel feel to the apartment, exactly as I'd hoped. It's not that the place was crowded with plasticky junk—it wasn't. But Amanda Austin was obviously a devotee of Native American souvenirs. I call them souvenirs because I'm not qualified to know whether they were genuine tribal items or what, you know? Scattered around the room I noticed a rough blanket with zigzag motifs, a cowrie-shell rattle, a pueblo drum, and about half a dozen wooden flutes that had been stuck together to make a lamp base, topped by a thong-laced paper shade.

A painting of a half-woman, half–she bobcat defending three terrified kits from an ugly white man in a lumberjack coat dominated the wall between the large windows that overlooked the street. Other pictures showed bare-chested braves dandling cute papooses on their knees in front of the campfire, dream catchers protecting sleeping families from miasmatic evil spirits, and mustangs running free.

Well, that explained the shopping-channel feel: The pictures were so stunningly inauthentic.

To be blunt, Amanda was what I'd been hoping for: a Native American wannabe. You know, a non–Native American person who finds something attractive and deep about Native Americans, and attempts to adopt their spiritual practices and customs—the appealing ones, anyway. Someone who thinks *Dances With Wolves* was a good movie and has never eaten government-commodity cheese, nor used it to weigh down a drying pelt. Needless to say, real Indians can't stand such people.

And it would seem she had been a wannabe for some time, if she'd gotten her thunderbird shoes before her spinal injury. I didn't know when that was, but it was evident that she'd become accustomed to her disability. The apartment had been modified for her, and the work didn't look brand-new.

Clearly this interview would take some work, but I'd prepared myself on the walk over, and was willing to give it everything I had.

"I have need to talk about Beverly," I said, taking a seat and continuing to talk in the fake-formal way that New Age types go mad for.

Amanda flipped her eyes sideways, then into mine, with a look that was both sly and excited. She searched my eyes for a clue.

I smiled conspiratorially. "The people in town speak very highly of you. Not so highly of Beverly, I fear, though such is not surprising. People warned me that you are very protective of your sister." A corner of her mouth turned up; she was fighting smiling back at me. "Well," I went on, "I mean her no harm. If I did, I would not reveal myself to you, like a blundering coyote. I would keep away from you the way a snake avoids prey more powerful than itself."

Her lips parted as she listened, and an expression of awe and still greater excitement came over her face. "*Who* spoke of me to you?"

I gave her a coy look that conveyed, *Don't bother about that; we're in on the same secret.* "It matters not," I said. "You are a distinctive personage around town, moving about in your chariot. People feel warmly toward you. They feel you have a special power: extraordinarily positive, good energy, like a she-bear when the new sprigs of berry canes peek up from the snow in springtime."

She almost laughed with pleasure at my bullshit.

I went on, "And you try to help people on their unique paths. This is plain." She liked that too.

I paused. "I knew Beverly in Detroit, but a twelvemonth has passed since my eyes last looked upon hers."

Amanda said, "I am protective of her, yes, and I'll tell you right now she's not in Idaho."

Shit. "Ah, yes, I see."

"Did you come from Detroit?"

"Yes."

"Are you from Detroit originally?"

In a haunted, hollow voice, I said, "My origins are unknown."

"You have a wonderful name: Stacy Wounded Deer. Are you of Original Peoples descent?" she asked compassionately.

"Of course your mind wonders. In a way, I am definitely descended from the great native tribal people of this land. The fact is, I was adopted. I was born to a wealthy white couple who abused me as an infant, then the government took me away. A medicine woman of the Chippewa adopted me and treated me kindly. I grew up largely among the rocks and trees of the forest. She taught me the old ways."

"Wow!"

The gist of Amanda was—how can I put it? There was a determined beneficence about her, something almost forced. Well, my God, how does a person cope with such a dreadful calamity as paralysis? You do the best you fucking can, and if that includes pretending to be a Sioux fortune teller, so be it.

She suggested, "Perhaps we can talk about the old ways."

"Perhaps," I answered, "but first—"

"Most of the people who've come asking about Beverly want something from her."

"I have heard such. But I am not one of them. In fact, I wish to give something to her. My surprise is great that you would permit I, a stranger, into your home."

"I'm not afraid!" she exclaimed. "I love people—*all* people. Since my accident I've become totally fearless. Because I've put myself in the palm of...in the palm of the Great Spirit." Plainly, her trust was broad, but I wondered whether it was very deep.

I nodded.

She added, "Everybody knows the Great Spirit in their own way."

"You said it."

"I find that more love comes to me when I say yes to everything. What's the worst that could happen, really? Somebody tries to rape me? Honestly. Somebody steals my possessions? Come on."

"You are a most impressive lady, Amanda Austin." She loved hearing that, looking down modestly and grinning like crazy. I said, "The fact is that Beverly owes me no money—it is I who owe her money, a large amount of money. I wish to pay her back on behalf of myself and two other individuals from Detroit. Together we did some...work. You understand?"

She nodded, lips parted, but of course she didn't know what the hell I was talking about, since I didn't myself.

"An argument occurred," I continued, "and we went our separate ways—to the four winds—but three of us were unfair to Beverly."

"Well, that's the first time I've heard anybody say they were unfair to Bev, instead of the other way around."

"Yes. There is a great deal more goodness in Beverly Austin than for which ordinary people give her credit."

She caught that 'ordinary' and nodded again. "That is so true."

"If you do not wish to help me return the money that belongs properly to Beverly, it is all right. I will find her sooner or later."

"Well—I—I'm not saying I—" She stopped and looked at the gifts in her lap. "I love my sister, you know?"

"Clear that is to me."

"It hasn't been easy." She glanced away regretfully.

"Clear that too is. The light from Sister Moon falls, and we must catch it in whatever vessel we have." I made a sweeping, horizon-to-horizon gesture.

"You are so right, Stacy, you are so right."

"My real first name is Cloudrunner, but only do I reveal it when in the company of a special individual. You may call me Cloudrunner. I sense that you have studied shamanism?"

"I have, Cloudrunner, for months and months."

"You have much more to learn."

"Oh, for sure! Maybe you could—" She clasped her hands awkwardly, the stiffness in them evident.

"You have felt pain from the actions of Beverly, have you not?"

"You can say that again. Can I tell you what happened?"

"Please."

"A lot of people have been mad at Beverly. Okay, she used drugs, she stole, and she lied, okay? But since my accident I've made a super-big leap in understanding." She smiled gently and gazed out the window at the buildings across the street. "It's all about forgiveness."

"Ah, forgiveness—the badger and the anthill, you know."

She shifted her gaze back to me. "I'm not sure I—"

"No matter. Please go on."

"Well, if you know Bev, you know she's wild."

"Undisciplined."

"Yes! That's a better word. We grew up with the usual sibling rivalry, but when it came down to it, we loved each other. We both loved the outdoors—this state is so beautiful! We'd run along the river, go kayaking and rafting on them all—the Boise, the Snake, the lower Salmon. We'd ski, we'd go off-roading with older kids with Jeeps. It was great!"

As Amanda talked, she looked at me steadily with an anxious expression, and I saw that she was hoping to please me, to pass the test of my judgment as a more genuine Native American than she was, which was pathetic, but that's what I wanted. Further, I saw her struggling with a growing desire to cooperate with me.

"Well, our parents split up when Bev was twelve and I was sixteen. She took it hard. The fact was, our dad was a jerk and our mom finally got up the guts to throw him out, but I think Bev used that as an excuse to behave badly. Mom had to go to work, so we were alone a lot. I used the time to do more homework for extra credit, but Bev hooked up with the wrong crowd, the hoodlum crowd."

"Understandable choice—such a group seems so much smarter than teachers and parents."

"Yes, yes, exactly."

"And yet hoodlum life is all empty, like a milkweed pod after an autumn gust."

"*Yes,*" Amanda breathed. "You have the most *beautiful* way of—"

"Go on, please."

"Well, Bev developed quite a drug habit—pot, cocaine, crack. Then she started using heroin, and I got scared. She was stealing. She stole from me, from our mom, from anybody. She'd borrow and never pay back. After high school I got a job guiding raft trips on the Snake. I was in better shape then." She looked down at her useless legs, then brightly up at me. "I used to be quite the athlete!"

My stomach clenched with pity, but I only nodded.

"I got Bev jobs too, sometimes," she went on, "but she'd work a little bit, then spend what money she made on partying. I'd get mad. I tried like heck to get her away from drugs. With our mom gone so much, I felt responsible for her, you know. I got involved in a pen-pal program for incarcerated people, and it was neat writing letters to convicts and getting some back. So I showed some of the letters to Bev, and she got interested. We were both writing to convicts for a while—young girls in Idaho writing to hardened criminals in penitentiaries!"

"Beverly corresponded with convicts?"

"Yes. In retrospect I realize it probably wasn't such a good idea, but you know, they censor those letters and you can't talk about drugs and sex and things."

"Right," I agreed.

"Well, all I know is that later she went to Michigan to see one of those guys."

A housefly zoomed into the room and headed for Amanda's face. She batted it away, then it buzzed toward me. I cuffed it in midair and it fell to the floor.

I asked, "Was he in the federal facility at Milan?"

"No. Somehow I think he was in one of the state prisons there. I don't remember which one."

"I see."

"I'm getting ahead of myself." She looked at the fly writhing on the floor. I put it out of its misery with a tap of my sneaker.

She looked at me.

I said, "I am on good terms with the spirits of vermin. Please resume."

She nodded, liking my style, liking the hell out of me. "Well, this drug thing went on for years. A couple of times she got arrested for robbery, but she got off with just probation. This went on for *years*. She could straighten out when she really wanted to—it'd always be after some disgusting boyfriend gave her a black eye or something. She'd stop using, start eating better, she'd gain weight—when she was using she'd get so skinny, you know?"

"Yes." I was thirsty but didn't want to interrupt by asking for water. I think Amanda was waiting for me to come up with a nature allegory, but I couldn't think of one, so she went on.

"But she could never stay clean. Like I said, she went to Michigan to meet this guy, then she came back and it started all over again—the degradation of drug addiction. Finally, I launched an all-out attack against her drug use. I began threatening to turn her in to the police when I knew she had drugs on her. She didn't like that! But of course I didn't really want to see her go to jail; I wanted her to get help."

A clock under a glass dome with one of those swirly mechanisms let out a little gong. I glanced at it on the table next to me and saw that the glass dome was decorated with squiggles and dots meant to look primitive or something—those "natives" and their painted-clock collections. I noticed shadows creeping across the floor, shadows from the branches outside Amanda's window, as the sun dropped slowly to the west.

She twitched the control on her chair and moved a bit. "The sun was in my eyes," she told me. "I want to see you." I nodded solemnly, acceptingly. "I learned about interventions, you know," she went on, "where friends and family get together and confront the person about their addiction, and they make them go into treatment. I organized an intervention for Beverly. I had such a good feeling about it—I got our mom involved—and that was a hard one, let me tell you—and our old school chums, and I even told some of her hoodlum friends about it and they promised to keep it quiet and help us! We had a date set and everything, and Bev had no idea."

"She had no idea? When was this?"

"None. It was eighteen months ago, almost exactly. Well, the *very day before* the intervention I had my accident. The timing couldn't have been worse."

"A terrible coincidence. What happened?"

"I got hit by a car. And it ruined everything. I mean, don't get me wrong—I accept my paralysis as a gift from the Great Spirit. But at first I was devastated."

"You were run over by a car?"

"Yes, hit-and-run. I never saw it coming."

Twenty-Four

I listened carefully, silently. Amanda continued, "I had a break between river trips, and I was out jogging on my usual route before dawn. I always ran down to the river and back—three miles: a good run, uphill on the way back, a good test for the spirit. Well, I never knew what hit me."

"Did the person stop?"

"No. They panicked, I guess. Maybe they were drunk and didn't even know they hit me."

"Any witnesses?"

"There was a paperboy who heard the impact and saw me go flying, but he was too shocked to memorize the car. He saw it race away, but he couldn't describe it beyond the fact that it was a car. So the police were left with nothing. It's okay. It really is."

"And nobody came forward."

"Nope. But that's not the point of this story, Cloudrunner. Listen. When I woke up in the hospital, the first person I asked for was Bev. I wanted my sister. My mom was there, and all my friends came to give their love and support. But no Bev."

"No Bev." I closed my eyes. *Holy hell. Holy everloving hell.*

"No Bev. Even my boyfriend came to see me a few times before he dropped me." Amanda gave a bright, who-cares little laugh at that. "I could deal with the fact that he did that, but when Beverly didn't come, that hurt worse than having my back broken. I don't usually expect people to understand that, but you're different. That's how it was. Can you understand what I'm saying?"

I swallowed and pulled myself together. "The velvet clings tightly to the antlers until violence occurs."

She considered what I said. "That is so true."

"So Bev disappeared when you were injured," I prompted. "Yet you say she's not in Idaho, so you at least know where she is *not*, so you must have experienced some form of commu—"

"I'm getting to that part. It's true I haven't seen her since." Amanda bowed her head in sorrow and, it seemed to me, shame. "I still don't know why she ran out on me when I needed her most. Well, that was hard—that was real, real hard. But that brings me to who I am today. See, I stewed over my feelings of abandonment for a long time. I sulked and pouted about being paralyzed like a little child whose candy has been taken away!"

"I don't know as I'd quite equate—"

"But then I got back to studying Native American ways. I'd begun reading about them in high school, and talking to Native-blood kids. Plus, some of my fellow rafting guides were into Native stuff too. Well, I eventually realized I'd never been all that worthy of Bev. I'd always held myself above her, which was wrong."

"To my ears, Beverly Austin behaved like a piece of dung, in opposition to your honest ways."

"Even dung can teach us things!"

I considered that. "Yes," I agreed wisely. "Yes."

"It was wrong of me to look down on her. It was wrong!" Amanda's eyes snapped. "I realized I would only truly heal if I forgave whoever ran me over, but *most important*, if I forgave Beverly for running away. Some friends of mine helped me do an Anasazi forgiveness ritual, where you pulverize the bones of a mouse and smear the—well, you probably know all about that. After that ritual, I felt incredibly much better. I felt truly clean and healed, like I was filled with light and a real spiritual, natural love."

"That's amazing," I managed to say.

"And I've been getting more and more into the Native cultural thing. I really respect and admire them, not in a superficial way but in a really deep way. They've got tons and tons of wisdom that the white people threw away a long time ago."

"Wisdom flies like time on the tongue of the trout," I agreed. "So you forgave Beverly for running you—uh, running out on you," I corrected hastily. "Uh—and you've decided to protect her from—"

"I decided I would never betray her. All the people she screwed and skipped out on owing all kinds of debts—well, they've tried to get at her through me, but I decided that if I wasn't going to make her pay her debt to me—her debt of pain—then I'm not going to help anybody else collect their debt either. As far as I'm concerned, everybody can try to do what I've done: forgive."

Amanda Austin picked up one of the leaves I'd brought and stroked it with her fingers, which on her left hand were almost gnarled with the paralysis. *Dear God.* I looked at her, this animated, sincere, if not terribly bright soul desperately trying to make sense of her life.

She looked up at me. "But you know what? It's so beautiful that I forgave her because now she needs me."

"She needs you?"

"Yes, it's true, and it's so beautiful. She called just a few days ago—let's see, it was Friday morning and, well, you know Bev."

Friday morning. I was looking for her, my guts churning, shouting her name in Porrocks's ruined house that morning. "What is the current situation?"

"She needs a passport. She can't use hers for...*reasons,* so she asked me to get one for myself and send it to her. I've never gotten one—have no need for one, you know. I never was a world traveler! Well, she wired me the money to get it, plus extra for expedited service, which was sweet. I went and got my picture taken and sent in the forms yesterday, and now I'm waiting for it. Soon as it comes, I'll send it to her. It's supposed to take two weeks or less with the special processing."

"She must be in great trouble."

"I don't make that assumption. She's in a hurry to go somewhere. Could be she's in trouble, but it could be there's some special opportunity for her overseas somewhere."

"Maybe so."

"I hope so. I really hope so."

It was time to close in. I took a deep breath. "It is good of you to protect your sister. Amanda Austin, I wish to tell you a story, one passed on to me by my spirit mother, the one called Rainbear, medicine woman of the Chippewa. She told me this story one night when we were traveling along a high river bluff, searching for powerful herbs that bloom only at night."

To my gladness, I saw that Amanda was just intelligent enough to realize I wasn't changing the subject. She straightened in her chair, clasped her hands over my gifts in her lap, and listened.

"Long ago," I began, "during the season of short white days—that is to say winter—there was a brave she-cougar who moved silently and powerfully through the forest. The forest was dark but never was she afraid. A special cougar was she, a cougar who had made mistakes in her life but was basically very good, deep in her heart.

"One day, however, as she was hunting for food, she heard a *snap!* and felt a terrible pain. She was caught in an illegal leghold trap!"

Amanda shook her head knowingly. "Bastards. White male bastards."

"The cougar cried out for help. She called to the animals of the forest, but the other animals feared greatly to help her. After all, she hunted, killed, and ate them whenever she got the chance."

Amanda interjected, "She had to feed her cubs."

"Right, her cubs were small. Back at the den, they had no idea. So this brave she-cougar anticipated a slow death, not of hunger, for she had just eaten, but of thirst. At that time a she-raven flew overhead and saw what had happened. The raven too was a special bird, with great sensitivity and caring, and she could see that her sister cougar had stumbled into an unfair situation.

"She could not free the cougar, but she could help the cougar survive. She flew up to a cedar limb that was covered in snow, and scooped snow with her wings. She glided down to the cougar and delivered the snow to her parched mouth, thus providing critical hydration."

I rested my hands on my knees and paused. Amanda Austin was *hanging* on my words, gazing at me as people in televangelist audiences gaze at their televangelists.

"After two days," I continued, "the man who had set the trap came. The she-cougar pretended to be dead, but as soon as the man opened his trap to remove his prize, she turned and snapped his neck with one movement of her powerful jaws. Ever afterward she walked with a limp, but she never forgot the kindness of the raven. That is the end of the story."

Amanda was silent. "Thank you," she murmured at last, "for telling me such a magnificent story."

"Amanda Austin, have you been given your spirit name yet?"

"N-no, but it's something I've been dreaming about."

This was the acid test right now. *God forgive me, God forgive me.* But I understood this woman well enough to manipulate her, and that's exactly what I did. She was a natural-born follower, a weak-minded, good-hearted seeker who was not ready to imagine her sister being a psychopath. If I pretended to a position of superiority over her and did it well enough, she would do what I wanted.

"Amanda Austin, approach the one who is called Cloudrunner Wounded Deer."

Eyes locked on me, she instantly tweaked her toggle. She motored to my chair across the plain of her living room. I took her hand, fastened her eyes with mine, and said, "What do you dream, Amanda Austin? What do you dream for yourself?"

She opened her mouth and whispered, "This is a pivotal moment in my life."

I nodded.

"I—I dream about being free," she whispered. "I dream of flying." She licked her lips and swallowed. Her hand trembled in mine.

"From now on," I said, "you will call yourself Snow on Raven's Wing. Fleeting, evanescent, strong, light, kind. Never forget your name. Remember who you are until the mountains around us again meet the sea. That is to say, forever."

"Thank you, Cloudrunner," whispered Snow on Raven's Wing.

Oh, God forgive me.

"Now do you understand what is happening?" I asked.

With an expression of joy and relaxation on her face, she said, "I must permit you to pay your debt to my sister. You have nothing to forgive her for but wish to help her."

"You are a deeply spiritual person, Snow on Raven's Wing."

"And you are yet more deeply spiritual than I, Cloudrunner Wounded Deer. You have helped me see to the next level of spiritual deepness. I will never be the same. I will tell you where you can send the money."

I am a shit. I am a shit. I am a shit.

Twenty-Five

I was a shit all right, but I was going to track down Beverly Austin. I bought a phone card at a drugstore on my walk back to the Boise bus terminal. I was very tired and hoped to take a nap on a bench there—or be lucky enough to catch immediately the correct bus out of town. As it happened, I had a four-hour wait. Something told me, though, to make my phone calls before buying my ticket. Thank God my credit card was still good, though only God knew how I was going to pay the bill.

I called Lou's cell number first, and she picked up while driving her city animal control truck. I heard the tinny hysteria of three or four dogs cooped up in the back.

"Oh, yeah, Lillian, I got everything under control," she said offhandedly. Normally, whenever somebody claims to have everything under control, the opposite is true. But with Lou it invariably was the case. She was one of the most can-do people I knew. "The walls," she said, "aren't painted, but at least they're intact."

"*Owooo!*" hollered her cargo. "*Yatta yi yi!*"

She told me she'd checked a Time-Life home-repair book out of the library, studied the drywall part, hauled materials and tools to

Porrocks's house, and on very little sleep put the place back together. "Her sister helped me. Yeah, she got in yesterday. And the place is clean."

"How's Erma doing?"

"Great, really great! They're gonna release her this afternoon, they said. And since Connie's here—that's her sister—she'll be fine at home. You won't believe this, but they're getting her to use a walker already right in the hospital."

"No way!"

"Way! She's doing marvelous. So I finally told her what happened at the house, like you said, then that cop, uh—"

"Stonehauser?"

"Yeah, Stonehauser. He came over to see her. You should call him— you know what he said? He said they found a clump of fuzz from Erma's sweater stuck in the grille of that rental car."

"Oh, my God—the rental car? You mean the one that I found the receipt for over at—"

"That's all he said: 'the rental car.'"

"Holy crap."

"So if you're doing your own investigation on this, Lillian, he's probably gonna tell you to lay off and let the police—"

"Right. How'd Porrocks take the news about her place?"

"Well, she took it pretty good, actually. I mean, she's a big girl and all that, but, uh—"

"But what?" I asked.

"I'd say she's pretty mad at you."

"Yeah. Yeah, well, that's okay. I gotta live with that."

"She sort of turned her head and muttered something about you that I didn't thoroughly catch."

"*Hauuurup! Rrup! Rowrooo!*" went the dogs.

"Lordy, Lou, how do you stand it?" I said.

"Stand what?"

"That racket!"

"Oh! I love dogs."

"Okay, well, I'll let you—"

Lou broke in, "One more thing, Lillian?"

"Yes?"

"You know—I really like Erma."

"Yes, I know."

Lou cleared her throat sharply. "I mean, I really, really like her."

"Yes, Lou, I know. I'm aware of that."

"Well…" She heaved a long, gusting sigh. "Well, I sort of, uh, *hinted* about my feelings for her, you know, uh, but, uh, well, she did- n't seem too receptive."

"Oh, Lou. When somebody's hurt and helpless like that, that's just not a good time to declare yourself. It's just not. You've gotta wait, hon. And Christ, moreover I don't even know if Porrocks is gay or bi or straight or what. I really don't. My God, Lou—"

"Well, what I want to know is, would you do me a favor?"

I pushed my forehead against the wall next to the pay phone. "I *owe* you, Lou. I owe you, okay? But if you're going to ask me to, like, *advocate* for you to Erma, I just—"

"No! I don't want you to advocate for me, I just want you to tell her I'm a good person, you know, and that I'd treat her like a queen. That's all."

"Lou, did you tell her you love her?"

Lou answered something very quietly.

"What?" I half shouted. "The dogs are making so much—"

"I said yes! Yes! Okay? I love her and I told her so!"

"Aw, Lou! I would not call that *hinting*, I would call that—"

"Lillian, you've got to help me convince her!"

"No. I'll do anything for you, Lou, except get in the middle of your love life. If you'll remember, we've been over that more than—"

"Lillian, *please.*"

"Look, pull yourself together. What did she say when you told her you loved her?"

"She just said 'oh' and looked surprised."

"I'll bet."

"Then she said she couldn't really talk about a subject like that right now."

"All right. Well, Lou, 'oh' doesn't necessarily mean 'no.' But you have to let it drop at least for a while. You gotta be patient, okay?"

"It's hard. It's so hard."

"I know, hon," I told her.

"When will you be back?"

"That's what I've got to tell you—I'm not coming back to Detroit just yet. I've got to get back on the bus and follow up on something."

"But shouldn't you let the cops—"

"Goodbye, Lou. I'll be in touch."

Next I called Billie. I had no intention of talking to Stonehauser just yet.

"I'm so glad you called," Billie said. "Why don't you have a cell phone? Nobody can ever reach you when—"

"How's Todd?"

"Lillian, he's failing."

"I'll be there tonight."

"I took him to Dr. Metz, but there really isn't anything they can do for the little guy. He looks around for you and won't eat."

"All right. Thanks, Billie. I'm coming. Keep him…" I couldn't go on.

"I'll do everything I can."

I walked out of the depot and motioned for a taxi.

"Take me to the airport, please."

I crouched in front of the nest-like box Billie had fixed up for Todd. Softly, I said, "Hey, Toddy boy."

He opened his eyes. I put my hand out for him to sniff. His ears perked up only slightly, but he coiled his haunches and awkwardly rose to greet me. "Ah, that's my Todd. That's it."

"He's been taking a little water but no food," Billie said. "I mashed up some good alfalfa with warm water, but he wouldn't have any of it."

"And Dr. Metz said, uh—"

"He said he's nearing the end. He's old, and his systems are just shutting down. Do you hear him grinding his teeth?"

"Yes." My faithful pet was definitely thinner, his movements stiff and effortful. When they're upset or in pain, rabbits grind their teeth. I picked up Todd and cradled him in my arms: I thought he felt hotter than usual, as well.

"And you know, Lillian, the doctor said it's getting about time to…help him."

"Oh, Billie."

"You shouldn't let him suffer," she said gently.

"I know, of course not."

"I think he's in some discomfort."

She was plainly right. And yet…

"Why don't you take him home tonight?" she suggested. "Let him be with you tonight. Then take him to Dr. Metz in the morning. I could drive you if we go early."

I swallowed. "That's a good idea." But something was stirring in the back of my mind. "Uh…"

"Are you all right? How 'bout a ride home?"

"Oh, I don't want to trouble you. You've done so much—"

"No trouble, I gotta go over to F&M anyway for a major shop."

"Okay. Well, okay."

That night Todd and I hung out together. On one hand, he was the same old Todd: calm, dignified, intelligent. Yet on the other, he'd lost his inquisitiveness. He'd lost his zest. He moved about very slowly, making one circuit of our flat, then returning to me. I put him on my lap and sat on the floor in the living room. I didn't feel hungry either. I petted his soft brown fur and told him how much he'd meant to me over the years. Boy, had he ever been there for me.

Granted, we'd gotten off to a rocky start, there in the nearly deserted rabbit quarters at the state fair, where, as the late-afternoon sun slanted in through the ventilators, he'd bitten my finger almost in half. But the old man had sexed him wrong, entered him in the wrong category, and now did not want rabbit W-46 around anymore to remind him of his ineptitude.

I took him home, gave him a name, and thus we began a relationship of mutual respect and support. I provided food, warmth, protection, and ear-mite medicine, and he provided friendship and immeasurable steadiness. I loved him and I like to think he loved me, but of course one can never tell for sure the things a rabbit keeps in his heart of hearts.

With his kodo drum–like, single floor thumps, Todd had alerted me to danger more than once. He had served as my silent partner, my sounding board, and occasionally my oracle. (Don't ask.) On one memorable occasion he gnawed his way out of a heavy leather golf bag (again, don't ask), startling a murderous maniac into a suicidal lunge for glory (ditto).

Todd was no apron-string rabbit, though—he could be willful and naughty. Sometimes he wanted nothing to do with me. But we always worked out our differences, and our friendship strengthened by the year.

The day faded, and the glow of the streetlight came through the blinds and lay in soft lines on the carpet.

I sat and stroked his back and ears and discussed many things with him.

He seemed to feel worse after a while; he trembled and gnashed his teeth. He looked up at me. He was in distress from something deep inside.

The thing that had entered the back of my mind at Billie's now popped into the front. I remembered I had once promised Todd that I'd never let anyone hurt him. It was on a dirty staircase in a parking garage, just after I'd abandoned him in fear of my life. Fate had reunited us, and such a promise was the least I could have done on that occasion.

Well. You can make the case that euthanizing a suffering pet is not the same as being cruel to a pet. It's the right thing to do when it's clear the animal is at the end of the road. Out in the woods, old slow Todd would have been snapped up by a hawk or a coyote by now, his suffering cut short by nature. His suffering was my responsibility. I had made a special promise.

Therefore I could not take him to Dr. Metz.

I prepared a hot water bottle and wrapped it well in a towel. Todd nestled into it and closed his eyes, though his trembling did not stop. I kissed the soft fur behind his ears.

It was about eight-thirty, past the McVitties' dinnertime but well before their customary bedtime. Mr. McVittie answered my knock.

"Is Mrs. McVittie available?" I asked at some volume, given his increasing hearing loss.

"Yeah! Mildred!" he yelled.

His wife tottered across the shag carpet into the living room. "Yes, dear? Come in."

"Just for a minute, thank you. Mrs. McVittie, I need to ask you a favor."

Her husband broke in saying, "If it's about the rent—"

"It isn't," I said quickly.

"What can I do for you, dear?" Mrs. McVittie brushed past him and took my shoulder; she could see the look in my eyes.

I said, "I'd like you to give me one of your insulin syringes. Do you have enough? A used one would be all right," I added.

"Yes, I can give you a new one, of course, but I'm wondering, ah—"

"Todd is dying," I said.

"Oh, my dear."

Mr. McVittie cried, "And you think you can cure him with insulin?"

"No," I said. "No."

Sweet Mrs. McVittie took me into the bathroom and got out one of her syringes from a huge multipack on the counter. "Do you know how to use it?"

"Yes, I had to give my uncle injections of anticoagulant for a week last winter."

"All right, dear. Do you want me to fill it?"

"No, thank you."

"You have something…?"

"Yes."

She hugged me, her bony arms circling me like twigs.

Back upstairs I got out the codeine pills I had left over from getting my last wisdom tooth pulled. I put two of the tablets in a heavy ceramic bowl and pulverized them with the butt end of my potato masher, then took the resulting white powder, along with a stainless soup spoon, to the bathroom. I found a candle and matches and brought them in as well. I left everything next to the sink, then went to be with Todd again.

I took my mandolin from its hook and played old plain songs: "Bonny Doon," "Cumberland Gap," "Little Pal," "Take a Drink on Me." Todd opened his eyes but didn't move from his place next to the hot water bottle. His hind legs began to convulse. I picked him up for a while, and the spasms passed.

Slowly, I played "Wildwood Flower," his soothing favorite. I played it, then I played it again with some easy variations. I returned to the melody and finished the song.

I went to the bathroom and lit the candle. I removed the syringe from its plastic sleeve and took off the needle cap.

I scooped the pill powder into the spoon and held it over the candle flame. The powder melted almost well enough; I added a few drops of water, then drew the milky liquid into the syringe.

I blew out the candle and took the syringe into the living room where Todd was.

Twenty-Six

I dropped an envelope into the post box outside the downtown Greyhound terminal, then went in to buy my ticket. I got a cup of coffee out of a machine and drank it as I waited but for once didn't care how bad it tasted. The last of it had turned cold by the time the bus rolled in.

Carrying a fresh change of clothes in my gym bag, I climbed onto the bus to continue my pursuit of Beverly Austin. I'd spent barely more than twenty-four hours in Detroit.

That morning the McVitties had kindly permitted me to bury Todd in their backyard beneath their raspberry bush, an occasional leaf from which he loved to munch. The dawn weather was bitter, but the ground was still pliant for me to dig a deep-enough hole. In bunny heaven, the rabbits chase the dogs, you know. I thought I smelled snow in the air.

The bus lumbered onto the street and accelerated down the ramp to I-75 south. My ticket said Fort Lauderdale, Florida, the place college kids call Fort Liquordale in tribute to the thousands of gallons of tequila, vodka, and schnapps that flow down their teeming gullets every year at spring break. The beach there is wide and pretty, the road along it lined with bars, restaurants, and places to buy T-shirts. I'd been there only once, when my good friend Duane invited me along on a business trip.

I was in for another tedious journey, but I'll spare you the anxiety and boredom of it. Actually, I was too sad to be bored; I mourned Todd, looking out the window at the flat grayish farm country of northern Ohio, remembering so many good times. I didn't sit there sobbing; I just felt empty. And lonelier than I'd felt in a long time.

After Dayton and the first of the rolling country that gradually drops you down to the Ohio River, my memories and self-pitying brain waves got crowded out by worry. I had to prepare to meet Beverly Austin.

Me: Okay, so prepare.

Me: Well, I have to, uh, decide how to approach her.

Me: No, you don't, all you have to do is decide what you want from her.

Me: Right. Well, I want the truth, of course.

Me: You already know the truth.

Me: Yeah, but I want to hear her say it.

Me: That is so unrealistic. You've learned that before.

Me: I know. I'm sure I'll have to settle for something far less—like one good minute alone with her before I call the police. I want to know what she ever felt for me, and I want her to know *I* caught her. I want her to know you can't get away doing such shit to me.

Me: Don't you think you should at least clue in Stonehauser in advance or at least Tom Ciesla, who could advise you a little bit?

Me: Of course I should. But I'm not going to, because I don't want anybody—

Me: Blowing it for you?

Me: Right.

Me: You're thinking about a citizen's arrest here, aren't you?

Me: Yes.

Me: Oh, great.

About the only good thing about that bus trip was the finale of *Encounter in Borneo*, fortunately the longest of all the Calico books to date. I'd forced myself not to finish it on the way to Idaho so that I'd have something to sustain me in a dark hour. I opened the book around Lexington, Kentucky, and immediately found peace.

So Calico Jones, the awesomely strong and beautiful professional international sleuth and avenger of injustice on behalf of those who can least handle injustice being inflicted on them, finally arrives at this crazy scientist's lair in the absolute dead center of Borneo. I can't begin to detail what she goes through *after* she bests the headhunters, but I'll say the journey involves expert marksmanship against grenade-throwing poachers, gymnastic feats to evade bloodthirsty jungle panthers, and the obligatory anaconda wrestling. I say obligatory as if it were a cliché, but all I mean is you're *always* hoping for a good constrictor-grappling scene in a book like this.

And you usually get it, but in this case it's an exceptionally good one. Calico's tangled in this barbed vine and can't get away from the snake, so she grabs a passing peccary and kills it with her *bare hands*—have you ever seen one of those? They're terrible, brutal jungle pigs with jaws like a pit bull's and teeth swarming with unsavory microbes. Okay, so she kills this passing peccary as *bait* for the anaconda, which goes, *Hey, fresh meat,* and stops advancing on Calico. But she's not totally off the hook yet, though, at which point—well, I shouldn't tell that whole part.

Between Knoxville and Chattanooga, I read how she finally locates this laboratory and shoots the guards with silent blow-gun darts dipped in sleep-inducing plant sap, which the headhunter queen showed her how to obtain—you remember the headhunter queen—

and gets to the heart of the building to find these enormous vats holding billions of mutant insect larvae aswim in liquid nutrients, which this evil scientist is raising to fill a series of small rockets, which if launched into the troposphere will fragment, releasing these bugs whose chemical makeup and genetically-determined excretory habits would permanently alter the earth's climate for the worse. I'm not talking about reversing things to the way they were before the cotton gin; I'm talking about a new and sudden Ice Age. Plus it's obvious he's not considering all possible complications, including the effects of high-altitude nuclear testing by rogue nations on larvae that are *already* mutant.

The truth is, the guy's a dangerous jackass who intends to transform the governments of the world into his dues-paying hostages, or else. He discovers Calico Jones as she's mixing up a batch of simple Clorox and mineral oil, which if properly administered will kill the mutant larvae. Then the team of *good* scientists from the countries that signed the Ottawa Climate Petition will have enough time to finish their safe, tested climate-adjustment project involving harmless activated charcoal and synthetic emeralds, you'll remember.

Well into the state of Georgia I got to the part where the evil scientist meets his end. There's no way I saw it coming. First of all, Calico Jones doesn't want to kill the son of a bitch (because then she has to write a longer report), but he forces her to by attacking her first, and boy, is his death grisly. I won't reveal the surprise, but suffice it to say it involves mutant insect larvae, Clorox, and mineral oil. Then of course you just know Calico's going to get a reward administered by the fabulously gorgeous, intelligent, and loving Swedish doctor Ingrid.

Somewhere on the outskirts of Macon, I finished the story and closed the book with a sigh of satisfaction. Those books are just so good. That author knows how to tell a story up one side and down the other. I wondered whether I'd be able to find the next in the series at John King, my favorite dirt-cheap used bookstore.

I felt that Calico Jones would approve of my plan of action.

Even though I had no time to waste, I'd resisted the temptation to fly down to Fort Lauderdale. Number one, my credit card was nearing max out, and I had more spending to do. Number two, I was certain I had enough time for a slower trip: I was no Calico Jones, but I could beat the U.S. Mail. Moreover, number three, I wanted the U.S. Mail itself to help me locate Beverly Austin's exact whereabouts.

How to conjure Florida for you? People like to call Florida Michigan's third peninsula because so many pasty Midwesterners go there on winter vacation. Then there are the retirees. So many people tell me they hate Florida that I'm always prepared for it to be a dreadful, ugly place full of sunburned, wrinkled golfing persons who've never heard of pesto or Susan Sontag or IKEA. But the reality, as the Greyhound stopped at the state line and us passengers piled out to go to the toilet and drink free cups of orange juice proffered by a shirt-sleeves-clad employee of the tourist board, was so different. At least the reality I experienced.

The main thing about Florida is that when you get off the bus, the air is moist and gloriously warm, in stark contrast to the cold, dry situation you left 1,100 miles behind. The air is full of oxygen emitted by all the green grass and trees, plus all that thick roadside vegetation that looks unstoppable until you realize that they manage to keep the ditches open *somehow*. The smell of green in Florida is deeper than the smell of green you get during a Michigan summer. It is a serious, wet green that stays even when you turn the air-conditioning on.

Florida is flat, which people seem to hold against it. Yet when you make your way to the ocean, you know it's coming. It's hard to explain, there's just this sense of the sky opening bigger and bigger, drawing you ahead, and then the signs and motels and bait shops stop but the flat-bottomed clouds keep going, from where you are all the way across the ocean to the horizon, and then a pelican flaps by, and you smell shrimp cooking somewhere and you want to run across the sand to the water and jump in, and you do.

In addition to its beach, Fort Lauderdale is famous for its complicated network of canals that connect dozens of marinas and little lakes. You can dock your boat in a slip a mile from the ocean, and when you want to go see the blue horizon, you motor slowly through, essentially, people's backyards for half an hour or so.

All those canals and marinas are part of this thing called the Intracoastal Waterway, which is a nautical route along the Eastern Seaboard that threads along, hugging the lee side of barrier islands, avoiding the open ocean, so that practically anybody can jump in a boat and just go. You can see the biggest yachts in the world tied up in the swanky marinas served by water taxis and floating convenience stores, but most of the boats in Fort Lauderdale are ordinary cabin cruisers or fishing boats or sailboats.

The bus pulled into the Fort Lauderdale terminal around seven in the morning. I'd dozed in my seat, but I felt creaky and tired. In town I rented the cheapest car I could find, which turned out to be a tiny white Hyundai. I bought a detailed map at a grocery store, along with a three-dollar pair of sunglasses and some provisions—four apples, an orange, a bag of Doritos, a brick of cheddar, a box of Triscuits, a six-pack of Pepsi (on sale over Coke), a box of Ziploc food-storage bags, a small bottle of sanitizing hand gel, and a pack of Camel Filters.

Now, even though my appetite hadn't been too hot lately, I was well fixed for my stakeout. I put on my Vietnam-surplus sun hat that I'd packed in my gym bag, added the sunglasses, and checked myself in the Hyundai's rearview mirror. The brown plastic wraparounds and floppy khaki hat made me look like an extra in an Elvis movie, but I didn't care.

Yes, my stakeout. Amanda Austin had written "Barbara Anders" into my notebook, explaining that that was Beverly's current code name. Beneath it she'd copied out, "c/o Kendall Marine Supply" and an address on a numbered street in this town.

Therefore, Beverly would only pick up mail there, unless she was living on a cot in the stockroom.

It was just after nine A.M. when I cruised past Kendall Marine Supply, a small business that looked grimly unprosperous. Kendall Marine's sign had sagged all cockeyed, and the paint was peeling off its concrete-block walls. The windows were dirty, and the only vehicle in the small parking lot was a Toyota pickup truck that looked as if it'd been dredged up from one of the canals. Kendall Marine had a good location, though, situated smack between two massive marinas that ought to have represented so much business for it. The boats in the marinas were arranged in rows more or less according to size. I'd never seen this much white fiberglass in one place, never.

The morning was lovely, maybe seventy degrees out, with clear sunshine streaming down between breaks in the cloud parade—fluffy, friendly clouds.

I parked the Hyundai across the street, adjusted the rake of my seat to ease my back a little, and began to watch and wait.

Twenty-Seven

The envelope I had mailed from Detroit before boarding the bus was a large flat one containing only a piece of cardboard, addressed to "Barbara Anders" at Kendall Marine Supply Co. It was bright white, and the cardboard made it rigid.

The delivery of it could prompt one of two scenarios, either one advantageous to me. Beverly Austin could show up to pick up the envelope, or someone could take it to her. I'd made the envelope conspicuous by choosing an eighteen-inch white one; the cardboard made it unlikely that someone would fold it smaller. So, even if it was delivered in a large stack of mail, or bundled with catalogs, I should be able to see someone carrying it out.

I could have merely waited for Beverly Austin to pick up her passport whenever it got there from her sister in Idaho. The main problem with that, however, was that the wait could be a long one—up to two weeks, given mailing times and so on. And the longer the wait, the more the chance that something could change. Beverly could decide to move on; she could call her sister with a new address; she could abandon the passport plan altogether. My nerves couldn't take a two-week stakeout anyway.

My envelope could realistically be delivered today, tomorrow, or next day at the latest.

I'd asked Amanda Austin not to tell Beverly about my visit, if she phoned her sister; I wanted my payment to take Beverly by pleasant surprise. I asked Amanda to promise on the red leaves I'd brought, and she did so, her hands lightly touching their dryness as she gazed needily into my eyes. "Good news is best delivered strong," I murmured.

"Yes," she breathed.

I sat in the Hyundai all day. I ate some of my food and drank my Pepsi and smoked half the pack of Camels. I never smoke that much, but when you're on a stakeout you've got to smoke. You just gotta.

What about going to the bathroom? Ah, that's where my Ziploc bags and sanitizing gel can came in handy. It isn't just guys who can pee anywhere: If you're a resourceful, agile, and above all careful girl, you can do an all-day stakeout with the best (or worst) of them. Thank God my last period had trickled to an end just before I started work on Porrocks's boathouse.

I fiddled with the radio and scrutinized everybody who came and went. They all appeared to be customers, walking in empty-handed and coming out with a coil of rope or a box of hardware or a jug of varnish. I perked up when the postal truck swung in and a big-assed mail lady carried two small boxes and a stack of mail inside. I couldn't tell whether my envelope was in the stack. Nothing happened after that—no Beverly, no nothing, just a few more customers.

Kendall Marine closed at six P.M., when a pug-nosed guy wearing shorts and deck shoes came out and locked the door, got in the scrofulous Toyota pickup, and drove off. I followed him to a beachfront bar and then had to decide whether to go in. My feeling was the risks outweighed the possible benefits, so I stayed put. I really could've gone for a cold beer right then, but I just swigged another Pepsi and drummed my fingers on the steering wheel. I was very tired, but the caffeine kept me going, aided by my adrenaline. When you're watching people, you never know what's going to happen. That makes it fun when something does.

An hour and a half later the guy came out, belched so loudly I could hear it from my spot in the farthest corner of the parking lot, and hauled himself into his truck again. I followed him to a marina about half a mile south of Kendall Marine, where he left his truck in the parking lot and walked out to a metal gate that led to the boats.

You know those marina gates on the ends of piers? When I was a kid they didn't exist—people never bothered other people's boats. Now everywhere you go you see these wide steel gates that stick out over the water and have spikes or razor wire on them. The few ruin it for the many.

The pug-nosed guy opened the gate with a key and walked through, letting it slam shut behind him.

I killed the Hyundai's engine and jumped out, keeping him barely in sight. I hurried up to the gate and tried the handle for the sake of thoroughness, but of course it had locked behind him. The marina was essentially a square basin with four long docks running into it like fingers. The boats, maybe a couple hundred of them, were tied up shoulder to shoulder. I turned away from the gate and walked quickly down the side of the basin, watching the guy as he slipped in and out of sight between the boats along one of the middle docks. At last I saw his head bob up as he hopped onto a boat, then he must have gone below because I didn't see him again. I memorized the shape of the boat's bridge and sighted it along a light pole from where I stood so that I could fix in my mind exactly which slip the boat was in. I walked along the basin from the pole, counting the parallel slips. Number 21 on the left, second row from the parking lot.

The sky was wide here above the masts and antennae bristling from the boats. Beyond the boats lay one of the pencil-line barrier islands, then beyond that the ultramarine Atlantic.

The marina was fairly well tricked out, with a nice new building, a smooth parking lot, and a little golf cart with a security shield painted on it, idle now next to the building. A sign told me that the building housed the office, plus telephones, showers, laundry, and vending machines for the boaters.

I wandered around. A few sailors were out and about, working on deck or pushing carts of supplies. A pleasant breeze came up, rattling the halyards on the masts of the sailboats. I guessed about half the boats were sailboats ranging from twenty-five to thirty-five feet in length; the rest were speedboats or fishing cruisers about the same size.

One guy was testing his rudder or something. motoring in a slow, tight circle at the end of a dock. He wore a bright-red polo shirt, and he waved to me as I stopped to watch. The daub of his red shirt was so nice to look at against the pretty blue sky and the white deck of his boat. I stood there wanting a boat and a red shirt too.

I sniffed the air. Was Beverly Austin here? I thought so. The vibe just came to me. Well, vibe or no vibe, it was simply damn likely.

The place had a feeling to it—how to put it? In spite of the nice building and sturdy gates, this marina felt a bit scuzzy. Was it the brackish smell to the water lapping the oily rocks that lined the basin? The larger-than-usual proportion of boats that looked like rust buckets? While it would be hard to accuse any place in Fort Lauderdale of being cheap, this place was definitely low-end.

Was it the people? Maybe so. The red-shirted sailor looked washed and possibly educated, but some of the others looked more like deadbeat dads hiding out from Friend of the Court. I'm sorry, but a beer gut covered by an undershirt paired with the briefest of bathing trunks—please. Add dirty bare feet and a scraggly ponytail and you've got yourself one prime cut of a blind date.

The pug-nosed Kendall Marine guy, whose age I pegged at about forty, didn't come across as being that hopeless, but he didn't look as if he'd enrolled for harpsichord lessons lately either. The look on his face was smarter than average, and he carried himself with the rolling gait of a barrel-chested guy with bad knees.

The couple of women I saw all had that hard-baked precancerous tan you'd expect. But their tans overlaid flabby arms and jouncing butts, which signified a lot of time spent sitting around boats and none on the high seas furling tops'ls or reeling in fighting marlins or whatever the hell athletic things people are supposed to do on boats like these.

What I'm trying to say is, the place looked like a no-questions-asked kind of place. Perfect for the likes of Beverly Austin.

Needless to say, all that water access plus proximity to places like Cuba and Central America is why the Miami–Fort Lauderdale area has been so attractive to drug dealers, desperate illegal immigrants, and all the ancillary services that go with them. Most of the drugs these days go by air into Miami, but the coastal customs agents still have plenty to do. A cop once told me that U.S. agents intercept only ten percent of the drugs coming in. Big money in that business. Big risk too, but money, money, money.

Plenty of people will do anything for money, and a lot of them live in Florida.

I hung around for about an hour but saw nothing else of interest, so I drove to a dumpy motel I'd noticed nearby, checked in, and fell asleep before I'd pulled up the covers on the damp-smelling bed.

I woke early and showered, feeling quite refreshed in spite of the motel's mustiness. That's another thing about Florida: if you don't keep on top of the mildew, it'll eat you alive.

I stopped and got a McDonald's breakfast on the way to the marina. I sat and ate my Egg McMuffin, potato thing, and coffee as I listened to a salsa station and waited for Kendall Marine guy. I had the feeling he'd come out with someone this morning—with Beverly Austin. I was wrong, though. He came out alone lugging a plastic garbage bag over his shoulder Santa-style. He flung it into the bin behind the marina building, then got in his truck and drove directly to Kendall Marine. He opened it up for business; it was nine A.M.

I waited and watched and after a while ate an apple. I decided against going back to the marina and doing some Dumpster-diving on this one: I couldn't really see how it might help me. Besides, I'd caught a whiff of that Dumpster, and you don't even want to—well, never mind.

Traffic chugged by, the cars and delivery vans and boat trailers flicking the sun around the buildings like faceted gems. There are quite a few luxury cars in Fort Lauderdale: a lot of Mercedeses and Lexuses, not so many Rolls-Royces and Ferraris as in Los Angeles. I watched the omnipresent gulls whirling and crying over the street, the buildings, everything. They stood flat-footed on light poles and awnings; they padded between parked cars looking for French fries and crackers, their heads so smooth and beautiful you can't believe they live on garbage. You want to avoid parking your car over a patch of gull droppings. Because soon the patch of droppings will be on top of your car. Check your environment, glance up and down before locking and walking away: That's my advice.

The mail truck came at ten minutes to eleven, and I perked up again. I saw a large white envelope at the bottom of the stack lugged in by the fat-hipped carrier and had to wait only twenty minutes before all the rest of the action got underway.

Someone on a bicycle whizzed past my open window at top speed and careered across three lanes of traffic into the Kendall Marine parking lot. Beverly Austin hopped off the bike, dumped it next to the building, yanked open the door, and strode in. She was wearing sunglasses, navy Capri pants, sneakers, and a white shirt that looked like the one she'd lent me, ages ago. She moved so fast I almost missed her.

Twenty-Eight

As I watched from my spot across the street, I fired up the Hyundai's meek engine and nursed it with gas to warm it. Beverly Austin walked slowly from the marine supply store holding the envelope, her face contracted in thought: I knew the postmark was puzzling her. I had to admire her discipline in not opening it immediately. She tucked it beneath her arm and picked up her bike, one of those folding jobs you see in pictures of European commuters. As she mounted the bike I saw her shake off her puzzlement, or at least put it off until she could open the thing in private. She pedaled away with alacrity in the direction she'd come from.

I followed in the Hyundai, hugging the curb about a block and a half back. I watched Beverly's rear end shift from side to side on the bicycle seat, and thought it a shame that such a juicily inviting butt should be attached to a criminal.

And yet…when I first saw her, my heart leaped. Do you believe it? I swear it's true.

She turned the corner into the same marina pug-nosed guy lived in.

I decided to approach her as she was opening the gate.

As I say, I was following slowly. Well, the speed limit was thirty-five miles per hour, and of course I was only going about five. I had a mere block to go before the turnoff into the marina when traffic thickened and the car behind me honked impatiently. I gestured for it to go around, adding an I-can't-help-it hand motion, but the driver must have thought I gave him the finger, because in an instant he swerved around, cut between me and the car in front, and slammed on his brakes. I barely stomped on mine in time to avoid smashing into him.

The guy stopped his car, an older Ford station wagon with a crunched-in hind end. I wondered how many times he'd made this particular maneuver. My bumper was an inch from his, and traffic backed up behind me as I saw him open his door. I hastily hit the lock button and rolled up my window as the guy got out.

"Hell," I muttered.

He wasn't a big guy. In fact, he was a thin young dude, a black kid, but he had a fierce Ayatollah-like look in his eyes. Perhaps I was the tenth person today to have dissed him, and he was going to take his revenge on me. Perhaps he hated Hyundais. His girlfriend in the passenger seat turned around and gave me a resigned look.

The guy took two strides toward my car, then stopped, staring.

"A *woman!*" he spat. "Shit!"

He flung himself back into his car, threw it in gear, and zoomed off.

And they say chivalry is dead.

By the time I got to the marina, Beverly Austin had passed through the locked gate; I saw her in the distance wheeling her bicycle down the row of boats.

I sat and thought, then rooted in my pocket for the drug-smuggler's bracelet I'd found in Porrocks's boathouse. I slipped it on my left wrist above my watch. Although the bracelet was too big, my Timex kept it from sliding off. The gold felt smooth and nicely heavy on my arm—outlaw swanky.

I waited for someone to come along to the gate, but nobody did for at least fifteen minutes. My nerves got edgy. I thought maybe I should just swim out to the dock, but that would be a more conspicuous move than I wanted to make right then.

Fortunately, one of the marina rats I described before happened along, carrying a case of Corona on one shoulder. He looked about ten years older than me, not a bit drunk yet this morning, and tremendously bored.

"Hi." I stepped toward him, leading with my right side, to hide my left wrist.

"How ya doin'?" he said in an automatic voice. Then he noticed me.

Believe me, I am no prize, but I'd taken off my sunglasses and Vietnam hat, and the breeze was riffling my hair. I was wearing jeans, a yellow cotton blouse, and my Chuck Taylors. I'm skinny, okay, but I do have boobs, which I now accentuated with a shoulders-back, Hepburn-neck posture (Audrey or Katharine, take your pick). My face—well, it's an ordinary one, but my teeth are good, and I can make my eyes look quite warm when I want to.

Practically any woman can get a lonely guy's attention. Everybody knows that.

I adopted a languorous gait. I smiled and moved toward this fellow another few steps until we were no more than an arm's length apart.

He stopped, balancing the beer case on his shoulder. His mouth fell very slightly open. He sniffed the air as if trying to catch perfume.

I said, "You're a strong one, aren't you?"

He flushed instantly red through his dark tan. "Oh, not so very, I guess." He smiled back with stained but intact teeth. He squinted lopsidedly into the sun over my shoulder, one eye squinching almost closed.

"Oh, I bet you are."

"Uh, want a beer?" he offered, swinging the case to the ground. He wiped his hands on his Rolling Stone tongue T-shirt.

"No, thank you. But maybe—later." I extended my hand. "Hey, I'm Lillian."

"Hey, I'm Pete." He took my hand, bowed over it, and kissed it.

I was astonished; no one had ever kissed my hand, except Lou once after three rum and Cokes. Pete gave me a close look, and I saw him trying to figure out if I was a hooker.

"Look, Pete, I have two favors to ask you. And I'm willing to—well, let me just tell you what they are."

He waited, trying to be guarded but smiling brainlessly and ogling my chest.

"One," I went on, "is huge, just absolutely huge to me. I want to walk through that gate with you."

He exhaled. "Well, sure—why'd you even—I mean, half the people here've lost their keys and they just go in with other people, or get the security guy to let them in." His voice was deep, but he didn't mumble; there was definitely a measure of coastal drawl in it, maybe elsewhere in Florida, or maybe slightly upward into Georgia or the Carolinas.

I glanced at the little golf cart, still parked next to the marina office.

"Yeah, where is that guy?"

"I think he's on vacation this week. They don't have but one guy. It's pretty casual here, you know." Pete's hair and eyebrows were caramel-brown and bushy, not quite out of control. He wore similarly lush sideburns, which gave him a look of seventies cool.

"Right, well, I wanted to be open about things. Plus there's this other, uh..." I lowered my voice. "Um, my boyfriend's in Buenos Aires this week making a buy."

"Oh, yeah?"

"Yeah, and I'm meeting my girlfriend on her boat for lunch today." I turned so he could see the bracelet. He noticed it. I held it up. "Ever seen one of these?"

Respect lit Pete's eyes. "I sure have. You get it from your boyfriend?"

"Yeah, actually I call it my mad money!" I laughed warmly.

Pete chuckled along with me.

Do you know what mad money is? When I was thirteen, my Aunt Rosalie gave me a ten-dollar bill and told me to keep it in the farthest recess of my wallet and not spend it. She explained how when you go on a date, it's good to have your own taxi fare home. "That way if the boy misbehaves, you don't have to put up with him unless you want to. See?" I saw.

"So," I said to Pete, "my girlfriend's expecting me. The thing is, though, I might need a boat in a little while, a day or two, and hers isn't running now. I wonder if you—"

"Mine's not running either," he interrupted sadly.

"Oh."

"I blew my engine two weeks ago and I'm waitin' for my cousin to come down from Tallahassee to help me fix it."

"Oh." There went my backup plan. "Well, Pete, never mind. But how 'bout I stop by for a beer later? 'Kay?"

"Or," he suggested, "I could join you ladies for lunch!"

"Naw, we got some girl talk to do—you know."

"Oh, sure."

I took his arm and squeezed it. "Pete, you're a prince."

He laughed and touched my hand. "Well, Lillian, if you need anything until then, just holler. I'm aboard the *Miss Behavin'*, D-6."

"The name of your boat is the *Miss Behavin'*?"

He leered gently, proudly.

"Fun name," I said. "D-dock, number 6? Thanks very much. See you later. I have a feeling I'll be thirsty."

He picked up his case of beer and managed to open and hold the gate for me with one hand.

"Thank you, Prince Pete."

"You're welcome, Princess Lillian."

He wasn't a bad guy, really.

What the hell *was* my backup plan? All I knew was, if your quarry has a boat, you ought to line one up too. It was as half-baked as that.

But I had another reason for making contact with Pete or whomever happened to be walking by.

I hate to actually come out and say it because it sounds melodramatic. But I wanted someone to witness me walking through that gate. I wanted Pete to hear my real name and remember me, I wanted him to take a good look at me and what I was wearing, bracelet and all.

Because I wasn't so stupid as to think I wasn't about to do something dangerous. And I wasn't so confident as to take for granted I'd come out of it alive.

Twenty-Nine

Boat owners are crazy for puns, do you know that? This marina was particularly bad: for every ordinarily named boat there were two or three with the kind of names a seventh-grade hillbilly would come up with, painted stylishly on their transoms. That is, for every *Sarah Ann* there was an *Oar-Gas-Um* and a *Lazy Daze*. For every *Dauntless* there was an *Aye Sea U* and a *Gator Baiter*. I hadn't really noticed this before Pete said the name of his boat, but that's the way it was.

The temperature was holding nicely at seventy-five degrees or so, but the clouds had thickened and lowered. It didn't feel exactly like thunderstorm weather—that quiet heaviness—but the stiffening breeze blew straight onshore from the sea, and I noticed a distinct chop coming up on the water beyond the marina. The salty wind smelled cool and metallic, like water in a new tin cup.

I strolled down B dock counting the slips until I came to number 21 on the left. The boat's bridge was the same as I'd memorized while watching pug-nosed guy. The boat, about a twenty-seven-footer, was named the *Lady Valiant*, which I approved of. Beverly Austin was not on deck.

I took a good look at the vessel, a cabin cruiser with some deep-water fishing features—a bait well, rod holders, fold-up outriggers, a gaff hook clipped to the starboard gunwale, and a socket in the cockpit that I guessed you'd set your fighting chair into. There were built-in lockers under bench seats for your tackle, life jackets and the like, topped with blue vinyl cushions. The *Lady Valiant* was fairly tidy, her white fiberglass skin clean and unpitted.

I glanced up into the shade of the covered bridge, a step up from the deck. It was a hut-like space just big enough for the skipper to sit in the padded seat and run the boat and use the radio. The chrome steering wheel gleamed in the shade. The ignition key, attached to a tiny yellow float, was inserted into the console.

As I say, Beverly Austin was not on deck, but she was below, behind the closed cabin door; I heard her voice spilling up through the open ports, angry and fast. I listened closely but couldn't make out her words. No one was answering her; however, so she must be on a cell phone, or just ranting to herself.

I thought it prudent to take possession of that ignition key. Very quietly, I leaned forward and grasped the railing. I stretched my left foot out from the dock, set the sole of one of my Chuck Taylors on the gunwale, and gradually put weight on it. The boat very slightly rocked in response, until I was balancing on that foot. I lifted the other one and brought it up. I crouched on the gunwale.

A couple of gulls skirmished on the nearest piling, squawking their atavistic song of hate, or love. Two gray mantle feathers floated down, then away in the breeze. I couldn't tell whether that was a good omen or a bad one. My blouse was clammy with sweat, even though the wind had strengthened even more.

Beverly stopped ranting. The gulls settled down. The world was quiet but for the rushing of wind.

I eased into the cockpit with catlike precision, just as Calico Jones would do. I wished I had a honking .45-caliber semiautomatic strapped to my hip, but people in hell wish they had ice water, don't they?

I'd have made it to the bridge, except that in my concentration on the key I didn't see a piece of crinkly clear plastic—a wrapper from food or bait—until the wind skittered it in front of me and I stepped on it.

Keeruncha! said the plastic.

I heard a bumping from the cabin. The door burst open, and Beverly Austin stood shading her eyes against the noon sun.

"Hello," I said genially.

"Oh, my God," she said. "Oh, my God."

She was a textbook cutie, as you know. The pixie face—little cleft in her chin, did I mention that?—the bouncy hair, the pleasantly swelling chest and hips, you know all about it. But the thing was, at that instant she was not cute at all.

Seeing her standing there in the cabin doorway, the color draining out of her face, I saw that she was what she had always been: a schemer. A casual destroyer of other people for the sake of money. Someone who felt entitled to what someone else had if she could merely figure out a way to take it. The taking of the thing entitles her to it: That is the philosophy of such a person.

I blurted, "Audrey, I love you."

The cockpit was a large one for a fishing boat, but only about seven feet by seven at that. Ours was to be a close-order encounter.

I watched her brain sort frantically through possibilities. I saw her tell herself not to panic. Her head snapped around, looking up and down the dock, sweeping around the neighboring boats.

"I'm alone," I said.

She tucked her chin, relaxed her neck, and swallowed. "What are you doing here?" Her voice was barely steady.

I smiled desperately. "I had to tell you I love you no matter what you've done. I almost hate myself for it, but I love you and I can't change that."

"How did you—"

"I love you, I love you, I love you!"

"Shut up! How did you—"

I reached to her with a cupped hand. "I can't bear to be apart from you," I said tenderly. "I don't have much to give, but—"

"Please shut up. How did you find me?"

"After a kiss."

She dropped her arms and I did it. So help me, I gathered her and pressed my pelvis into hers and kissed her as passionately as I could, and the first time we'd kissed came flooding back to me, so sweet and exciting. I made sure to close my eyes, knowing she'd keep hers open to check my sincerity. Her lips were warm but tense.

I released her and flung myself onto one of the cushioned locker tops.

Beverly sat on the short bench at the transom, facing the bow, sideways to me. Our legs stretched into the cockpit at right angles. She looked at me, waiting.

I said, "It's irrelevant how I found you."

"Did you—did you talk to—"

"All right. Truth be told, I didn't *find* you! I never lost you—because I followed you!"

"You what!"

"I never left town that morning." I kept smiling.

"You—you—"

"You're not that hard to keep track of, you know. Hey, sunshine, relax! Got anything to drink around here?"

"Then who—"

"I've been enjoying just making sure you're safe. I love to watch you, you know? Everything you do is exciting. Oh, it's definitely been a voyeuristic thrill, Audrey. It definitely has."

She was totally, thoroughly flummoxed, and it was a great thing to see. She decided to go with the flow, which of course was *my* flow. I saw her relax a fraction; it was evident I was alone and unarmed, and she had time to deal with me. Perhaps she could make use of me.

I saw all this in her eyes.

She glanced casually at the boat's controls, then leaned back on the cushioned bench and stretched her arms along the transom. "Lillian, what made you decide to let me be alone in the house?"

"Just a feeling I had. I'm very good at getting feelings about things. Audrey, I know you're freaked out, me showing up here like a *stalker* or something." I touched her cheek softly with the back of my fingers. "Don't be," I whispered.

The breeze whipped at our hair, and the strength of it felt good to me. The planet carries on its business regardless.

"I have to say," I went on, "I was hurt—disappointed, frankly. I mean, Audrey, you did behave badly. You can admit that, can't you?" I wanted to lunge for that ignition key, but she was watching me like a lizard.

"Well," she said, "I'm sorry you felt—"

"But I blame myself."

"Uh—"

"If only I hadn't drawn you into that situation. If only I'd just kept my mouth shut about what Drooly Rick found in that wall—if I'd just tried to handle Porrocks's avarice and dishonesty on my own, if I had-n't put all that temptation right in front of you. Hell…" I looked at her. "But then, you wouldn't be so flush as you are now."

She sought a new handle on me. "So you want—"

"I don't want a penny." I moved to the end of the bench seat and took her hand. Our knees touched. I held her hand in both of mine as I'd held her sister's.

She wouldn't look up.

"Audrey, please meet my eyes."

She lifted her head. Her eyes showed controlled fear.

Now I could ask it. "Please, tell me what you ever felt for me."

After what seemed like an hour, she said, "It wasn't you. I've never loved anyone."

"Not even your sister?"

She made a sound in her throat but turned it into a cough. She knew then I'd come for justice.

I think I was in a bit of denial about the situation I'd created because when she said, "Let's go fishing!" I thought it'd be a nice way to have a quiet talk about everything, the way I did with my Uncle Guff. Everything out in the open.

A second later I realized what a bad idea it would be.

But Beverly Austin had me.

She quickly flipped off the stern line and took her place at the controls. She pressed switches and turned knobs. "Cast off that bow line, will you?" It was her turn to smile.

I hesitated. If I jumped off the boat and let her go, well, she would be gone, God knew where. I could dash to the public phone and call the police, but the time it would take me to explain the situation, them to reach Stonehauser and confirm it, then to get a pursuit boat or helicopter or plane on the job—all but hopeless. I didn't even know whether she could skipper a boat, but she appeared to know what she was doing. Well, if you spend time in Florida now and then, get a boyfriend with a boat to do some intermittent money-laundering for you, you can see how you might gain some skills yourself.

If I stayed aboard, she would try to kill me. Therefore, if I stayed aboard I would have to figure out a way to neutralize her. Not kill her, of course—just get her to let me tie her up or something. *Oh, Christ.*

I went up and cast off the bow line.

Beverly Austin piloted the *Lady Valiant* out of the marina in a few minutes, then throttled it up until we'd rounded the barrier island, then she pushed the throttle even harder and pointed the nose due east, out to sea. The blotty gray sky was huge. The heaving water was huge. Everything was huge except for our boat and little old us. I give her credit for bothering to smile as she did all this, in a transparent effort to charm me back into the cluelessness I'd left behind in Detroit. She kept one eye on the water and one eye on me the whole time.

But never mind cluelessness: It was all I could do to hold on as the hull smacked the mounting waves. *Wak-cha! Wak-cha! Wak-aka-cha!* Salt spray stung my face as I clung to the port railing. Small craft were headed in, their skippers glancing over at us as we rushed out with the tide.

Soon we were out of sight of other boats, and the Florida coast was only a dark ruff on the horizon, the tall hotels of Fort Lauderdale and Miami Beach mere serrations.

I thought about the fishing equipment and tackle. In movies you see people fighting on boats with the most imaginative weapons. One thing I did know was that when you go hunting for big fish you take along a billy club, to make sure the fish is dead before boating it. Therefore practically every boat in the world has a billy club handy because every fisherman believes he'll haul in a record-buster sooner or later.

I realized that if I could knock Beverly overboard, I could throw her a life jacket and a line and tow her safely in, radioing ahead to the authorities.

Yes, that was a plan.

She cut the engine and turned toward me. I'd hoped she'd try one last seduction—you know? I'm ashamed to tell you that.

The boat's momentum slowed abruptly, and Beverly Austin wasted no time. I saw her hand flash into a compartment next to the radio and thought, *Lord, she's got a gun*, but it was a knife she came up with, a sheathed filleting knife. I can't say the sight of it made me much happier.

Thirty

I judged the blade to be about seven inches long. She threw away the sheath as I picked up a blue vinyl seat cushion and braced myself. She leaped at me, her eyes as cold and empty as caves. I thrust the cushion to meet the blade, hoping to knock it out of her hand. At the same time I aimed a stomp at her instep, but missed as the *Lady Valiant* lurched in the waves.

The knife more or less glanced off the firm cushion.

I saw she was surprised at the force of my counterstrike.

"I had a feeling you might do that," I managed to grunt.

The thing to remember during a dirty hand-to-hand fight—I tell you this just in case!—is that to surprise your opponent you must do more than one thing at once. That is, you must not only parry a blow, you must deliver one at the same time, or nearly instantly. You must punch with a hand and kick with a knee, all the while screaming curses at the top of your lungs. You must become a frenzy of unstoppable violence. I'm not saying I'm great at it, but I know that much.

Beverly shrieked wordlessly and came at me again. Again I lunged at her knife hand with the cushion, which she grabbed with her free hand. My heart hammered in my ears.

Was she stronger, or was I?

My reach was certainly longer, but she outweighed me. Moreover, she was a killer.

This time the knife pierced straight through the cushion, its tip popping out right in front of my nose. I yanked the cushion hard sideways and threw my elbow at her head. But she retained her grip on the slim knife handle, withdrew it, and struck again.

I felt something hit my upper left arm and thought she had punched me, but then I saw the knife handle still in her fist. The blade was stuck in my biceps, such as they were. I smacked her in the face with my right fist as hard as I could, hoping to break her nose, and I think I did, because I felt something give and heard a satisfying *crunk!* She screamed and fell back, stunned. Blood poured from her nose.

I grasped the knife and pulled it from my arm. I didn't feel the wound.

The boat, engine idling, propeller disengaged, lurched randomly in the whitecaps. It was impossible to anticipate the movement of the boat; our fight must have looked like a drunken one to the gulls.

"You're not gonna kill me, you psycho bitch!" I hollered. "God damn you! Stay back!" I neither wanted an explanation nor thought I'd get it, but I said, "That money wasn't yours."

"Finders keepers," she grunted.

"You killed Rick."

"I'll kill you."

"You killed Vic Toretti with heroin, and you ran over your sister and Porrocks."

"I hate you."

"I'm devastated."

Beverly came at me again, hurling her whole body in an attempt to knock me down, and did. I couldn't believe she'd run right into me like that while I was holding the knife. That was my key failure. She was astride me in a microsecond. She grabbed my right wrist with both hands and slammed my hand on the deck, once, twice, *bam!* I watched the knife fly out of my grasp. Then, as the boat heaved, it slithered away, trailing my blood, into a scupper and out of sight. Blood dripped from Beverly's nose into my eyes.

"No!" I screamed. "Let go!" I rolled onto her knee, and she grabbed my hair and triedd to bang my head on the deck. I levered my leg against her hip and managed to flip her off me, losing a fistful of hair in the process, but gaining a second of action time.

She scrambled to a locker and snatched it open. I leaped to my feet and grabbed the gaff hook and tried to roundhouse it on her, but the arc took way too long; she sidestepped and pointed a short red tube at me. It was a flare, but I had enough time, seeing it sizzle to life, to duck. The fiery clump of phosphor shrieked past my head.

"Hah!" I said, blinking.

Next she came up with the billy club—what did I tell you? This one appeared to be a foot-and-a-half piece of hickory, its handle wrapped in black tape. She rushed me. I ducked, but a lurch of the boat threw my head into the path of her club.

The rock-hard wood split my scalp—I felt that—but she hadn't generated enough force to addle me or knock me down.

"*Shit!*" she hissed, scrambling to face me again.

I thought, *Well, it's worth a try*, and swiftly took my Case knife from my back jeans pocket. I snapped open the humble three-inch blade, which she disregarded. She sprang, and I thrust it into her upper abdomen as she reached me. At the same time I blocked the club with my left hand. It would not make a fist.

"Huff!" she said, and wavered, staring into my face. She dropped the club.

I held my little knife into her, and her body sagged forward. Her warm blood flowed over my hand. Her eyes clawed my face. I felt the twitchings of her insides, transmitted by the handle of the knife.

I dared hope it was over, but with a surge of energy she leaped backward off the knife. My hand was slippery with her blood, but I was ready and held on to my trusty knife.

Beverly lunged sideways for the club just as I thought to kick it away. She came up empty and much slower, but determined to attack me with her bare hands.

I had plenty of time to meet her with my jackknife, driving it in roughly the same place, this time angling it upward. I felt the hinge give slightly, but it was in up to the hilt, and stayed in.

My bloody pixie lover collapsed onto me, her mouth wide, screaming airlessly, her eyes rolling back now. I stepped aside and let her fall to the deck.

Thirty-One

Before I would go to sleep that night, I would clean my hands and wrap a towel from the boat's galley around my punctured arm and tie it off using my teeth. I would take a sleeping bag from one of the berths and spread it over Beverly Austin's corpse. The wind would whip it half away and I would use a tackle box and a small ice chest to hold it down, in lieu of dragging the body below.

I would search the *Lady Valiant* and find sixty-four banded packets of hundred-dollar bills equaling $320,000 in a storage compartment in the prow.

I would put the boat in gear and figure out how to work the radio and tell the Coast Guard what happened, and I would let them know I was following the compass due west, back to shore. The storm would finally break, and rain would lash down until I would make out the running lights of the Coast Guard cutter, all blurry at first.

I would receive medical attention and explain everything to the police, then wait in the crappy motel reading newspapers until they would tell me to board the Greyhound for Detroit. Porrocks would wire me $200.

Back in Detroit I would visit Lt. Stonehauser and receive a severe talking-to. I would phone Tom Ciesla and receive a severe talking-to. I would place a timothy nugget on Todd's grave and shed a tear for my beloved little friend. I would sit over coffee with Mrs. McVittie and eat some of the gingerbread she would bake for me and feel a little better.

I would visit Porrocks at home, attended by her sister, and receive a severe talking-to. Then Porrocks, lying back on her couch and asking her sister to leave the room, would ask me worriedly for advice on how to discourage Lou from being so attentive, and I would counsel her to be gentle and know that Lou is one of the best humans ever to walk the earth. I would suspect that one day I would see them holding hands at a movie or a café.

Porrocks's doorbell would ring and I would answer it. The two guys she'd hired to bust out the wall in the boathouse would be standing there wanting to know if she had any more walls that needed busting. They wore new Rolexes, we would notice, and had hangovers, and after questioning by Porrocks would admit that they'd found $28,000 in the wall and had gone to Atlantic City, had a rousing time, and were now broke except for the watches.

I would have a quiet dinner with Billie. She would offer to give me a puppy, and I would say no thank you.

All this would occur, one thing after the other, until one day I would be alone in my apartment with nothing to do but think about what to do next.

But in the meantime I stood on a boat in the Atlantic Ocean, shifting to keep my balance on the heaving deck, looking down at Beverly Austin as she lay staring up at the jagged sky. I looked at her and knew what it was to take a life in hot blood. I knew I was a different person now. Exactly what kind of person I'd become, I didn't know. I wondered whose business it was to forgive me for what I'd done.

I wasn't sorry.

I lifted my head and slowly and deeply breathed the clean ocean air.

"I'd do it again," I said to the wide world, and wondered whether I'd ever have to.